The Whisper Theory

Amber Albee Swenson

WESTBOW
PRESS
A DIVISION OF THOMAS NELSON

WestBow Press books may be ordered through booksellers or by contacting:

WestBow Press
A Division of Thomas Nelson
1663 Liberty Drive
Bloomington, IN 47403
www.westbowpress.com
1-(866) 928-1240

Because of the dynamic nature of the Internet, any web addresses or links contained in this book may have changed since publication and may no longer be valid. The views expressed in this work are solely those of the author and do not necessarily reflect the views of the publisher, and the publisher hereby disclaims any responsibility for them.

Any people depicted in stock imagery provided by Thinkstock are models, and such images are being used for illustrative purposes only.

Certain stock imagery © Thinkstock.

ISBN: 978-1-4497-3344-5 (sc)
ISBN: 978-1-4497-3345-2 (hc)
ISBN: 978-1-4497-3343-8 (e)

Library of Congress Control Number: 2011961845

Printed in the United States of America

WestBow Press rev. date: 12/12/2011

Also by Amber Albee Swenson

Bible Moms—Life Lessons from Mothers of the Bible

To my husband, Steve,

and our children

Sage, Simon, Audra, and Addy

My prayer is that God is your guide
during your high school and college years
and that as Max Lucado says so beautifully,
your heart is so hidden in God
that any potential spouse
has to seek Him to find you.

and

Mabel Carrie Albee who taught me everything I know
about being on "the farm," introduced me to Amish Bread,
and supplied many meals and as many laughs to me while
I was in college.

Preface

The Bible studies are intended to show what God's Word says about each topic. It is not the author's intent to put a heavy burden on Christian teens, nor to in any way portray the idea that keeping these commands "earns" you a place in heaven. Salvation is a gift (Ephesians 2:8), and all of us—youth group leaders and teens alike—stumble and struggle. If anything, the law and our inability to keep it shows us all the more our need for a Savior.

These studies are meant to equip Christian teens so they aren't blindsided by the culture and to prepare them to deal with the temptations they will likely experience at some point.

"Therefore, I urge you, brothers, in view of God's mercy, to offer your bodies as living sacrifices, holy and pleasing to God—this is your spiritual act of worship. Do not conform any longer to the pattern of this world, but be transformed by the renewing of your mind. Then you will be able to test and approve what God's will is—His good, pleasing and perfect will" (Romans 12:1–2).

Acknowledgments

Thank you, Lord. Let my words help them fall more in love with You.

A sincere and heartfelt thank you to Armin Panning for his editorial review and comments.

Thanks also to all of you who took the time to read this in manuscript form and gave me suggestions and encouragement. A special thanks to Jillian Albee, whose interest prompted me to finish writing this, and returned the manuscript with a collage of Post-It notes in just the right places.

And to all my favorite Christian musicians: Thanks for making great music to point us to our Hope and Strength, and thank you for inspiring perseverance in a broken world.

Contents

Preface   ix

Acknowledgments   xi

Chapter One: How Could You Forget?   1

Chapter Two: A Wonder to Behold   15

Chapter Three: The Raisin   27

Chapter Four: The Whisper Theory   47

Chapter Five: Lily Menteen   61

Chapter Six: Chilled   77

Chapter Seven: The Blond No One Knew   91

Chapter Eight: The Right Move   107

Chapter Nine: Good-bye for Now   121

Chapter Ten: A Reason to Give Thanks   143

Chapter Eleven: The Road Trip   157

Chapter Twelve: A New Start   179

Chapter Thirteen: Deal or No Deal   195

Chapter Fourteen: The Best and Worst of Times   215

Chapter Fifteen: Out with the Old   237

Chapter Sixteen: I Do   263

Resources   285

Chapter One: How Could You Forget?

The late August storm that hit Evanston my first night there ushered in oppressive heat that stayed for a week. Sweat clothed everything, right down to the toilet, and my roommates and I languished, finding no reprieve.

We sauntered to the Henry Crown Sports Pavilion/Aquatic Center, or SPAC as we called it, passing manicured lawns outlined by solar lanterns. A few hours earlier, students likely had played volleyball and Frisbee in the park-like student area behind the building, but it was abandoned now, except for a few who sat on the boulders stacked into a retaining wall next to the lake. From our perch, we watched Chicago's lights reflecting on Lake Michigan. The only sounds came from waves roaring and then fading in splashes on the rocks beneath where we sat.

"When I'm gone, I'll miss this," I said, trying to breathe in the atmosphere of the night.

"You just got here. How can you talk about it being over?" Carol asked.

"I won't miss it," Jeff said. "I'll be too busy looking for a rich woman to marry."

"Marry Carol," I said. "Her parents are loaded."

"Would you marry me, Carol?"

"Not a chance," she snapped, as she took off her sandals and stretched her legs.

"I don't know how to get these sounds into my mental picture," I said.

"Why are you so consumed with remembering?" Jeff questioned.

"It's so beautiful with the lights and the waves …"

"And us," Carol added. "How could you forget?"

"She could end up with Alzheimer's," Jeff said, "but then she wouldn't know she had forgotten, so it wouldn't matter."

"Just adopt Jeff's approach and drag college out for five or six years," Carol said. "Then you won't have to leave next spring."

"It won't take me six years," Jeff protested. "If I take summer school, I could finish in five…maybe."

"I can't afford the nine months I'm here," I said.

"I wish I would have known I could take college classes in high school," Carol said. "I would have done that, too. I hated high school and there were colleges nearby."

"I hated high school, too," Jeff said. "I would have left in a heartbeat."

"What changes in the months between high school and college to make such a difference?" I wondered. "One month pretty people run the school, and three months later, no one cares."

"Maybe it's because you pay for college," Carol suggested. "Or having brains actually matters."

"And you can move away from the people who made the last twelve years of your life a dark and lonely existence," Jeff added.

"Well, whatever it is, I'm glad I got out when I did," I said. "Two years was enough for me."

"Remind me of that when I have kids," Carol said. "Keep them out of high school at all costs."

"Great idea, Carol. Raise a bunch of dropouts," Jeff snorted.

"Boarding school is more her style," I said.

"But then she'd have private school brats."

"I went to private school," I reminded him.

"I rest my case."

"I would have gone to a Christian high school if there had been one nearby."

"We can all be thankful there wasn't," Jeff said. "I can't imagine how overbearing you'd be."

I sighed, not willing to start another argument. "We should look for that lighthouse."

"I'm tired," Jeff said, shoving his baseball hat down to cover his eyes.

"I don't think it's far," Carol mentioned.

I turned around to determine which way was north. "It's got to be somewhere over there," I decided.

Jeff hung his head and groaned.

"We'll be fine," I said. "Don't feel like you have to protect us."

His head popped up. "Is that what you think? I stick with Carol because I know no one will mug her."

"What makes you think that?"

"If you answer that, I'll punch you," Carol said.

Jeff turned to me. "Need I say more?"

We followed a trail to the lighthouse. It was attached to a little white house with dingy windows. Overgrown trees nearly hid a garage. A path wove around the garage to a hill of knee-high grass. From the top of the hill, we heard water.

"Don't wake me up," Carol mused.

We listened to waves colliding onto sand and felt the tall grass swaying against our legs. I imagined the lighthouse, solemn and dark though it was now, beaming across the lake.

Carol started toward the wood fence at the bottom of the hill where the grass turned to sand. Jeff and I followed.

Jeff stayed on the beach. When Carol and I left our sandals next to him, we were only going to wet our feet, but the water danced against our ankles and in no time we were in up to our shoulders.

We were used to seeing Chicago's lights from the beach where we had swum the last several nights. Here we had only the light of a sallow moon.

"We'd better turn back," I said to Carol at last.

"I know," she said. "It got deep all of a sudden."

"And cold," I said, turning in the direction of her voice. "Imagine that. After sweating all week, I'm talking about being cold."

She didn't respond.

"Carol?"

I felt the hair on the back of my neck bristle.

By the time I felt the current, it was too late. It sucked me under and swept me across the bottom of the lake, grinding me into the pointed tips of rocks and sand and broken shells.

Just as suddenly as I had been sucked under, I was spit out, and pushed up, leaving me sprawling in knee-high water. I wobbled backwards, coughing and trying to catch my breath.

Carol called my name.

"I'm here," I sputtered.

She called again. I summoned my strength and yelled louder.

She came through the water toward me. "What happened?"

"Are you okay?" Jeff asked, running to the water's edge.

"I got pulled under and dragged across the bottom of the lake."

"Can you walk?" Carol asked.

"I think so. I'm just freaked out," I said.

Lights appeared at the top of the grassy knoll.

"Now I'm freaked out," Jeff said. "Let's get our stuff."

Carol helped me to my feet and I followed her back to our sandals. We'd just put them on when two officers arrived, dressed in shorts and short-sleeved uniforms. They didn't look much older than we were.

"What's going on?"

Their lights hit us like spotlights.

"We're just leaving," Jeff said.

"This beach is closed," one officer said. "All beaches close at dusk, and this beach is restricted use only."

"Sorry," Jeff said. "We didn't know."

"I don't suppose you could read the signs in the dark," the other officer barked.

The first officer to speak focused his light on Carol and me. "Swimming here is not very smart. There's an undertow. You get caught in that and it will spin you in circles until something pulls you out. There've been dozens of deaths here over the years."

"Sorry," Carol said. "It won't happen again."

"Let's get you off the beach," he said.

We followed the first officer and the other officer followed us. When we reached the sidewalk, we apologized again and headed for the apartment.

"Between my heart pounding and my legs shaking, I'm not sure how I'm managing to walk," I said.

"I feel like I could puke," Jeff said. "When I saw those lights, I didn't know if it was frat boys or cops. I'm glad it was cops."

"That could've been a bad situation," Carol said.

"We could've been raped," Jeff said.

"Who would want to rape you?" Carol asked.

"I don't want to know what goes on during rush week, but finding three undergrads alone on a beach with no one around for blocks ..."

"Thank God my parents pray," I said.

Back at the apartment, Carol changed into dry clothes, while I took a bath to get the sand out of my wounds. After putting on my pajamas, I went to the living room and lowered myself gingerly onto the end of the couch opposite Jeff. He stretched my legs over his lap.

"You've got some serious road rash," he said, surveying the damage.

"My back took the worst beating," I said.

"Lift up your shirt," he said.

"Yeah, okay, Jeff," I muttered.

"I'm serious," he said. "Let me see it."

I turned over and lifted the bottom of my shirt.

Carol moaned. "I'll get some triple antibiotic cream."

When she came back, she dabbed the cream on and taped gauze across the lower half of my back. She handed me the tube. "You can get your legs."

I thanked her and turned over, repositioning the pillow behind me so I could recline. She went to the kitchen to wash her hands and returned with a plate of watermelon.

"Want some?" she asked, offering the plate to Jeff and me.

"I inhaled all the water I need for tonight," I said.

Jeff passed, too. He grabbed the cream from my hand and started dabbing it, first along one leg, then the other.

"A lot of people do extraordinary things after a near-death experience," he said. "Maybe you could clean Carol's room."

Carol guffawed.

"I'm glad just to be ordinary."

"Let's not exaggerate," Carol said.

"Maybe you could get a T-shirt made that says, 'I survived the undertow.' "

I closed my eyes. Breathing seemed almost too great an effort. "Where do you come up with this stuff, Jeff?"

"Years of nothing to do but watch Comedy Central."

"All that time wasted," Carol said, "and you're still not funny."

"I could have gotten into a whole lot more trouble, I know that."

He nudged Carol with his foot. "Turn on the TV."

He rubbed cream over the last of my scratches, put the top on the tube, and handed it to Carol.

"Thanks," I said, leaving my legs on his lap.

"I put lotion on the old people at the nursing home all the time."

"I'm sure they're grateful."

"Hey, Carol," Jeff said, "Are you seeing how Meghan's God-works-all-things-for-my-good works?"

"Shut up," she said.

"Maybe he's working it for *our* good. Maybe she'll wise up a little."

"If there wasn't a God, I would be getting pulled out of the lake by divers tonight, Jeff." I shifted my weight. "I don't think I've ever hurt so much."

"When I heard that officer talk about the undertow I had goose bumps," Carol said. "I can't imagine calling 911 to say you hadn't gotten back to the beach. That's the first time I've witnessed something like a miracle."

"Not you, too," Jeff groaned. "Carol, you have above average intelligence. Please tell me you don't buy into this God crap."

"I graduated near the top of my class," I said. "Just because I have faith doesn't mean I'm an idiot."

"If you say so," Jeff said.

"It takes just as much faith to not believe," I said. "Anyway, Darwin was a racist."

"The apostle Paul supported slavery, so I guess we're both following flawed men."

"I follow Jesus, not Paul," I said. "And Paul reminded masters their slaves were equal to them before God."

"Not quite the same as, 'Slavery is wrong. Free your slaves.'"

"He wasn't trying to create a new social order. He was concerned with how people would spend eternity."

"Carol, she's babbling. I think she's in shock."

"I'm in shock, too," Carol said.

"Some day you'll know the truth, Jeff," I said. "It might not be until you're dead, but you will know."

"You Christians are so arrogant," Jeff said.

"Confident," I corrected, "because whatever else happens, we know in the end we win."

He pushed my legs off his lap and stood up.

"Meghan, I'm glad you're alive."

"That was nice," Carol said.

"I couldn't afford the rent without her," he said, giving me a wink.

"You're a hard nut to crack," I said, "but I think there's hope."

"Leave my nuts out of it," he said, walking out of the room.

7

I looked at Carol, and we laughed.

"I don't know if I can sleep. I thought I was done. I've never felt so small or alone. It makes me think of that old woman downstairs who sits in the window all day."

"I think Earl brings her groceries," Carol pointed out.

"I bet the days crawl for her," I said.

"I wonder if anyone would notice if she died," Carol contemplated.

Jeff came into the room eating out of a bag of chips. "If she died in the window we might."

"It doesn't seem right to die like that," I said.

"There are a lot of things that aren't right about dying," he muttered.

"Would you rather live like the people you take care of in the nursing home?"

"I don't want to live that way," Carol said.

"You'll never make it to old age, Carol. Someone will kill you first."

Carol spit a watermelon seed at him, but it fell short.

"I've thought about killing you myself," he said.

"If you do, I'll come back to haunt you."

"You haunt me now."

"I can feel the love," I said.

"You could find love in a concentration camp," Jeff retorted.

"Desperate situations have a way of making people bond," I offered.

"Didn't you learn anything from tonight? Your optimism is unrealistic."

"Would you rather I was pessimistic?"

"I'd take realistic."

"Reality is for those who lack imagination," I said.

"You're setting yourself up for despair," Jeff warned. "When things don't work out, you'll be crushed."

"Who said things won't work out?"

"Am I sober, Carol? I can't believe this nonsense. I think I need to go beat my head against the wall."

She looked at me and shrugged.

He disappeared, leaving Carol and me to an open window and the warm breath of a humid night. Another night I might have greeted the heat with disdain, but that night I welcomed it—even embraced it—because I was alive and could feel it.

Bible Study Chapter One

In this first chapter, we're introduced to the narrator Meghan and her roommates. Who are her roommates?

What did Meghan, Jeff, and Carol hate about high school?

Especially in youth but all throughout your life, there will be people who will judge you by your looks, your sense of fashion, your hair style, or the shape of your body. Some people won't care what you know. Some people will exclude you. Look up the following Bible passages. What does God have to say about the things Meghan, Jeff, and Carol hated about high school?

God's concept of beauty (pretty people ran the school)

Look up 1 Samuel 16:7. What is God looking at when He looks at you?

Read 1 Peter 3:3–4. What does God find attractive in a woman?

How valuable is that to God?

How long does this beauty last?

Think of what you do to make yourself attractive. A haircut might last six weeks to two months; fingernail polish stays on maybe a week; makeup needs to be applied every day. The things God finds attractive in a woman don't fade. That's worth investing in!

How much time do you put into your appearance every day? How much time do you put into becoming the person God wants you to be? That is going to require time in His Word and time with Him …praying.

Read 1Timothy 6:11. What character traits are valuable in a Christian?

How do the qualities in verse eleven differ from what our culture teaches are attractive attributes?

What word does Paul use for what we should do to attain these traits?

The word "pursue" insinuates these traits are not going to just fall into your lap. You will need to work at these to have them.

The origin of knowledge and wisdom (brains didn't matter)

Read Proverbs 1:7. Where does knowledge come from, and how does it differ from wisdom?

My Bible says wisdom includes skill in living—following God's design and thus avoiding moral pitfalls.[1]

Read James 1:5. How can we attain wisdom?

Read 1 Corinthians 2:13–14. When you are a Christian who believes in creation and justification by Christ's sacrifice (in other words, that the Bible is true), some people are going to find you ignorant. It may be a high school teacher or a college professor. It may be your friends.

Why can't those who think Christianity is foolish understand the things of God?

How is it we know and believe the things of God?

Favoritism and how do I deal with the unbelievers in my life? (they made my life a dark and lonely existence; they excluded me)

Read James 2:1–13. How should we feel about the way the world groups people; i.e., the preps, jocks, dirtballs, etc?

Think back to the passage we looked up in 1 Samuel. What should you be looking at when you look for friends?

In 1 Corinthians 15:33, Paul says, "Do not be misled: 'Bad company corrupts good character.' " While it is important that we exclude no one—and by that I mean we should be nice to everyone—it is also important that we don't deliberately put ourselves in a crowd of people whose morals are different from the ones we want to hang onto. Subtle ideologies from our friends can easily creep into our thinking, allowing us to believe things the Bible doesn't teach. Choose your friends and companions carefully!

Sometimes we don't have a choice as to who our companions will be. People are often put into groups for classes. Freshmen in college are often assigned roommates in the dorms. Peter wants us to be sure we're aware and ready for the fact that some people will put us down for believing in God. But he gives us the right attitude and a good course of action to take with those who confront you for your beliefs. Read 1 Peter 2:11–12. If you end up sharing a dorm room with someone whose morals are completely different than yours, how should you live?

Read 1 Peter 3:15–17. Your beliefs will likely be tested at some point. Should you respond, and if so, how?

Read 1 Peter 4:1–5. Should you go along with the crowd, participating in activities our society deems acceptable for youth... drinking, having sex, being irresponsible?

Why not? (v. 2)

How are people likely going to feel about you if you don't go along with the crowd (v. 4)?

Living under God's protection

When Meghan, Carol, and Jeff talked about going to the lighthouse, the idea of a man protecting a woman came up. Meghan told Jeff she didn't need a man to protect her, but before the night was over she was glad Jeff was along. Ladies, do you harbor an attitude of resentment towards men who try to protect you?

Read 1 Peter 3:7. The word weaker here refers to physical strength. Are you cognizant of the man's role in protecting women, whether in a large coed group of friends or on a date?

Read Psalm 91:9–16 and Luke 4:9–12. If God says He will protect us, does that give us permission to live dangerously?

Jesus clearly showed that it was a sin to purposefully put yourself in harm's way and expect God to save you from disaster. Did Meghan purposefully put herself in harm's way by swimming at the lighthouse at night?

Chapter Two: A Wonder to Behold

"School stinks," Jeff said, walking into the apartment.

I put my notebook down. "Of course it does. That's why we pay an enormous amount of money to attend. I do anyway."

"I just spent two and a half hours at a lead writing workshop. You know what I did? I wrote one sentence."

"How could that take two and a half hours?"

"There's only one way to write it. The right words in just the right order with perfect punctuation. I might not make it as a journalist."

"Yes, you will. How many people were still working on leads when you left?"

"Half the class."

"So all things considered, you did pretty well?"

"By some standards."

"I bet it will take you half the time next time, and by the third time you'll do it in two or three tries."

"I can't think about next time."

"How about a back rub?"

"I'm too tense."

"Isn't that the point?"

Jeff shrugged.

"Sit down."

He settled on the floor between my knees.

"Your muscles are in knots back here. I don't know how you made it home."

"In a stupor."

"I'm glad I was here. How's it feel?"

"I forgot what it felt like to be touched by a woman."

"Don't get weird on me. We're roommates."

"You are a woman, aren't you?"

"I'm your friend. Leave gender out of it."

"So you look at me as gender neutral?"

"I know you're a man, but you're off limits, the same as if you were married or dating someone."

Jeff turned to face me. "You've never looked at me and wondered what it would be like to date me?"

"Honestly? No."

I turned him back around and ran my fingers the length of his back.

"So you wouldn't be jealous if I was dating someone?" he asked.

I paused. "Would you be jealous if I was dating someone?"

"Not if it were just a date. If he were coming out of your room in the morning, maybe."

"So it's a sex thing? You don't care if I date someone, but it would bother you if I slept with them?"

"Maybe."

"You don't have to worry about that."

"Why?"

"I'm not sleeping with anyone till I'm married."

He turned back around to face me. "You're a virgin?"

"You're not?"

"There aren't many people our age who are."

I grabbed his shoulders and turned him around again. "Just like the bees. Each year there's fewer and fewer."

"Excuse me?"

"My dad gardens. He says the bees are disappearing. Not as many people have flowers in their yards. Too much work."

"Great analogy."

I pushed him forward. "Backrub's over."

"Are you mad?"

"Now that you have something to occupy your mind you don't need me."

"You think I'm going to think about you all afternoon?"

"Are you?"

"I think it's great you're a virgin. It shows you have..."

"...morals?" I offered.

"Legs of iron."

"So I haven't dated anyone strong enough to pry them apart?"

"Yeah."

"And I was afraid you didn't understand me."

"Let me rub your back," Jeff said.

"I don't think so."

"Come on."

"Nope."

"*Plleeeaassseeee*,"

"Oh, alright," I said, trading places with him. "But stay away from my scrapes."

He pulled up a corner of my shirt.

"How's it look?"

"It's scabbing over. Still looks pretty gnarly."

"If feels pretty gnarly."

"I think you should reconsider your dating policy," he said after a while.

"Which part?"

"The roommate clause."

"Why?"

"I'd like to take you on a date."

"The only reason I'm living with you is that I promised my parents I wouldn't date you."

"They don't need to know."

"I'm an open book. When someone in the family wants to know something about someone else, they call me."

"You can't keep a secret?"

"I won't lie."

"So as long as they have no reason to ask, you wouldn't have to lie to cover it up."

"A lie of omission is still a lie."

Jeff sighed. "Do you want me to ask you on a date or would you rather go through the logistics all afternoon?"

"You didn't hear a word I said, did you?"

"Would you go on a date with me, Meghan Marie Shanahan?"

"My middle name isn't Marie."

"Sue?"

I turned to face him. "Mabel. After my great-grandmother."

"Is that a yes, Meghan Mabel?"

"No. It isn't."

"If you need convincing..."

He leaned in to kiss me, but I put my hand over his lips and pushed him back.

"Are you asking me out because I'm a virgin? I wouldn't sleep with you either."

"I'm not trying to get in bed with you."

"I don't kiss on the first date. We haven't even been on a date."

"I'd bet you know me better than most of your first dates."

"Doesn't matter," I insisted.

He leaned back against the chair. "So where do you want to go?"

"I never said..."

"Tell you what. Think about it."

He picked up his bag and went to his room. When Carol came home a few minutes later I asked her to go for a run with me.

"If it's a short one," she said. "I've had a long day."

We ran the seven blocks to the beach and halfway to the pier before Carol gave me the signal she'd had enough.

"Are you too tired to walk?" I asked.

"No," she said. "A walk would feel good."

It was late afternoon and the waves were choppy. Students dotted the beach, sunbathing and reading and hanging out with friends. We started on the path, but between the bikers zigzagging around pedestrians and the dawdlers, we opted to walk through the parking lot instead.

"What made your day so long?"

"Wednesdays are always bad. I have three classes in the morning, lunch, then my three-hour ethics class."

"I think I'd like that. Is it an honors class?"

She nodded.

"Who teaches it?"

"Dr. Curtler."

"And you like him?"

"If he was thirty years younger, I'd marry him. I'm still pinching myself. This year is so much better than last."

"You mean as far as classes?"

"That and our apartment. Dorm life reeked."

"Have you met any guys?"

"I'm not looking..."

"At the students," I corrected.

She smiled. "I've got three years of school after my Bachelors."

"Someone asked me out, but I'm not sure I want to date him."

"Not your type?" she asked.

"He's friendly enough, but I don't want to start anything. It's nice to be unattached and concentrating on classes."

"Tell him that. If he wants to go to a movie, or dinner now and then, fine, but you're not looking for a husband."

"Do you think it can work, just hanging out?"

"We hang out with Jeff all the time."

"But when you're dating, just the two of you, doesn't it seem men want more?"

"I've never dated anyone, Meghan. I went to prom with a friend and my cousin. I could make something up, but I have no experience to counsel you with. If you want to stay unattached, tell him. You never know, he may turn out to be a good friend, maybe more."

"Are you sure you haven't dated?"

"I think I'd remember if I had."

We were just about to the pier when a man came up behind us and grabbed Carol's waist. Her scream drew stares from across the beach.

"Don't ever do that again!" she yelled.

The man laughed. "Paranoid, Carol?"

"Yes, when I'm attacked from behind."

"Next time I'll stomp my feet so you hear me coming."

"Or just say hi like the rest of the world."

"I'm Meghan," I said, holding out my hand.

"Daniel," he said, giving my hand a firm shake.

"Nice to meet you," I said.

"You, too. How are classes, Carol?"

"No complaints. How about you?"

"I'm in my program now. I love it. Why haven't I seen you in Allison?"

"I'm not on campus anymore."

"Nice. Moved out as a sophomore, huh?"

"It is."

"Well, if you get hungry for dorm food you know where to find me. Nice to meet you," he said, waving to me.

"You, too," I said.

"So?" I asked as we started back to the apartment.

"He worked in Allison Hall as a Food Service Worker. He dished my meals last year."

"And?"

"And he has a habit of coming up and grabbing me from behind."

"He likes you."

"Well I don't like him. I nearly drop dead every time he does that."

"You never know, he may turn out to be a really good friend, maybe even...."

"Don't say it."

"You said it to me."

"That's 'cause you're the type of woman men want to marry. Not date necessarily, but marry."

"What's that mean?"

"Just what you said. College guys are looking for a good time. You're more of a commitment person."

"For someone with no dating experience, you seem to have this figured out."

"I grew up with lawyer parents. That's got to be good for something."

"They gave you an analytical mind…a wonder for all to behold," I announced.

"At least I have something someone wants to behold."

We laughed and headed back to the apartment.

Bible Study Chapter Two

The concept of consecration

Read Numbers 33:51–52; 55–56. What two things were the Israelites to do when they took possession of Canaan (v. 52)?

When the Bible says the people who inhabited the land before the Israelites had carved images, cast idols, and high places, it means they worshiped false gods. Today our culture worships all kinds of things, but they aren't necessarily objects. What are some of the things our culture worships?

What did God warn would happen if the people didn't drive out the inhabitants of the land (v. 55)?

Read Deuteronomy 7:1–6. Why did God warn the children of Israel to not marry the heathen living in the land (v. 4)?

Look at the words God uses to describe His people in verse six. We are _____ to the Lord. He has _____ us out of all the people. We are His _____ possession.

My Bible explains holy as "separated from all corrupting people or things and consecrated totally to the Lord."[2]

God knew if the Israelites lived with people who did not know or follow God's laws, it would be likely the Israelites would fall into the sins of the other nations (which is exactly what happened when you read the Old Testament). Because of this, God wisely warned the people to set themselves apart so they weren't tempted.

Have you taken consecration (setting yourself apart from the world) seriously, or do you think you can be part of the world without it affecting you? Jesus told us to be in the world but not of the world. (John 15:19). Is that how you are living?

Boundaries— how should we feel about them?

Read Psalm 78:4–7. Who established the law? Who told parents to teach their children the commandments?

Read 2 Timothy 3:1–5. Think of your favorite TV shows, books, music. Do they glorify any of the behaviors Paul lists? If they do, what does Paul warn you to do? (v. 5)

Read Ephesians 6:1. Why should Meghan obey the boundaries her parents have set?

Read Ruth 3:1–6. Does the fourth commandment put a time frame on how long children should honor their parents or parental figure?

Read Colossians 3:20. Which of our parents' rules should we obey?

Did you notice a disclaimer in that passage about as long as you think the rule is fair, or as long as it doesn't mean you are the only one of your friends that has to do something? I didn't either!

Why didn't Meghan go to her parents for advice about whether or not to go on a date with Jeff?

Being trustworthy and the reason for dating

Read Proverbs 22:1. What does it mean to have a "good name"?

Where does keeping your promises and being a person who keeps her word fit into a "good name"?

Can you be trustworthy if you break your word often?

What is the ultimate purpose for dating (beyond meeting people and having something to do)?

Isn't the purpose of dating (for Christians) to find a spouse? Secular society will tell you to date to have a good time, to fulfill your sexual desires, to have someone to go places with. But, if

God tells us to save our sexual experiences for marriage, then we need to be careful of who we date, since spending time with people often leads to intimacy. It's important to look at each date as a potential husband or wife. What traits do you want in your future spouse?

Is Jeff what Meghan is looking for in a husband? Should she date him?

Chapter Three: The Raisin

The next afternoon, Jeff knocked on my door. I threw my notebook on the bed and went to see what he wanted.

"Are you busy?" he asked.

"Just trying to come up with an image for an airline ad."

"Can I come in?"

I hesitated.

"To talk."

I opened the door.

"Want a seat?" I asked, motioning to my computer chair.

He grabbed the chair, spun it around, and sat down on it backwards. "Nice chair."

"Thanks."

I sat across from him on my bed.

"Have you considered my offer?"

"For a date?"

"Yes."

"It would be helpful to know what you're looking for. I like hanging out with you, but then we don't need to go on a date for that."

"I want to get to know you better."

"But we live together. Your room is fifteen feet from mine."

"Why is that a problem?"

"What if we hit it off? Don't you see the temptation?"

"Not really. You can have sex anywhere. The couch could be a temptation. But if it would make you more comfortable, we just won't go in each other's room."

"That might be good."

"So...?"

"So let's go somewhere and not call it a date. Then I don't have to feel like I'm lying to my parents."

"Okay, we'll go on a raisin," Jeff said.

"A raisin?"

"Like a date, but not a date. I know just where I want to take you."

"Where?"

"It's a surprise. What time are you done with school tomorrow?"

"Two."

"We need to leave by four."

"What should I wear?"

"Clothes, I guess, although if you'd rather not, I won't object. Might have to change where we go, but ..."

"Ha ha. Casual?"

"Casual's good."

Jeff stood, turned the chair around, tucked it under my desk, then started walking toward the door. I stood to follow him. He stopped abruptly and turned around.

"We seem to keep finding ourselves this way," I said, my face inches from his.

"Maybe it's a sign. I was just going to take a last look...at your room that is, since I won't be seeing it from now on."

"Don't let me get in the way."

"No really, I think I like what I'm seeing better, anyway."

I smiled.

"Do you have class tonight?"

I nodded. "I have to leave in ten minutes."

"I'll let you get ready."

Jeff didn't seem the type to plan a secret date. Where would he take me? No time to waste wondering. I combed my hair and got my books together before going to the kitchen to make a sandwich. He was at the table.

"What time are you done?"

I grabbed the bread and headed for the fridge. "Nine."

"Do you want me to meet you?"

"Why?"

"So you don't have to walk home alone."

"You don't have class tonight, do you?"

"No, but I could do some research at the library."

I threw a couple pieces of deli turkey on my bread and considered. "You can if you want."

"I'll see you at the library at nine," Jeff said.

"If you're sure."

"I'm sure."

"See you then."

I took my sandwich and my bag and headed out the door.

"How was class?" Jeff asked, stomping his cigarette into the cement.

"Same old thing. You get the syllabus and wonder if it's possible to get it all done. How'd the research go?"

"I didn't do any. I have an assignment due tomorrow that I'm still working on, so bigger irons in the fire."

"You just got here?"

"Yep."

"That was nice of you."

"It's seventy degrees, and I went for a smoke break. I don't think I'll earn a halo for it."

"Not that halos can be earned or that they even exist for that matter, but even so, you won't be out here in January is what you're saying."

"Hard to say what January will bring."

I let my mind wander for a minute. As if reading my mind and willing me to stop, Jeff ran ahead to the next light post, grabbed it with both hands and hoisted his body so he was completely horizontal to the sidewalk. Except for his hands, he looked like he was lying sideways on the ground, but he was four feet in the air.

"Show off," I said, as I came to where he was.

"Let's see you do it," he said, letting himself down.

"How many bones do you think I could break trying?"

"You wouldn't break any bones."

"Well, you've impressed me. I've never seen that before."

"The first of many things you'll experience with me."

"Are you implying sex?"

Jeff kept walking, but when I didn't follow, he turned around.

"Sorry. Won't happen again," he said.

"I get the feeling you see me as a conquest," I said.

Jeff sighed. "Not true."

"Why should I believe you?"

"Because I just walked you home." He came back to where I was. "Or at least I walked you to within three blocks of our apartment."

"I don't know if I can trust you," I said.

"Well, I know one thing. I won't be waiting out here for you to make a point when it's thirty below zero."

"Play your cards right, and you won't have to," I said, starting to walk.

"Here we go."

"What's that mean?"

"Let the games begin."

"I'm not playing games."

"Stopping in the middle of the sidewalk to make a point isn't a game?"

"You're making comments about sex before we've been on a date!"

"Okay, okay. Best behavior. Got it."

At the apartment building, he opened the door. I went in but stopped after the first flight of stairs.

"What?" he asked.

"Just checking to see if you're looking at my butt."

"That's never bothered you before. Do you want me to go first so you can look at my butt?"

"Not really."

He motioned and I started up the steps.

I stopped at the next landing.

"Thanks for walking me home," I said.

"You're welcome."

"Are you glad you did?"

"I'll let you know."

We laughed and went down the hall to the apartment.

"Where are you going?" Carol asked, standing in my doorway as I got ready to go out with Jeff.

"I've got a..." I hesitated, putting on my blush.

"Date?!" she squealed.

"I thought I'd give him a chance, like you said."

Jeff came out of his room wearing jeans and a long-sleeved button-down shirt rolled at the sleeves and opened to show his tucked-in tee underneath. He came to my door and stood beside Carol.

"Where are *you* going?"

"I'm going to hang out with a friend," he answered.

"Male or female?" she prodded.

"Female."

"At quarter to four?"

"If I want any chance of sex on my sorry budget I need to get her to happy hour when it starts. Hopefully she'll be feeling loose by six."

"I haven't seen any women coming out of your room," I said.

"That's because you guys are always around."

"I doubt Jeff needs much room," Carol said. "There's not much to him. I doubt he needs much time either."

I put on a necklace and matching earrings.

"So, where are you going?" Carol asked.

"I don't know."

"You're going out with a guy you barely know, and you don't know where you're going? That doesn't sound too safe."

"I've got my phone."

"You could be killed before you get a chance to dial."

"I'll walk her downstairs," Jeff said. "Then I can check out this guy and threaten him if she's not home, untouched of course, by what? Eight, nine o'clock."

Carol clapped. "Very gentlemanly of you. Just try not to foam at the mouth, or drool, or frighten him away."

I grabbed my purse. "I'm off."

"Have fun," Carol said, "and remember if he's an octopus, go to the bathroom and give me a call. I'll come get you."

"You're awesome, Carol. See you later."

"Bye, Jeff," Carol called. "Remember to cover up your little guy so you don't bring anything funky home."

I stopped. "Caroline Nichols. You did *not* just say that!"

"We share a shower with him, Meghan. Who knows what the women he dates have."

I shook my head and followed Jeff out the door.

"What is it with you and Carol?" I asked, as we hurried down the stairs.

"Sibling rivalry."

"What are you fighting over?"

At the bottom of the steps he held the door and shrugged.

I went to the sidewalk and stopped. "Which way?"

He pointed to the left. "We'll take the train to Chicago."

The El stop was three blocks from our apartment and up two flights of stairs. Several other students were going into Chicago, too.

We sat next to each other on a bench along one side of the train, looking out the windows on the opposite side of the aisle. Tall apartment buildings lined the tracks. At one time they were probably nice, but now the paint was faded and the facade was dreary.

"I wonder about the people who live in these apartments," I said. "It wouldn't be bad if you were single or newly married or retired, but I can't imagine raising children here."

"After my dad died, I figured out where we lived wasn't nearly as important as being together. Sometimes having a place to call your own is enough."

"I always had a yard to play in...somewhere to sled and make snow forts in the winter and explore and do dance shows in the summer."

Jeff's face brightened. "Dance shows?"

"You know...dance around the front yard in front of a pretend audience. It's a little girl thing."

"You think you could do one of those dance shows for me later?" he asked.

"You bet. I'll get my baton and do cartwheels. Trust me, there's nothing sexy about it."

He looked back out the window. "I'd guess growing up in the inner city is a whole different ball game."

"I wonder how different I would be if I had grown up somewhere else."

"You'd be the same. You have a strong family. Lots of my friends in high school came from broken homes. Life gets more complicated when you factor in divorce or absent parents."

"None of my friends' parents were divorced. Do you suppose we migrate to people who have lives similar to our own?"

"Not in the case of Carol, you, and me."

"Seems unreal the way we ended up together, and that we get along despite the obvious differences."

"We all want a place that feels like home. Carol didn't have that growing up because her parents were always gone. Home for me was insecurity and trying to have enough food and money to make ends meet every month. You actually had a home that functioned like a home, and now you bring that to the apartment."

"There was a time when I was searching, too, when home wasn't enough."

"That surprises me."

"Everybody goes through something. I didn't think I was pretty enough."

"Not every guy wants Barbie"

"You might have told me that in tenth grade."

"You didn't ask."

We looked out the window.

"What are you looking for now?" Jeff asked.

"Nothing, really."

"You aren't, are you?"

"Not yet. Someday I'll be looking for my Prince Charming."

"Prince Charming doesn't exist."

"I don't mean literally.... I just mean I'm waiting for the guy who's perfect for me."

"If you're looking for perfection, you'll be waiting your whole life. And trust me, you'll never find it." He put his hand on my knee. "I'm looking better all the time, aren't I?"

I grimaced.

At our stop, Jeff stood and put his hand out for me to go first.

"You never told me what you're looking for," I said when we were off the El platform and walking down the street.

He shrugged. "I'm not sure."

"That's too bad."

"Isn't it?"

He grabbed a light post and hoisted himself up.

"Pathetic."

He slid back onto his feet. "I'm glad you have such a high self-esteem."

I smiled. "Just trying to be helpful."

"You're helpful, all right. You'll help me right off the dock."

"What dock?"

He pointed ahead several blocks to where the Chicago River flowed through the city. Jeff bought tickets, and we went down a ramp and onto one of the boats. A canvas canopy shaded us from the afternoon sun.

"This is better than anything I would have thought to do."

"I've seen these boats cruise along the lake and always thought it would be fun."

"If we're just hanging out as friends, I should pay for myself."

"We're on a raisin, and it's my job to pay for you. It may be old-fashioned and lower-class, but that's how I was raised."

"My dad says men should take care of women, too."

"Not many women want to be taken care of."

"Oh, I don't know. We do and we don't."

"So fickle."

I smiled.

"I'm glad you find that entertaining," Jeff said. "Try being a man and figuring it out."

We listened as the guide began the tour. The September afternoon cooperated with a calm that might be stifling in July, but on that day, the slight breeze on the open water was nothing short of perfect.

When the tour ended, the boat docked, and we climbed the ramp. Jeff led me through the streets to an Italian restaurant tucked into the corner of a building. It was sectioned off into quaint, dark little rooms, lit only by the candles on the tables.

"I guess we won't notice if we get a hair in our salad," I said as my eyes adjusted. "I wouldn't have had to wear makeup."

"You didn't need to put makeup on anyway. I usually see you without it."

"That's something I've never had a guy tell me."

"You don't wear much anyway," Jeff continued. "Makeup I mean. Unless we're skinny-dipping, and then you weren't wearing...well, anything."

"I'm remorseful about that," I said.

"As you should be."

"You never saw anything did you?"

"What?"

"When we were skinny-dipping. I never looked at you or Carol. Did you look at me?"

"Umm..."

"You've got to be kidding me."

"I'm a guy, Meghan."

"What did you see?" I demanded.

Our waitress approached the table. "Can I get you something to drink?" she asked.

Jeff looked at me.

"Chocolate milk," I said.

"I'll have a beer, whatever's on tap," he said.

The waitress checked his ID and left.

"Front or back?" I insisted.

"Chocolate milk?"

"It's my favorite drink."

"Well, this date is just full of firsts, isn't it?"

"You've never been with a date who's ordered chocolate milk?"

"I don't know. Maybe in third grade."

"You didn't answer my question."

"What question?"

"Front or back?" I demanded.

"You mean skinny-dipping?"

"You know what I mean."

"Side."

"Profile?"

"Yeah."

"When?"

"On the beach when we were getting dressed. I just happened to look in your direction as you put your shirt on."

"Wasn't it dark?"

"Of course it was dark."

"Then how did you see anything?"

"It must have been because you had the lights of the city behind you."

"I feel like I've been raped."

Jeff lowered his voice. "Don't even joke about that."

"You broke a trust."

"I glanced over to make sure you weren't being attacked."

"If that isn't the lamest excuse I've ever heard, I don't know what is."

The waitress came with our drinks and took our order.

"Don't be mad," Jeff said when she left.

"I didn't look at you," I said.

"Of course you didn't. You didn't know I existed until yesterday."

"Still, that's not fair."

"Well, I'll tell you what. I'll make it fair. When we leave here we can go somewhere, and I'll take off my pants."

"Ha. Ha."

"I'm serious. I don't want to have an unfair advantage."

"Jeff, I live with you and I don't even know if you wear boxers or briefs."

"Boxers mostly...."

"That's not the point," I said. "Don't you think I could know that if I wanted to?"

"I'm not following."

"I respect your privacy. I don't look when I'm not supposed to look."

"Line a thousand men up on the beach and tell them to get dressed next to a naked woman and three-fourths of them will sneak a peek. The other fourth are gay."

"I don't believe that."

"I do."

"I think there are some men who have enough integrity to not look."

"Okay. One out of a thousand would not look, and he'd go home and read his Bible and pray."

"He'd go home and have sex with his wife who respected that he hadn't been looking at other women."

"So you do have a sex drive?"

"Wouldn't you like to know?"

"Yes. I'm very interested to know about that."

"Is this the way you always treat women on the first date?"

"Well, this isn't a date. It's a raisin, and honestly, by now I usually know all about the woman's sex drive."

"Can we stop with the raisin?"

"Are you starting to loathe it?"

"I am. And a raisin by any other name is still a date."

Jeff laughed.

"What kind of women do you go out with anyway, that you know their sex drive immediately?"

"Human ones, mostly, who flirt and laugh and maybe even let me touch their hand."

"How do you know they aren't just playing the dating game? They might not like sex at all."

"How do I know you'd like sex?"

"Why aren't you with one of those girls tonight?"

"I don't know."

"I don't know either."

He took a long drink of his beer. "You intrigue me. You rant and correct and..." his tone softened, "care and think about other people."

I sighed. "To know me is to love me."

"Time will tell."

"I'm going to find the bathroom."

When I washed my hands, I paused at the mirror and turned sideways. How could I be so stupid? There was little of Jeff I hadn't seen, and yet.... I shook it off and started back to the table. As I sat down, I was thankful for the dark and for our food which had arrived and gave me something to concentrate on. When I looked up, Jeff was looking at me.

"What?" I asked.

"What are you thinking about?"

"The beach."

"And?"

"I've never seen a man naked, that's all."

"I didn't mean to look," he said turning back to his food.

"Yes, you did, or you wouldn't have."

"You're right."

"Would you do it again if we were on the beach tonight?"

"There's no good way for me to answer. If I say no it's an insult, and if I say yes it's an insult."

"Just tell me the truth."

"I'm very attracted to you."

"That doesn't answer the question."

"If we were on the beach tonight, after this conversation, I'd think about it but probably wouldn't."

"That's not an insult," I said.

"Whew," Jeff said, reaching for his beer.

Carol was on the couch when I walked in the door. Jeff said he'd walk around the block a couple times to keep her from getting suspicious.

"How'd it go?" she asked.

"It was awesome."

"Seriously?"

"We took a boat ride around the city. I'd go again, if you want to go. The tour guide talked about the history of the waterfront buildings and the city itself."

"No way!"

I nodded. "After the cruise, we went to eat at Cicero's."

"Where's that?"

I shrugged. "Downtown somewhere. It's an Italian place with awesome food and it was all dark except for candles. It was just like being in a little village restaurant."

"What'd you eat?"

"We had salads and split a pizza."

"You split a pizza. How romantic!"

"We split pizzas all the time, Carol."

"Yeah, you're right. Then what?"

"Then we took the El back and he walked me home."

"You took the El?"

"Yeah. Why?"

39

"I guess I thought he'd pick you up. Did he kiss you good night?"

"Yes. On my forehead, right after giving me a hug. Very gentleman-like, don't you think?"

"See if he has a brother."

"I'm not going to get too excited, but it was fun."

"What did he say when he left?"

"That he'd see me soon."

Carol snapped her fingers and sang, "Meghan's got a boyfriend. Meghan's got a boyfriend."

"No, I don't. It's been one date, and I don't want Jeff to know."

"Oh, yeah. Definitely keep him away from Jeff. Did Jeff know him when he walked you out?"

"Jeff knows him."

"And he knows you live with Jeff?"

"He knows."

"Do you ever wonder if we did the right thing letting Jeff live with us?" Carol asked.

"I didn't have anything to do with it."

"I told him he could stay the summer," she said. "You didn't fuss about him being here, or I probably would have looked for another roommate."

"The only reason I'm here is I assured my parents he wasn't my type."

"I'll agree with that. He's so …what's the word?"

"Masculine?" I offered.

Carol squinted. "Yeah. Kind of. He represents all the crap women don't like about men."

"I think he does it just to get under our skin. But I could be wrong. Time will tell."

The door opened, and Jeff came in.

"Hey," he said, plopping into the chair.

"Hey?" Carol said. "That doesn't sound like a greeting from a guy who just had sex."

"I'm curious, Carol. How does a person greet their roommates if he's just had sex?"

"Oh I don't know, a little pep in your step and badda bing to your ring."

"Were you listening to Snoop Dogg while we were gone?" I asked.

Jeff smiled at me. "How was your date? Did you come home with a little badda bing to your ring?"

"No. He was a dud."

"Really? A dud, huh?"

"Nothing for you to worry about. I'm going to bed."

"Good, cause I need to talk to Carol."

"It's no good," I said walking past him and giving him a wink. "I already told her not to tell you anything. If you want to know anything about my date, you'll have to come to me."

"You're so vain. What makes you think I was going to ask about you?"

"Sorry," I said, going to my room. I shut the door and fell on my bed. When I assured my parents I wouldn't date Jeff, I was telling the truth. At that point I never thought I would. It hadn't even been a month, and I'd already broken my word.

I rubbed my face. This wasn't happening. How was it I had been charmed by someone who seemed such a far cry from what Prince Charming was supposed to be?

Bible Study Chapter Three

The double-minded person and freedom in the law

In this chapter, we see Meghan oscillating between doing what's right and not holding to what she's been taught. She pushes Jeff to set the rule to not be in each other's bedrooms, but breaks her word to her parents about dating him. She doesn't let Jeff kiss her, but we read that she's been skinny-dipping with him.

Read James 1:6–8. What does the Bible have to say about "double-minded" people?

James makes a distinction between knowing the Word and actually doing what it says. James 1:25 says that the law gives what?

Keep a bookmark in James and flip to John 8:34. If the law is a set of rules how can it give you freedom?

Have you ever considered that the rules in your life are keeping you from becoming a slave to sin? Smoking, drinking, using drugs, gambling, pornography, etc. can all be very addictive. I tell my children that the key is to not do those things the first time. Once you start, you may become a slave to it. Not being addicted is freedom from it.

Go back to James 1:25. Write down the last part of verse 25. "The man who looks intently into the perfect law that gives freedom, and continues to do this, not forgetting _____

_____

_____."

There's another way that following the law gives freedom. It gives you freedom from guilt and worrying about being caught!

The Devil and his goals

When the Devil came to Eve in the garden (Genesis chapter three) what did he use to convince her to sin?

One of the ways the Devil is still leading us astray today is by having us question the sanity, the fairness, the effectiveness of the rules we have in our lives—rules designed to protect us. He's been doing this since the beginning of time!

Read 1 Peter 5:8. What is the Devil's goal?

Read 2 Corinthians 11:13–15. I think our biggest misconception is that evil comes in dark packages, that we'll be able to sense an ungodly person a hundred miles away. What does this passage teach us about evil?

Make note of this: A non-Christian is no more or less evil than we are, but a non-Christian lives by different rules. They live to please their sinful nature. Christians live to please God. Anyone can be funny, beautiful, or even caring. Do not think that an unbeliever will not have very alluring traits!

Guilt—it's purpose and how to deal with it

Meghan's conscience leaves her feeling guilty after her date. Read Hebrews 8:10–11. What gift did God give His people?

Read Romans 1:21–25. Does everyone have a conscience, and can the conscience be dulled or ignored?

Read Psalm 38:4 and 18. Why is feeling guilty good for us, and why does the Holy Spirit convict us?

Read Psalm 32:5 and fill in the blanks with the words forgiveness, guilt and repentance. One word needs to be used twice!_____ leads to _____ and _____ leads to _____.

Read Isaiah 6:1–7. Should we hold on to the guilt we feel over our sins? Why or why not?

Read Isaiah 30:15. Where is our salvation? Where is our strength?

Did you notice guilt wasn't included in this equation? Once we have repented (turned from our sin), we can put our guilt to rest. In quietness and trust we can believe our sins are forgiven—our guilt is gone and that gives us the strength to go on. If we continue on in our sin, our guilt should remain, convicting us to hopefully turn away from that sin.

Read Psalm 103:11–14. When we humble ourselves and have repentant hearts, how does God feel about us?

If Meghan was going to be obedient to her parents and God, what should she do about Jeff?

The consequence of sin

Read Numbers 13:26–14:4 and 14:26–35.

What was the consequence of the people not trusting God to give them the land of Canaan?

Read 2 Samuel 11:1–5 and 2 Samuel 12:13–18. Was David forgiven? (v. 13)

What was the consequence of David's sin with Bathsheba?

While it is true that God forgives our sin and takes away our guilt, there may be consequences for our actions that we have to live with. If you drive while you are drunk and get into an accident, the consequence may be living with your injuries. Meghan is feeling guilty about her choices. She had been skinny-dipping with Jeff, and she broke her word to her parents by going on a date him. She is just starting to realize some things can't be taken back. Once a person sees you naked, you can't take that back. Many people send provocative pictures to their boyfriend or girlfriend. It may seem to be not that big of a deal at the time, but once you send it, you have no control over it from there. Choices have consequences. When it comes to your body, it's best to keep it covered until you are in a situation where it is appropriate to show it. That situation is in the confines of marriage.

Think of some other common situations in high school and college where the choices you make have lasting consequences.

Chapter Four: The Whisper Theory

"I believed in God until my dad died," Jeff said, pulling another swatch of my hair into a braid.

"Seems to me that's when you needed Him most."

"What I needed was a dad."

"God is the perfect father."

"He can't play ball in the back yard."

"Didn't you have an older brother?"

"Two."

"So God provided...ouch! Are you trying to pull my head off?"

"Sorry. You have a snarl."

I handed him the comb.

"I can't imagine what you've been through, Jeff. And I'm not trying to minimize your pain."

"I appreciate that."

"But, blaming God isn't the answer. If your lifestyle is any indication of his, he was lucky to live to forty-nine."

He gave me the comb. "I didn't think you believed in luck."

"I don't."

"A lot of people live the same way and make it to eighty."

"A lot of people don't wear a seatbelt. That's fine if you don't get in an accident. A lot of people have unprotected sex. That may work a few times, but the next person has an STD. Is it God's fault they got it?"

"I'm not blaming God. Since Dad died, I haven't seen any evidence God exists. He certainly hasn't helped me. I've always had to work harder than everyone just to get the same things."

"You've always had a place to live and food to eat, clothes to wear."

"Secondhand clothes to wear, the generic food from a food shelf to eat."

"It kept you alive. God promises us daily bread, not steak and lobster."

He put an elastic in the braid and started on the other side. "Why would God let Mom struggle so much and work so hard just to get what she needed to raise her kids?"

"God didn't make your mom struggle. Living in this world is where the struggle comes from."

"He could have made it easier on her."

"He never said life would be easy. I worked two jobs all summer, and I already have my application in to be a professor's assistant. Likely, I'll still end up with loans." I thought for a couple seconds. "How does your mom feel about God?"

"She doesn't miss church."

"Because she's seen God answer her prayers."

"You give God too much credit. The government, not God, provided our food. People with plenty of money cleaned out their closet and gave their clothes away. That's not God."

"The government can't make food grow."

He groaned.

"But you're right. God isn't responsible for everything. He wasn't responsible for my swimming at night, but I *do* think He or one of His angels kept me from drowning."

"Not that you can prove that."

"You heard the officer. If you get caught in the undertow you'll spin until something pulls you out. I prayed, Jeff. That's all I could do when I was underwater. I'm not going to explain it away as coincidence. Faith is seeing with your heart, not your eyes. I bet God's spoken to you in many ways and at different times, but you've dismissed it as coincidence or fate."

"I do hear voices, but they always tell me to find a way to shut you up. Do you think that's God?"

"No. I don't."

"Then how can you be sure it's God talking to you?"

"God has always spoken to His people throughout the ages. Moses spoke to God face to face. Elijah heard a whisper in the cave. God spoke to Joseph in a dream."

"And you believe God speaks to you?"

"I do."

"Do you have to go in a cave to hear him whisper?"

"You have to be in the Word to hear Him whisper."

The door opened and Carol came in.

"What's up?" she asked.

"Meghan's trying to convince me that God's been talking to me," Jeff huffed.

Carol dropped her basket of laundry, spilling a shirt onto the couch. She walked over to where we were.

"Meghan, this is Jeff. Jeff, this is Meghan. When it comes to religion you have no common ground."

"I'm just trying to help Jeff see God's hand in his life."

"I've felt His hand. It's usually slapping me."

I shivered as he put an elastic in the braid on my neck.

"Thanks for making me pretty."

"I don't perform miracles, Meghan. I just braid hair."

"Are you saying I'm not attractive?"

"She wants to make sure you aren't gay," Carol added.

"You think I'm gay because I'm home on a Saturday night braiding my roommate's hair? I had a younger sister. It's called slave labor. Besides, what do you have against gay people? Carol's gay."

"I'm not gay, you idiot."

"Really? We didn't know."

"Don't drag me into it," I said.

"Is that why you never braid my hair?" Carol asked. "All this time, I thought it was because you had a crush on Meghan."

"I did, too," I said.

"I love you like I love my cigarettes." Jeff said, sliding his hands up my back and around my throat. "I can't live without you, but I know someday you'd kill me."

"Carol knows CPR."

"If you two start having sex, I'm moving out," Carol said.

"You can't move out. The lease is in your name," I reminded her.

"Meghan doesn't believe in having sex."

"You don't?"

"Not before marriage."

Carol looked at Jeff.

"She time-traveled here from the 1950s," he said.

"She can stay," Carol said. "You on the other hand..."

" ...will be living a life of celibacy until I find some loose chick with her own apartment," Jeff finished, then added under his breath, "God help me."

"How can you pray to a God you don't believe in?"

"I wasn't praying. I was using a figure of speech."

Jeff pushed me forward so he could stand up. "I'm going to the library."

"Why?"

"I have homework, and I can tell I'm not going to get it done here."

"I'll go, too," I said. "I have to start looking through ads for an assignment. Or did you want to be alone?"

"God, no. I might actually meet a woman."

"You shouldn't use God's name like that, Jeff," Carol said. "Meghan hates that." I nodded. "I do."

"Really?"

"It's disrespectful," I said.

"So God gets mad when I use His name?"

"Of course not. The sin is in misusing it, or using it like a curse word. How would you feel if your name was used that way?"

"That's the story of my life. Can we go now?"

"I'll get my stuff," I called, heading to my room.

"One of these days you should kiss her to shut her up."

"Carol, if I thought it would work, I would have already done it."

"Maybe you *should* have sex with her. She'd probably loosen up."

"You think?"

"I could hear you," I said, coming back into the room. "Carol, are you sure you don't want to come?"

"I'll get more done with you guys gone."

"Just what my mother always said," Jeff said. "Now if you'll excuse us, we're going to the library so Meghan can study and I can find new friends to live with."

We walked out and Jeff shut the door. "Did you know she wasn't gay?"

"Carol? She's just different," I said.

"I can hear you," she yelled.

We laughed and ran down the steps. Jeff nearly ran into a blond woman, a bit older than us, as we rounded the corner from the second floor. As we slowed to her speed, Jeff gave me a look that said, "check her out."

"She's probably got her own apartment," Jeff said when she went to her car and we turned toward campus.

"So you're hoping to move in with her? With her looks, odds are in favor of her already being spoken for."

Jeff lit a cigarette.

"How long have you been smoking?" I asked.

"About three seconds."

"Hilarious," I muttered.

"Six years."

"Have you tried to quit?"

"Have you tried to start?"

"It's one of my goals."

He handed the cigarette to me.

I put it in my mouth and sucked in. It burned all the way down my throat.

"You can have it," I said, handing it back to him.

"I never thought I'd see that," he said.

"If I can quit you can."

"Everything is easy to fix in your world."

"Just because your dad died doesn't mean you have to be miserable your whole life."

"I realize that."

I wrapped my arm in his. "I think you have the potential to be very happy."

"I know I do. I'm just not sure it will be with you."

I let my arm drop.

"Sometimes I wonder what we're doing," he said. "We couldn't be more opposite. This relationship has no future."

"I've told myself that a million times."

"Then let's keep this platonic."

"As in we date other people?"

"That's how it works."

"Will you be sleeping with other women?"

"It's a bit hard to say if I'll be sleeping with a woman I haven't met."

"You know I won't be sleeping with anyone."

"That's what you say now."

"I don't want platonic. If you want to date other people, then let's not date each other. I already feel I'm letting my parents down."

"The guilt that keeps on giving. That's religion for you."

"It's not my religion making me feel guilty. It's my conscience. Dating you is being duplicitous to my parents."

"That's not a word."

"It should be."

"But another tendency of religion. Make it up as you go along."

"If I made it up as I went along, I would have wiped out several people in my life a long time ago."

"We can all be glad you aren't God. You're far too flippant."

"When have I been flippant?"

"When haven't you? You move in with a guy, go skinny-dipping in the lake when you barely know me..."

"Carol was along."

"You have these high moral philosophies even you don't live up to."

"I could if you weren't always getting me into trouble."

"I didn't make you take your clothes off at the beach."

"You suggested it."

"Since when does a girl strip down the first time a guy suggests it?"

"Since the two nights previous she walked home dripping wet after swimming with her clothes on and the same person to suggest it also suggested no one could see in the dark anyway."

Jeff laughed. "You're so naïve."

"I should have listened to my mom."

"I like that you're naïve."

"I'm sure you do. Now stop using that word. I'm starting to loathe it."

Jeff opened the door to the library. "I hate the word *loathe*."

"I do, too."

We went to a study table at the back of the first floor. I set my bag on the table. Jeff sat across from me.

"As long as we're talking about my naiveté, did you notice the officer at the lighthouse checking me out?"

"Yep."

"Are you serious?"

"Are you interested?"

"I was shocked when Carol mentioned it and wondered if she was right."

"When you came out of the water, your shirt was glued to you and so were his eyes."

"That's nice."

"When you swim with clothes on, they stick to you when you get out. That's not a surprise to you, is it?"

"I have to quit swimming."

"Or at least wear a suit," Jeff offered, standing up. "I'm going to start my research."

"I'm going to find a rope."

"Were you planning on swinging from a chandelier?"

"Hanging myself."

"You're young," Jeff said. "You've got all kinds of embarrassment ahead."

"Thanks."

"What are friends for?"

"I'm starting to wonder that myself."

He grinned and walked away.

In frustration I wandered upstairs to the corridor of study rooms. There were several empty, so I went in one and shut the door. I took my phone out of my jeans and slid to the floor.

"What's wrong?" Mom asked.

"Jeff told me I'm naïve."

"I never saw that as bad."

"Great. You're agreeing with him."

"You're young and have a lot to learn. You probably *are* more naïve than Jeff. Think of all you've been protected from."

"I know. I just wish I knew how to act in situations so I didn't end up looking stupid when it's all said and done."

"Pray for wisdom," Mom said. "That's how you understand situations without experiencing them."

"I could use some of that."

When I hung up, I stayed on the floor praying.

"Where'd you go?" Jeff asked when I got back to the table.

"I called my mom."

"I've been worried about you."

"I'm flattered."

"Don't be. I'd be worried about any woman I brought somewhere only to leave for a few minutes and have her disappear. Especially if said person had just commented on hanging herself."

"Sorry. I'm just trying to figure out how to live."

He leaned across the table toward me. "Have I mentioned that I like that you're naïve?"

"A couple times, already."

"You're one of the few women on this campus that actually needs protecting. It makes me feel more like a man."

"I'm happy for you."

"I do what I can," Jeff said.

"You do what you can to what? Get me naked? Make me feel stupid?"

"It's all part of life."

"Part of life with Jeff Sanders, anyway."

"Take it or leave it."

"I may have to."

"Which?"

I shrugged and picked up my folder.

He shook his head. "Women."

I shook mine and huffed, "Men."

He laughed. "I think I like you."

"Of course you do. What's not to like?"

"Don't make me answer that."

At nine, we walked home. Jeff stayed outside the apartment to smoke. Carol was in her room, so I went to mine and got ready for bed. I waited till I heard Jeff come in before I turned out the light.

Bible Study Chapter Four

Hearing God's voice in our lives
Read Hebrews 1:1–2; and 2 Peter 1:21.

What is the one place we can always go and be absolutely sure we are hearing God's voice?

Does that mean we aren't capable of misinterpreting Scripture?

Read 2 Peter 2:1–3. Some people will explain the Word with their own interpretations. For instance, many denominations now say that the account in Genesis chapter one didn't really happen in six days, despite the fact that the Bible says, "there was evening and there was morning" to distinguish a twenty-four hour period. What does Peter call people who do this?

We don't want to start drawing our own interpretations from the Word and lead ourselves or others astray and become like the false teachers Peter was talking about.

Read John 14:26. Who helps us understand the Scriptures?

Read Acts 8:26–35. Who explained the Scriptures to the Ethiopian to help him understand what he couldn't?

Read Titus 2:1. Paul was writing to Titus, who was head of the church in Crete. What was one of Titus' main jobs as a pastor?

You'll find that not every pastor has been trained as a pastor. Some denominations require little or no training of their pastors. Some denominations do not believe the Bible is God's true, divine Word. It is important when you are seeking the advice of a pastor to know how he came to be a pastor. The same is true with those leading Bible studies. I've been teaching Bible studies for years. Part of my preparation for teaching is to study commentaries and studies from reputable people so I first make sure I understand what I'm teaching. My pastor or other pastors from my community have been instrumental in providing me with the materials I need to understand the Word better.

The more you study the Word, the more you will know the Word. The more you know the Word, the more you will be able to discern the influences in your life. Then you will more easily be able to recognize what has come from God's hand and what hasn't.

God's heart toward a perverse tongue

Read Proverbs 10:19–23. What is the lesson of verse 19?

Verse twenty compares a righteous tongue to choice silver. Is choice silver valuable? What is the flip side of that in the rest of the verse?

What do the lips of the righteous do? (v. 21)

How many people do they affect?

What does the Lord call a person who finds delight in evil conduct? (v. 23)

You are in that category, not just if you are the one to joke about perverse things, but if you find that type of joking amusing.

Read Proverbs 10:31–32. What phrase is used to describe people who speak perversely? (v. 32)

From these verses, we see God's heart toward perverse speech. He calls those who use it fools, wicked, and of little value, while those who keep their speech righteous are wise, nourishing, and of great value.

Read Matthew 12:33–37. What comes out of a person's mouth is an indicator of what? (v. 34)

Look at verse 36. Does God take perverse talk lightly? Should you?

Let's talk about sex

Read Ephesians 5:3–7. How much is too much when it comes to talking about sex or sexuality in a crude manner, or joking manner, or as a means of common conversation (v. 3)?

What is the warning in verses 6 and 7?

The footnote in my Bible says, "Although Christians live in normal social relationships with others, as did the Lord Jesus, they are not to participate in the sinful lifestyle of unbelievers."[3]

What course of action could Meghan take so as not to "partner" with her two perversely talking roommates?

Walking with the Lord requires time spent with Him

Read 1 Corinthians 10:12. Does Meghan feel strong spiritually?

Put a bookmark in 1 Corinthians, and turn to Joshua 1:8 and Psalm 1:1–2. In order to stay in tune with God, how often should we be in the Word?

Do you remember the lyrics to your favorite song four years ago? Can you rely on what you learned four or five years ago or more to keep you from falling into sin today? So many times, we study God's Word, get confirmed, but then fall into a spiritual desert. The problem with that is that if we aren't in the Word, we leave ourselves wide open to be brainwashed by this world. Since the Devil is called the prince of this world, we can ascertain that most of the concepts the world embraces are in opposition to God's Word.

Read 1 Corinthians 10:13. Being in the Word on a daily basis is how we stay strong spiritually. In addition to that, we also need to recognize temptation and steer clear of it. Where was Meghan's out with Jeff? Did she take it?

Do you think Meghan is in a spiritually hazardous situation with Jeff? Why or why not?

Chapter Five: Lily Menteen

"Where have you been?" Carol asked as I came into the apartment.

I looked from her to Jeff. "What did I forget?"

"The poetry reading," she said.

I looked at my watch. "If we run we'll only be a couple minutes late. Give me a minute to get my stuff."

"I'm leaving now," Jeff said. "I'm not a good runner."

"That's cause you always have a cigarette in your mouth," Carol said.

They were two blocks from the apartment when I caught up to them.

"Shall we?" I asked, jogging by.

"Fanatics," Jeff mumbled.

We were five minutes late and a little out of breath when we took our seats in McCormick Auditorium in the Norris University Center. A professor from the English Department was doing the introduction.

The poet was probably in his late forties or early fifties, with short brown hair and a graying, well trimmed beard. He offered simple language that danced and played and had subtle rhymes woven throughout. His even, confident, yet soft voice left us like full-bellied babies lulled into content. He left the stage and we rallied to move.

"Want to get a coffee?" Carol asked as the room cleared.

"It will be too busy here," Jeff said.

"We could go to Mel's."

"I can't stay long," Jeff said.

"I can't either."

Mel's Café, a coffee shop frequented by NU students, sat on a corner three blocks from Norris.

"I didn't know poetry could be so cool," I said, sitting at a table and rubbing my hands together.

"Are you kidding?" Jeff asked.

"The only poetry I've read was Keats and Whitman in freshman English," I said.

"Welcome to the twenty-first century."

"I would marry that man," Carol said.

"Not that you know anything about him," Jeff retorted. "He could be a whoring drunk for all you know."

She shrugged. "It would be nice to be surrounded by creativity."

"Poets need someone to inspire them," I said. "Maybe you're someone's inspiration waiting to be found."

"Wrong," Jeff interjected. "What poets need is someone to pay their bills."

Carol and I looked at him.

"I know lots of poets. Journalism majors and English majors are not exactly worlds apart—at least not until they reach the job market."

"Then set Carol up with a poet."

"It's against my morals."

"I wasn't aware you had any," Carol said, flagging down a waitress. "I need a coffee."

After the waitress took our order, Jeff elaborated. "Let's say I set Carol up with one of the guys I know pretty well. He ends up liking her—I know this is far-fetched, but bear with me—and she breaks his heart. Now I'm in an awkward situation. Or, what if I set her up with someone I know but not all that well, and he mistreats her? I'm in an equally awkward situation."

"Sounds like you've thought this out," I said.

"More or less."

"Or is it just too much work?" Carol determined.

"That, too."

"Hey," I remembered. "Aren't you wondering where I was earlier?"

"We were before," Jeff said. "Now we could care less."

"I went to see Lily Menteen."

"Who is Lily Menteen?" Carol asked.

"She's the old lady who sits in the window downstairs."

"I swear Meghan is a forty-year-old woman trapped in a nineteen-year-old's body," Jeff said to Carol. He turned to me. "How'd she know you weren't going to rob her?"

"I thought she might be suspicious, too, but she invited me in."

"Did her apartment look like Miss Havisham's mansion?" Jeff asked. "Minus the mansion."

"No. It's tidy, and modern. She said Earl repainted it and put new appliances in for her a couple years back."

"So if you live in Candlewood for thirty years, you eventually get new appliances? Good news, Carol—you only have twenty-nine to go."

Carol stuck her tongue out at him.

"She's only lived there for eight. Before that she lived with her husband in a big Victorian in downtown Chicago. I saw the pictures."

The waitress delivered our coffee.

"I never would have guessed that," Carol said. "I don't know why, but I had the same assumptions as Jeff."

"She had four children. One daughter, Anna, died in a car accident thirty-five years ago. Anna was married with two children at the time. One of the children died in the accident with her. Lily raised the other, her granddaughter Margaret, who is married to our prominent landlord, Earl."

"That's how she got the appliances," Carol surmised.

"It's all who you know," Jeff said.

"Then you better stick with me," I touted.

"And where are you going to get me?"

"Hopefully, heaven," I murmured.

Jeff sipped his coffee. "You want to comment?" he asked Carol.

She shook her head.

"I thought that was you," my friend Cindi said as she approached the table.

"Hey, Cindi."

"I saw you come into the reading," she said.

Jeff smirked and took another drink as if to say "you and everyone else in the auditorium."

"Jeff's always making us late," I teased.

Cindi smiled at him. "I can see that about you."

"Right," Jeff snorted. "Typical journalist, known for our inability to be on time, especially at Medill."

"More like anally on time," I said.

"*Anally* isn't a word," Jeff corrected.

"I didn't realize it was a word either...till I met Jeff," Carol said, giving me a fist bump.

"These are my roommates, Carol and Jeff," I explained.

"Sounds like you guys have plenty of fun," she said waving at a man rounding the corner from the restrooms. "Gotta go."

"See you Thursday," I said.

"How are you two friends?" Jeff asked when she was gone.

"She's in the graphic design program."

"She doesn't seem like your type."

"It's funny you say that. Girls like her blew me off in high school."

"She knows she's good looking, that's for sure," Carol commented.

"I don't care. Maybe she can see that about me. Anyway, she's got a boyfriend, Jeff, so you can quit staring."

"I want to get back to Lily," Carol said. "Why does she sit in that window all the time?"

I shrugged. "She reads a lot and crochets. Maybe it's the light."

"Maybe she's the neighborhood watch," Jeff suggested.

"Like *Rear Window*," Carol added.

"That's how she knew it was safe to let you in," Jeff concluded. "She's watched you more than you've watched her."

"I bet you're right."

"For once," Carol muttered.

"She'd like to meet you guys sometime."

"Tell her I work at the nursing home on Seventh, and she'll be there soon enough."

"She's a nice old lady, Jeff."

"Most of them are," he said. "Except for the royally witchy ones."

"Don't you wonder what those ladies were like in their day?" Carol asked.

"Nope. I just get them fed and put to bed."

"Are we talking about your work or your dating life?" Carol asked.

"I wish we were talking about my dating life."

"I would be interested to know if the crabby ones were always crabby," I said.

"I think it's medical," Jeff explained. "People who stroke out have personality changes, mostly for the bad, while a lot of dementia patients are happy-go-lucky and the Alzheimer's patients are more gruff, especially the men."

"You'll be a crab, Jeff," Carol said.

"If he makes it to old age," I added.

"Megan will be singing hymns and reciting Scripture, giving advice to all her caregivers," Carol said.

Jeff shook his head. "She'll be beaten to death by one of the Alzheimer's guys."

"Nice," I said, reaching for my coat.

Jeff looked at Carol and shrugged. "What?"

"Where's Carol?" I asked, walking into the apartment.

"She went to a play in Chicago. I made supper for us."

"What's the occasion?" I asked.

"I didn't know I needed one," he called as I put my bag and coat in my room. When I returned, Jeff handed me a glass.

"What's this?" I asked, sniffing it.

"Try it."

I took a sip.

"Do you like it?" he asked.

"It's not bad. What is it?"

"Cheap wine."

"I'm not legal for a year and a half."

"Don't worry. I won't tell."

"Where do you get the idea that as long as no one knows, it's okay?"

"No one waits until they're legal."

"Well, I have."

"Oh my…"

"Don't say it."

"I can't believe you've never drank."

"Well, none of my friends in high school drank and I lived at home during my first two years of college…which were also my last two years of high school."

"So you didn't have the opportunity?"

"Or desire."

Jeff dished meatloaf onto our plates.

"When did you have your first drink?" I asked.

"Prom, my senior year. I drank a quart of Schnapps."

"How'd that go?"

"It felt pretty good going down, not so good coming back up. Then again, I'm pretty sure that was the vodka."

"Did you puke on your date?"

"She had to go home right after the dance."

"You drank by yourself?"

"No. There were a bunch of us."

"Great meatloaf."

"It's my grandma's recipe."

I took a sip.

"How's the wine?"

"Good, regrettably."

Jeff dismissed the thought with a wave.

"Did you go to prom with your girlfriend?"

He nodded. "We dated most of our senior year."

"Was she your first?"

"Yep."

"How many girls have you dated?"

"Is that what you're asking?"

I smiled sheepishly.

"I've slept with two people."

"Did you date them long?"

"My last relationship lasted about four months. I dated my girlfriend from high school over a year."

"What happened?"

"We were young and finally realized we weren't very compatible. Have you dated?"

"I hung out with Eric during high school. I met Bill in college."

"And?"

I shrugged. "I'm still friends with both. I just don't see much of them anymore."

"Why?"

"College, I guess. They went their way, and I went mine."

"I always knew people like you existed."

"What do you mean?"

"You're so…"

I rolled my eyes. "Here we go again."

"Never mind."

We ate in silence for a minute.

"What are you going to do with your life?" Jeff asked. "Go into the Peace Corps, become a missionary…what?"

"I'm just trying to graduate. After that I'll figure it out."

Jeff stood and took our plates. I went to the sink and started filling it with water, but he reached behind me and shut it off. I turned to face him.

"No dishes tonight," he said.

He leaned in and put his lips on mine and held them there for just a moment before he put his hands on my face and began kissing me.

"This isn't your first kiss, is it?"

I felt my cheeks warm.

"Is it?" he persisted.

"I kissed a boy on the bus in seventh grade."

He leaned into me again and teased me with his lips, kissing me softly and slowly, before pulling away just enough to make me wonder if he was coming back. He lifted my face so I was looking into his eyes. I knew what he was asking and I knew how I should respond, and yet...

This time I pulled him to me. We were only kissing after all. There was no harm in that.

I went to my room right after morning classes. Jeff came and stood in the doorway.

"You might as well come in," I said.

"That isn't the way I meant for the night to go," he said.

"How *did* you plan for the night to go?"

"Just dinner, I guess, but you looked so good."

"I can't see you anymore."

"In my defense, I gave you the opportunity to stop."

"You were right."

"I was?"

"I can't trust myself."

He pulled me to him. I cuddled into his chest and he rubbed my back.

"I feel like I'm hanging onto my virginity by a thread."

"I've got a scissors if you want it cut."

"You all but did that last night. I'm just thankful Carol left the play at intermission."

"That was close," he said.

"I had no idea how powerful kissing could be."

"It is powerful."

"One more night like last night, and it's all over. Then you will have to marry me."

"I'm not getting married, Meghan."

I leaned back to look in his eyes.

"I don't want to lead you on," he said. "I've got two or three years left of school. I'm just hanging out with you till something better comes along."

I pushed him away, but he pulled me back into his arms.

"If you still want to date, it is with the understanding we are not going to do what we did last night."

"You need to loosen up," he said. "We kissed. We messed around a little. You're still a virgin."

"You're right. I think too much. I thought you were trying to have sex with me last night. You weren't. You were just trying to see me naked...again."

"Let's settle this right now," he said unbuttoning his pants.

"I'm not looking," I said covering my eyes.

"I shouldn't have looked at you that night on the beach. We're going to make it even."

I could hear him taking his pants off.

"I didn't look at you because of my integrity. That is still intact, though after last night barely. I think it would be best if you put your pants on."

He didn't move.

"I said I'm not looking."

"You had your chance."

I heard him stepping into his jeans. I let my fingers open just a crack.

"Caught you!" he cried.

"Congratulations," I said. "You might be able to have children some day. You saw me naked. What are you trying to prove by showing me your boxers?"

"Do you want to see the real deal?"

"Would you really show me?"

"If you want I can take these off right now."

"Get dressed," I said.

"Only if you're sure."

"I'm sure."

He buttoned his pants and sat down on my bed. "There's a vibe between us that blows my mind."

"Opposites attract. Now get off my bed."

He stood up. "I like feisty. It turns me on."

"It doesn't take much, does it?"

"Not with you," he said.

Bible Study Chapter Five

The elderly

Read Leviticus 19:32. How are we to treat the elderly?

Read Proverbs 16:31. This verse offers a very different view of old age than we're used to. What are some of the terms our society uses for those who are old?

Read 2 Kings 2:23–24. What was the sin of the young people?

You may read this and be appalled at Elisha. It's important to note that these were likely teens or young men who were not making an issue about the amount of hair on Elisha's head, but rather were rejecting him as Elijah's replacement, or a prophet at all. The "curse" he uttered was probably something like, "may the Lord deal with you." In that way he gave it over to the Lord who executed judgment on his behalf. Even if his curse was directly related to the mauling of the youths, the fact that the curse was fulfilled established him as Israel's prophet and God's representative, and serves as an example of the impending judgment that will come to any and all who reject God.[4]

Read 1 Kings 12:1–11. Who had the more godly advice, the elders or the young men?

Do you seek the advice of older people when you have a dilemma in your life?

Temptation

Read James 1:13–15. James describes three stages of temptation. What are they?

My Bible uses 2 Samuel 11:2–17 to illustrate this process. How is David first tempted?

When he sends someone to inquire about Bathsheba what is he told? (v. 3)

What does he do?

What is the motivation behind bringing Uriah home?

Notice the progression from desire to sin to death. Since David did not deal with his sinful desire, even ignoring his servant's words ("is this not the wife of Uriah?") the desire progressed to sin. Since he did not deal with his sin (confessing to Uriah what he had done, humbling himself before the Lord) his sin progressed to the point where David would do anything, even kill another man to cover his sin.

Contrast David's actions to Joseph's in Genesis 39:6–12.

Joseph shows us how to keep desire from conceiving and giving birth to sin. What did Joseph do?

Read 2 Timothy 2:22. What course of action does Paul give you to keep from sinning?

Paul doesn't say mosey away from evil. He doesn't say see if you can withstand the temptation. He says be like Joseph and *flee!* Don't look back!

What is the first rule Meghan broke during her evening with Jeff?

When she tried the wine, did she like it?

What has Jeff's theory been as far as why Meghan hasn't had sex or hasn't had alcohol to drink?

Did her actions prove him right or wrong?

Read 1 John 5:3–4. We've already talked in chapter three about the freedoms God's rules give us...freedom from emotional baggage, from STDs, from addiction. From this passage, why should we obey God's rules and boundaries?

Think again about Joseph's situation. He had opportunity to sleep with Potiphar's wife, but he didn't because of his love for God. God rewarded him richly for not sleeping with another man's wife. God saw Joseph's character and eventually put all of Egypt beneath him.

It's one thing to know the rules. It's better to determine why you are going to follow the rules before you are tempted, or, like Meghan, in the heat of the moment you may lose sight of what you're doing. It certainly is going to be easier, at the time, to break the rules. When everyone else is drinking, it is going to be easier to drink. When you're with someone who wants to have sex, it's going to be easy to go along with them and have sex. But if you trust God and love Him, you know He's got your best interests in mind, and you'll obey His laws because of it.

Dabbling with sin
Read 1 John 1:5–7. Is it okay to "try out" sins?

What are we living if we claim to be Christians yet partake in the sins around us? (v. 6)

Read John 3:20–21. What does it tell you about what you're doing if it requires closed doors or no one else around?

Is there such a thing as "just a little sin"? Jeff reassured Meghan that they didn't do anything wrong because they hadn't had sex. If she didn't have some of her clothes on, do you think they were being sexual, whether or not what we call "sex" happened? Jesus said in Matthew 5:27–28, "You have heard that it was said, 'Do not commit adultery.' But I tell you that anyone who looks at a woman lustfully has already committed adultery with her in his heart." It isn't just doing the sin that is wrong. Wanting to sin is just as wrong.

When you are living according to God's laws, do you ever have to worry about being caught?

What are some common sins young people in high school and college try?

What plan of action do you have to combat that sin when confronted with it?

Read Acts 19:13–16. This is a wonderful example of why we shouldn't thumb our noses at temptation or evil. The forces of evil are very powerful, and though we may feel we are able to withstand anything the Devil or this world could throw at us, we may just end up beaten and bleeding like the Jews in this account. If you don't want to fall into sin, avoid temptations and when they come upon you, flee from them!

Chapter Six: Chilled

Winter was officially two months away, but during a cold spell in late October, temperatures dipped to single digits and wind chills left little room for dawdling. With campus five blocks away, Jeff, Carol, and I bundled and we hurried, and hoped for warmer fall days.

"I'm going out tonight," I announced from Carol's doorway while putting on my jacket.

Carol looked up from a pile of books. "You're going out on a Tuesday?"

"Professor Hollis asked me out. He's hired me as his assistant."

"Where are you going?"

"Probably Ed's. He'll give me a ride home, I'm sure."

"Is he married?"

"I think."

"So what's with the skirt?"

"I was going for the professional look."

"It's a little short for that."

"It's just about knee-length. That's acceptable, isn't it?"

"When your office is a bar?"

"He's an old man, Carol. He's not interested in a college student."

"You've heard of dirty old men? They live for fresh meat."

"I'm sure this is strictly professional."

"If you start thinking otherwise, give me a call. I'll take a cab and pick you up."

It only took a few seconds to realize my mistake. Heels prevented me not only from running, but from moving quickly at all, and nylons offered little barrier from the cold. When I finally took a seat in the lecture hall, my legs burned from exposure. After class I went to the faculty offices on the second floor.

Professor Mark Hollis' office door was ajar. He was at his desk.

I knocked on the door frame. "Professor Hollis?"

"Come in and sit down. You look nice. And call me Mark."

"If I had it to do over again, I'd be wearing pants. This skirt isn't wind chill friendly."

He laughed. "Fashionable or sensible. Always a dilemma."

I sat on the brown leather loveseat beside his desk. Two framed pictures of Italy hung on the opposite wall.

"Look at this," he said, handing me a student's project. "Tell me what's profound about this."

It was a circle with "Brown printing" in it. Underneath it were the words "we print whatever you think."

I wasn't sure what he wanted me to say.

"A name in a circle is not a logo. It's a name in a circle," he said at last.

"I guess we've got a lot to learn."

"Some people have more to learn than others."

I handed the paper back.

He opened his briefcase and put the papers in. "Shall we?"

I nodded.

Each step I took echoed in the empty halls.

"I won't be sneaking up on anyone tonight."

"You don't get away with much in these halls early in the morning or late at night."

"Not that I'd want to."

"Nor was I implying."

Mark let me stay inside while he crossed the parking lot to his jeep. He pulled up to the door and moved a stack of papers so I could sit in the front seat.

"Do you want to go to the Silverado Hotel?" he asked. "They have a little bar there."

Hotel? Why would he want to take me to a hotel?

"How about Ed's?" I suggested.

"We could go there."

Ed's Attic was on the outskirts of campus. It was a two-story bar with dining on the first floor. Mark ushered me in the door and up the stairs. We sat at a table toward the back of the bar away from the pool tables and dart boards.

Mark knew the waitress, a woman closer to his age than mine.

"Are you staying out of trouble?" he asked her.

"Oh no," she answered with a raspy chuckle.

"That a girl."

"What are you drinking tonight?"

"Scotch," he said.

"And you?" the waitress asked.

"I'll have a strawberry daiquiri."

"Coming up," she said.

"You like the fruity drinks?"

"I don't drink much," I answered, thankful she hadn't asked for an ID.

We had barely taken our coats off when she returned with our drinks.

"Tell me about the job," I said, taking a sip.

"Don't worry. It's mostly secretarial stuff. Some weeks we'll have more for you to do than others. When you have extra time, I'll let you help me write grants."

"Write grants?"

"It's a lot of fill in the blanks."

"I was always good at fill in the blanks."

"Perfect."

Mark drank his scotch in a few swallows.

"Would you like another?" he asked, flagging the waitress.

"I've barely started this one."

"It's on me," he said. "What do you want…a screwdriver, sex on the beach?"

My cheeks burned.

"Give her a sex on the beach," he said. "I'll have another scotch." He turned to me. "Where are you from?"

"Just outside of Madison."

"Not much of a leap to Northwestern."

"My high school English teacher talked me into NU."

"Must have been a good teacher."

I shrugged. "He convinced me the extra money for tuition would pay off in the long run. To be determined, I guess."

The waitress brought our drinks.

"How is it?" he asked.

"Strong," I answered, catching my breath, "for a fruity drink."

He chuckled. Over the course of the next hour, he told me about his wife and two kids and about going to Italy every four or five years to teach. I finished my second drink and thought we were about to call it a night when he waved to the waitress and ordered me another.

"I don't think I need this," I said when she put it in front of me.

"It's on me," he said.

"And that makes a difference how?"

He laughed. "You're logical, aren't you?"

"I try to be. Anyway, you've stopped drinking."

"I have to drive. I can't afford a DUI."

"Who can?"

"Point taken," he said.

I debated if I should take a drink, but didn't want to be rude.

"I don't think I'll make it as a drinker," I said, after a taste.

He smiled. "Some tastes need to be acquired."

"I'm not sure that's one of my goals."

"What are your goals?"

"Graduate, get married, have kids."

He cringed. "You don't want to get married and you do not want to have kids any time soon."

"Why?"

He shook his head. "Have fun. Travel the world. You can come stay with me in Italy for a while. I'll show you around."

"I'm sure your wife would love that."

"She'd get over it."

When my drink was gone, Mark paid the waitress. I stood to leave and stumbled over my purse. He caught me.

"Thanks," I said, steadying myself.

He recovered my purse from the floor and held my coat. Once it was on, he motioned for me to lead the way.

"What are you guys doing here?" I asked as we approached Jeff and Carol at a table just a little ways from where Mark and I had been.

"Just out for a drink," Carol replied.

"Mark, these are my roommates, Carol and Jeff."

"Nice to meet you," Mark said.

"Are you going to be here long?" I asked.

Jeff looked at his watch. "I need to get home," he said.

"I might as well go with them," I said.

"Good enough," Mark said. "I'll see you tomorrow."

Carol slid over and I sat next to her.

"Were you spying on me?"

"How much have you had to drink?" Carol asked.

"Too much."

"I thought I was the only heathen in the abode," Jeff said.

"I'll go ask the bartender to call a cab," Carol said.

I let her out and unzipped my coat as I sat back down.

"Were you going to sleep with him?" Jeff snarled. "Or was this just about making me jealous?"

"Are you kidding? I came here to talk about my job. He's a married man."

"What are you doing dressing like that to go out with a married man? You've never dressed like that for me."

"Why would I put on a skirt and heels to go out with you?"

"If we hadn't come, he'd be all over you right now."

"I beg to differ."

"Why do you think he bought you all those drinks? If he came to talk, wouldn't you have had one drink and called it a night? Good grief, Meghan."

Carol came back. "It will be ten minutes," she said.

"Let's walk," Jeff said.

"It's too cold," I said.

"Maybe you'd sober up."

"I sobered up the minute I started talking to you."

"What's going on? Are you guys fighting because of Cindi?"

"Why would we be fighting about Cindi?" I asked.

"You probably don't approve of Jeff going out with her."

I glared at Jeff. "You're dating her?"

"No."

Carol gasped. "Are you kidding? Why not?"

"She's not my type."

"You couldn't keep your eyes off of her when we were at Mel's," Carol said. "I can't believe you turned her down. You're worried she'd talk to Meghan, aren't you?"

"That's it, Carol. You've figured it out."

"Cindi asked you out? What happened to the guy she was with?" I asked.

"She wouldn't have dumped him for Jeff, so he must have broke up with her," Carol said.

Jeff reached for his coat. "As fun as it's been watching Meghan dote over a man three times her age I think I'm ready to call it a night."

We went downstairs to wait for the cab.

I woke up and rolled over. It wasn't so much nausea I was feeling as the impression of going downhill on a roller coaster. In the bathroom I splashed my face with cool water and brushed my teeth.

Carol had made coffee. I turned the coffeemaker off and poured the bit that was left down the drain. Now I was nauseated. I put a slice of bread in the toaster and waited.

Jeff went from his room to the bathroom, then back to his room. He returned a few minutes later buttoning a flannel shirt.

I took a clean dishcloth from the drawer, ran some cold water on it, and put it on my forehead. "Tell me what happened with Cindi."

"She came up to me at Norris and asked if I would be interested in getting together."

"What did you say?"

"That I was dating someone."

"What did she say?"

"If it didn't work out to keep her in mind."

I grabbed my toast. "What a friend. She knows we're together."

Jeff leaned against the counter. "What was going through your head last night?"

"Apparently a fair amount of alcohol."

"You weren't drinking when you made the plans."

"He asked me to go out for a drink to talk about my job. What was I supposed to say?"

"That you aren't legal, and you could talk it over someday in the library, Norris, any other public place. And what were you thinking when you got dressed?"

"I wanted to look nice."

"You have no idea how men think."

"You've got that right."

"I'm just glad I came home when I did so we could come get you."

"I would have made it home."

"How do you know? You don't know anything about him. Who knows what he'd do with an attractive girl with a short skirt who couldn't keep her legs crossed."

"Excuse me?"

"You didn't in the cab. Why would you have in his car?"

"He has a Jeep."

"That's worse."

"How so?"

"More room."

"You've got to be joking." I ran the cloth under cold water again. "Then again, I guess you'd know."

He went to his room and shut the door. Immediately I regretted my words. It was the perfect way to start an utterly crappy day. Worse, it was the first day of my new job, and the last person I wanted to see was Professor Mark Hollis.

After my Print Advertising class the following Monday, Professor Oakly asked to have a word with me. She allowed the room to clear before shutting the door and leaning on a desk across from me.

"I heard you're Mark's new assistant."

I nodded.

"Mark does a wonderful job as the department chair. It's a lot of work, so he doesn't have to twist anyone's arm to hold the position, but there have been issues with previous assistants."

"What sort of issues?"

"He isn't afraid to cross any lines. Like you, the other ladies were old enough to make their own decisions, but he puts himself out there."

I felt queasy.

"You don't have to work in his office. There's a faculty room a few doors down. It has everything you could need, and it has the extra advantage of faculty coming in and out on a regular basis. As long as you set the boundaries, you won't have anything to worry about."

"Thanks for letting me know."

"You're welcome," she said. "Have fun. Just be careful."

Jeff and I had managed to avoid each other for almost a week. Carol must have felt like she was living in a revolving door. When one of us came in, the other left. In the moments we were both home, we stayed in our rooms with our doors shut. Thankfully we were far enough into the semester that we had enough to keep us busy.

When I got back to the apartment I knocked on Jeff's door.

"Come in."

He was on his beanbag, working on his laptop. I sat on his unmade bed.

"Apparently your suspicions about Mark were not unfounded."

"Who's Mark?"

"Professor Hollis. I've been warned he's not afraid to get involved with his assistants."

"You didn't put yourself in a very good situation."

"Thanks for coming to get me. I can't even imagine how awkward it would have been if he had tried something."

"You can't keep assuming everyone thinks like you."

I wanted to shift some of the blame from me. "Why didn't you tell me Cindi had asked you out?"

"Why are you friends with her?"

"I guess I hoped at some point I might be able to point her in the right direction."

"I don't think she wants to hear what you have to say."

"Most people don't."

"I don't always want to hear it, but you make me think."

I sighed.

"Carol and I fought the whole way to Ed's. I wouldn't believe you were there, especially with a married man. When I saw you drinking and flirting and dressed like that..." He shook his head.

"I didn't think I was flirting...obviously it was a lapse of judgment."

"You are mature in so many ways, and stupid in so many others."

"I know. I'm sorry about the jeep comment."

"I can't change that I've had sex. If you want, you can sleep with someone so we're even."

"Who would I sleep with?"

"There's always Mark."

"I'd have to be more than drunk. Unconscious maybe."

"That defeats the purpose."

"What's the deal with getting a girl drunk and wanting sex?"

"Drinking weakens your inhibitions so you let down your guard."

"That's sinister. Was that your intention the night we were together?"

"No."

"So I don't have to worry about you trying to get me drunk and in your bed?"

"You're already in my bed."

"You know what I mean."

"You are going to marry a nice man someday."

"You are a nice man."

He shook his head.

I walked over and kneeled next to the beanbag.

"You are a nice man."

"I'm glad you think so."

"Why don't you think you are?"

"Forget it. Let's get something to eat."

"It's cold out."

"Get used to it. It will be for the next four months."

"That's a cheery thought."

"I'm from Michigan. We're born with antifreeze in our veins."

"Remind me not to suck your blood."

He raised his eyebrows and logged off his computer.

"Jeff?"

"Yeah?"

"Do you want to date Cindi?"

"I'm not interested in her." He shut his laptop.

I leaned in and kissed him.

"What's that for?" he asked.

"For protecting me."

"Knock it off or you will need protection."

I helped him up, and we headed into the frigid air, walking arm-in-arm to Norris. For the first time in a week, I didn't mind the cold.

Bible Study Chapter Six

The effects of alcohol

Read Genesis 6:9 and Genesis 9:20–23.

What kind of man was Noah? (6:9) What happened to him when he drank?

Read Genesis 19:30–36. What did Lot do when he was drunk? Did he realize what he had done?

Both of these Biblical examples show how alcohol affects our judgment. Noah, an otherwise morally righteous man, forgot modesty. Lot unknowingly impregnated his daughters. If these two men had lapses of judgment when they drank, should we assume drinking would or could lead to lapses of judgment with us?

Read Ephesians 5:15–18. Fill in these blanks. Paul tells us to be wise and make the most of every _____. He tells us to understand the Lord's _____, not to get _____ on wine, but to be _____ with the _____. In comparison, foolish living will result in wasted opportunities for the kingdom of God and missed blessing in our lives.

Notice Paul's wording of verse 18. He doesn't say, "Do not get drunk on wine which *may* lead to debauchery." He said getting drunk *leads* to debauchery. What is debauchery?

What did Jeff tell Meghan she could have done differently to avoid the situation she'd been in with Professor Hollis?

Was that good advice?

God will work through anyone

In the book of Nehemiah, God used a heathen king to supply all the material Nehemiah needed to rebuild the walls of Jerusalem. In the book of Esther, God used a heathen king to save the Jewish people.

Read 2 Chronicles 36:22. Who moved the king's heart?

Who rescued Meghan from a bad situation that could have become even worse?

Sometimes God works through people who don't acknowledge Him to work for the good of the saints.

Modesty

Read 1 Timothy 2:9–10. Paul says to dress with decency, modesty, and propriety. My dictionary explains these terms this way: "not obscene, respectable, not vain or boastful, reserved, proper."[5]

Both Carol and Jeff questioned the way Meghan dressed to go out with Professor Hollis. What did they question about her outfit?

Dressing modestly means covering what parts of your body?

Was Meghan's outfit practical in light of the weather?

What was her reasoning for dressing the way she did?

Her outfit fell short of which of the terms from the passage above?

What does Paul say we should clothe ourselves with and why?

Read 1 Peter 3:3–4. When you try to impress people with your clothes, people will notice your clothes. It would be far more glorifying to God if they noticed what about you instead?

Chapter Seven: The Blond No One Knew

I was at my desk working on my laptop when the door to my room flew open and Carol shrieked, "Meghan, that girl from the second floor with the long blond hair is outside on the lawn, and I think she's dead."

"What are you talking about?" I asked, jumping from my chair.

She opened my shades. "Look! Cops everywhere."

"I didn't hear sirens."

"They don't put sirens on when someone's dead. She's covered up now! She wasn't a few minutes ago. Do you think we have a murderer in the building?"

"Why would you think that?" I asked, lowering my voice to a whisper. "The cops are talking to Jeff."

"They'll question anyone coming in or out of the building," she said. "They're sending him around back."

"I'm going to see Lily."

"What? Why?"

"She might have seen or heard something."

"You can't go alone."

"Why not?"

"If I've learned anything from lawyer parents, it's that you don't get caught up knowing anything and have it be your word against someone else's...especially when it comes to murder."

"Quit being so dramatic. Anyway, Lily wouldn't turn on me."

"Are you willing to bet your life on it?"

"Seriously, Carol," I mumbled, walking out of my room.

I met Jeff between floors.

"Where are you going?"

"To see Lily," I said. "Come with me."

"Do I have to?"

"I want to know if she saw anything."

Jeff sighed and followed me down the steps. An officer was posted at the exit and another was in the entry by the hall that led to the first floor apartments.

"Where are you going?" the officer asked.

"There's an elderly lady in this first apartment. With the excitement I want to check on her."

I knocked on Lily's door.

"Oh my," she said when she saw us. "What's the commotion?"

"Carol said that blond girl from the second floor is on the lawn...dead. Did you hear or see anything?"

"I heard shouting a while ago, but it only lasted a minute."

The officer came over. "Was it two women shouting?"

Lily shook her head. "A man and a woman. I didn't catch what they were fighting about. I just heard raised voices."

"When was that?" he asked.

"It must have been a half hour or so ago."

Earl walked between Jeff and me and put a hand on Lily's shoulder. "Did you see something?"

She shook her head.

Jeff nudged me and we excused ourselves to go back to our apartment.

"Did she see anything?" Carol asked when we came in.

I shook my head. "She heard a man and a woman fighting."

"I wouldn't want to get involved either," Carol said.

"I think she knows more than she's saying, too. She seemed to be thinking about something," Jeff said.

"As of right now, the only thing we know for sure is that two people got into a fight. It may not have even been her," I said.

"Or she was fighting with someone who decided to snuff her," Carol decided. "Hopefully it was her boyfriend. Better that than some crazy hanging out watching the people in the building. This whole thing gives me the heebie-jeebies."

"I feel bad we never knew her name," I lamented.

"After the news breaks, you'll never forget it," Jeff said.

I looked at my watch. "I've got to get ready."

"For?"

"I have class tonight. Do you want to come so I don't have to go alone or would you rather sit here and see what happens?"

"I suppose I could go to the library," Jeff decided.

"Let's go to the gym," Carol said.

"Who invited you?"

"I'm not staying in this apartment by myself!"

"With all the police, it's probably the safest it's ever been," I pointed out.

"I don't care. I'm still not staying here alone."

"This will change everything," Jeff predicted.

"How so?" I asked.

"When someone is killed in your building, things are bound to change."

"Do you really think she was killed? Maybe she overdosed."

"Why would she be in the front yard if she overdosed?" Carol asked. "Wouldn't she take her pills and go to bed?"

"If she was partying with a bunch of friends..."

"In the middle of the afternoon?" Jeff challenged.

The front entrance was roped off with yellow police ribbon. An officer directed us to the back door. When we came around the building we saw reporters and camera crews working from across the street, questioning police officers and neighbors.

"At least no one cares what we look like right now," Jeff said.

"My mom might be a little freaked if she turns on the evening news and sees me exiting the building where a murder took place today. I better call her," Carol said, grabbing her phone.

"*If* it was murder," I corrected.

"Do you think Earl did it?" Jeff asked.

"What?"

"Do you think Earl killed her?"

"Why would I think that?"

"He looked nervous."

"Of course he looked nervous. A girl died outside his apartment building today. He'll come under all sorts of scrutiny now. They'll look at the doors, the security, the condition of the building. Anyway, Lily would have recognized his voice."

"It was more than concern for his building. He was trying to act cool, but his eye was twitching and when he put his arm on Lily's shoulder, I saw a wet spot where he had sweat through his shirt."

"If he did kill her, we're all in trouble."

"Not necessarily."

My phone rang. "Hi, Mom."

"Your dad is watching the evening news. Did a girl die outside your apartment building?"

"Unfortunately."

"Did she live there?" Mom asked.

"Second floor."

"They said 'suspicious death' and 'foul play has not been ruled out.' "

"Really? That's what they said?"

"Do you think you should get a hotel room tonight? Dad and I will pay for it."

"Our building is crawling with police. It's never been so safe."

"What if someone in the building is preying on young girls?"

"We've got Jeff," I said.

"That's not going to matter if they sneak in during the night and slit your throat."

"You're making me feel much better."

"Meghan, this isn't funny."

"I don't think so either, Mom. Let's just see what the police find out. I'm on my way to class."

"Call me when you get home."

"Mom wants us to get a hotel," I announced.

"My mom says we should move," Carol said.

"If we break the lease you won't get the deposit back."

"Mom doesn't care. She wants me out."

"Where would we go?" I asked.

"Maybe we could start a neighborhood watch," Jeff decided. "We can get to know our neighbors, and if they hear a creak in the night they call us, and we can all go out and confront Earl together."

"Earl is not the killer," I insisted.

"Maybe Meghan's right and she wasn't killed. Maybe she tripped and hit her head," Carol suggested.

"If we find you dead on the front lawn some day, that's a plausible cause of death," Jeff said. "Pretty blond girl looked to be a bit more sophisticated."

"The news is reporting it as if it could be a murder. They're calling it a suspicious death," I said, stopping outside of Fisk Hall. "Where should I meet you when I'm done?"

"We'll come back," Jeff said. "What time do you want us here?"

"Nine."

"See you then."

I headed into the building and up the steps. Several people were gathered around the classroom door. As they cleared out of the way I saw the note.

Basic Design has been canceled.
Look online for your assignment.
Sorry for the short notice. Prof. Young

I raced down the steps and out the door, trying to determine which way Jeff and Carol went.

"Meghan, I'm glad I ran into you."

I turned around. "Oh, hi, Pastor Jon."

"I saw that a girl died today at your apartment. I was just on my way to the church to find your phone number to check on you."

"I'm fine, thank God."

"Did you know her?"

I shook my head. "I had seen her but never talked to her."

We chatted a few minutes more, then he left and I sat on the steps to call Jeff.

"Where are you?" I asked.

"Norris."

"Class was canceled. I'll be there in a couple minutes."

It was dusk and the smell of stale leaves hung in the air. I pulled my jacket tighter. Only a few leaves remained on the trees, trying not to succumb to their winter fate. I thought of the blond girl and how the night before, the few hours she had left had hung in the balance, too.

I found Carol and Jeff in Norris and sat down.

"Are you going to eat?" Carol asked.

"I'm not hungry."

"What's the deal with your class?" she asked.

"It was canceled. I had a nice talk with my pastor, though."

"About what?" Jeff asked.

"He invited me to stay with him and his wife if I didn't want to stay at the apartment."

"What did you say?" Carol asked.

"That I didn't want to leave you guys."

Jeff looked up from his burger.

"Then he was going to ask someone from choir to take in three college girls," I said.

"Uh oh," Carol said.

I nodded. "So I got to tell him I was living with the two of you."

"How'd he take that?" Jeff asked.

"Better than he could have."

"What are we going to do?" Carol asked. "Mom doesn't want me to go back."

"What are the chances Earl's going to murder someone else right away?" Jeff asked.

I cradled my chin in my hand.

"Look," Carol said. "It's on TV."

"Too bad we can't hear it," Jeff said.

Pictures of our building earlier in the day were shown before they switched back to a reporter live outside the apartment.

"I think Jeff's right. What are the chances the same person will murder again?"

"Maybe Mom has settled down," Carol said.

"Do you think we should go somewhere else?" I asked.

"Where would we go?"

I shrugged.

They finished their food, and we trudged back. An officer checked our IDs and verified we were tenants. We didn't have the nerve to peek down the hall on the second floor to see if officers were still there.

Once inside the apartment, with the doors locked, Carol and I went to our rooms to call our moms. I looked out the window while Mom and Dad talked. Most curtains in the building were pulled. The windows in the apartment above Lily's were uncovered and dark. Was that the blond girl's apartment? Could Lily be keeping something quiet? What if it *was* Earl? I was trying to convince my parents I was safe, all the while wondering if I was.

"Why don't you come home this weekend," Dad suggested.

"What about Carol and Jeff?"

"Bring them with," Mom said.

"Jeff works every weekend."

"Maybe we should come down there," Dad said. "Then we can check out the security in the building."

"We'll bring the air mattress and sleep on the floor," Mom said.

When I ended the call, I knocked on Jeff's door.

"Come in."

I left the door open and sat on his bed. He was in the beanbag with his laptop.

"My parents are coming this weekend."

"They are?"

"This really is the end of the world as we know it."

"Why do you say that?"

"They know me. They'll be able to tell we're dating," I whispered.

"For all we know, Carol's mom has been online and found a new place for her anyway, which may or may not have three bedrooms."

"How do you feel about that?"

He shrugged. "Mom's had to move several times and she's always managed to find something."

Carol came in and plopped on the other side of the bed.

"Are we sleeping in here tonight?" she asked.

"Fine, but no clothes allowed, except you, Carol. Meghan and I will take the bed. You can have the beanbag."

"Ha ha," I said.

"What did mommy dearest say?" Jeff asked.

"She's around criminal activity enough to know that the police have probably already concluded if this is a random murder or love gone wrong. The news will catch up in a few days and we'll go from there."

"Maybe we *should* sleep in one room tonight," I said. "I'm not sure I can sleep in my room alone."

"I can sleep just fine alone in my room," Jeff said. "Unless of course that wasn't what you were suggesting."

"I'll camp out with you," Carol said to me.

"My room or yours?" I asked.

"Go in Carol's," Jeff said. "All the crap on the floor is a natural booby trap."

"How do you know I have crap all over the floor of my room?" Carol demanded.

"You keep the door open all the time. I'm not blind."

"I'll sleep in yours," I decided. "Someone would have to go by Jeff's room to get to us. Keep your door open tonight," I said to Jeff.

"Fine," Jeff said, "but I sleep naked."

"You do not."

"I do."

"So when you get up to go to the bathroom in the middle of the night..."

"Naked," he said.

"No!" I cried.

"I'm very comfortable with my body."

"That's great, but my parents are coming this weekend, and if either sees you naked in the night, it will be over. I'll be moving out."

"Your parents are coming?" Carol asked.

"They want to make sure we're safe," I said. "You're kidding about being naked, right?"

"No, he's not," Carol said. "I've seen him."

"You have?"

"He left the bathroom to get a drink of water, and I came out to go to the bathroom."

"Nice," I said.

"That's what she said," Jeff said. "And I'm pretty sure she meant it."

I looked at Carol. She shrugged.

"You can't just walk around the apartment naked," I said.

"I wouldn't protest if you were doing it," Jeff said.

"How about me?" Carol asked.

"No problem. Just make sure you beep like a truck backing up when you walk around so I know to avoid going out of my room," Jeff said.

"Jerk," Carol mumbled.

"At the very least, wear underwear. When my parents are around, you need more."

Jeff stood up. "I think I'll get ready for bed now," he said, taking off his shirt.

"I'm out of here," I said, getting up.

"I'll stay," Carol said.

"Do you want a piece of me?" he asked.

I shut the door to my room and put my pajamas on. When I came back Jeff's door was shut, but I could hear that Carol was still in there. I opened the door, and they laughed.

"We wondered how long it would take you to come in," Carol said.

"I *would* move out," I said.

"Good night, Jeff," Carol said, going to her room.

"Good night," Jeff called.

"That hurt," I whispered to Jeff. "I can't believe Carol's seen you naked."

"I've given you several chances. Anyway, I was hoping I'd run into you."

"What did you plan on doing if I came out in the middle of the night and you were naked?"

He raised his eyebrows.

"Get some pajamas."

Carol had her pajamas on when I came in. I threw my pillow on her bed and sat against it.

"Would you sleep with someone if you were dating them?" I asked.

She shrugged. "It depends."

"On?"

"How much I liked them and if the relationship had a future. Are you really going to wait until you're married?"

"That's the plan. What about Jeff? Would you sleep with him if he came on to you?"

She sat on her bed. "Maybe."

"Are you serious?"

"Well," she said, "I don't know. Why?"

"I thought you thought Jeff was a pig."

"He *is* a lot of hot air, but you didn't answer the question. Why do you ask about Jeff?"

"No reason."

"You wouldn't sleep with Jeff, would you?" she asked.

"If he married me."

"Jeff isn't getting married anytime soon," Carol said. "Anyway he isn't your type."

"What is my type?"

"Christian."

"I won't be getting married anytime soon either," I said.

"You'd be married in a month if you found the right person."

"If you say so."

"I do."

I yawned and looked at my watch. Somehow I knew I wouldn't sleep. Not in my room. Not in Carol's room. Death seemed to loom in the apartment, and I wasn't sure it had anything to do with that blond girl from the second floor.

Bible Study Chapter Seven

Murder and hatred

Read Matthew 5:21–22 and 1 John 3:15. Have you ever wished someone was dead? In that moment your heart was full of hatred, and you committed the act of murder in your thoughts. Jesus and John tell us that hating anyone puts us in danger of what?

Read James 2:10–11. Which is worse in God's eyes, adultery or murder? What about stealing or wanting something of your neighbor's? Is a murderer a worse person than a thief?

Can you think of any godly men of the Bible who were also murderers? (Exodus 2:11–12; 2 Samuel 11:14-15; Acts 7:54–60; Acts 9:1)

Read Luke 6:27–31. How are we supposed to treat those people in our lives who hate us?

To live in fear or not to live in fear

Read Psalm 27:1; Psalm 34:4; and Isaiah 41:10. Does God want us to live in fear? Why or why not?

Read John 15:18–20; 16:2–3. If God loves us and protects us, should we expect that we will never be in any harm?

Every year Christians are killed because of their beliefs. Read Matthew 10:28–31. What does Jesus have to say about this?

Read John 11:25 and Revelation 2:10. When we die on this earth, what happens?

Read Psalm 31:15. Are we going to die one minute before God has determined it is our time to go?

Early in my marriage, a coworker of mine gave me two books to read. One was on the life of the serial killer Ted Bundy. The other was about FBI profilers. For months after reading those books, I checked my doors and windows to make sure they were locked. I was terrified at night if I was home alone. Eventually I came to realize you need to be safe but not petrified. You need to trust God. Even if you die at the hands of a murderer (heaven forbid!), no one can take your soul, and the next life is eternal. That's the one that matters!

The armor of God

Read Matthew 10:28. It would be a horrible thing to be tortured or killed for being a Christian, but Jesus tells us not to be afraid of that. What are we to be afraid of?

To my knowledge that's the only time Scripture tells us to be afraid. All of us, but especially women, learn all kinds of ways to keep ourselves physically safe—stay in groups, keep your doors locked, etc. Read Ephesians 6:10–18. What are your tools to stay safe spiritually?

Belt of _____; breastplate of _____;
Shoes (feet fitted with) _____;
Shieldof_____;helmetof_____;
and the sword of _____, also known as the
_____.

Paul's visual aid here boils down to reading the Word of God, believing the Word of God, and using the Word to destroy the lies and work of the Devil. The Word combined with prayer will keep you from falling prey to the Devil. If you've put on your armor, you have nothing to fear!

Read Numbers 22:1–6, 18. The Israelites were camped on the plains, totally unaware of what was going on around them. What did the king of Moab want the prophet Balaam to do to Israel?

If we were to read the next two chapters, we would see that Balaam went with the delegation of men who wanted Israel cursed, but every time he opened his mouth blessings, not curses, were uttered about Israel. Who was behind the blessings?

People planned evil for Israel, but God protected them. In this chapter, we see God protected Meghan from Jeff. In what way?

Was Meghan even aware of God's protection or the need for it? Isn't it wonderful to realize God is busy protecting us whether or not we realize it?

Can you think of a time God was protecting you when you didn't know it?

Chapter Eight: The Right Move

My parents arrived around one on Saturday. Carol and I had gathered all the newspaper articles since Tuesday. Saturday's breaking news and the headline for the *Chicago Sun Times* read TRACIE KIMBELL MURDER SUSPECT IN CUSTODY.

"Tracie was an escort for the last four years," I said, showing them the papers. "Apparently she had gotten into recruiting lately. She was killed, allegedly, by the father of one of the women she recruited."

"How did he get in?" Dad asked.

"He buzzed her and said he needed to talk. She met him in the doorway. They got into a fight and when someone came into the building, they moved outside where he apparently hit and killed her. The person from the apartment identified the man and that led to his arrest."

"How were they able to find him just by his description?" Mom asked.

"His fingerprints were on Tracie's call button, and his daughter's name was in Tracie's book."

"How sad," Mom said.

"Two families destroyed," Dad added.

"It's comforting to know he wasn't able to just walk in," I said.

"I think the place is pretty safe," Dad agreed.

"I'm just glad it wasn't Earl," Carol said.

"The landlord," I explained. "Jeff was sure Earl had snuffed Tracie."

"Why would he think that?" Mom asked.

"Because he has an active imagination," Carol said.

"Now if the news crews can find a different story to focus on," I said, "we won't have to worry about being on TV every time we walk out the door."

Dad stood and stretched. "I can't sit anymore. My back gets stiff from driving."

"Why don't you show us around," Mom suggested.

Carol declined our invitation to go along, so Mom, Dad, and I walked to the library, Norris, church, and finally the beach.

We stood on the pier, looking out at the lake. The sky was gray. In the distance, it was hard to tell where the water ended and the horizon began. The water gurgled and splashed as it hit the rocks below us.

"This is a beautiful campus," Mom said.

I nodded in agreement. "I love it here."

"How's it going, living with Jeff?" Dad asked.

I felt my face get warm. "Fine. Why?"

"There's another apartment open now."

"You're not suggesting..." Mom started.

"You want me to ask for Tracie's apartment?" I shrieked.

"Settle down, you two," Dad said. "What do you think they do when a person dies? You'd still be in the same building as your friends."

"Maybe Jeff could move down there," Mom suggested. "It is sort of odd that he's rooming with two girls, isn't it? Are him and Carol..."

"No," I interrupted. "He was only planning on living there through the summer, but it was working out so he stayed."

"That's an even better idea," Dad considered. "One of you should move. If not Jeff, then you."

He seemed to sense my disappointment. "It isn't that we don't trust you, Meghan."

"I know, but I like having roommates. There are always people around. It keeps everyone in check."

"In check how?" Mom asked.

"Like with dates," I said.

"You never invite a man to your apartment, regardless of how many people you live with," Dad said matter-of-factly.

"Once a person is in your apartment, it isn't always easy to get them out," Mom added. "Especially if their intentions are different than yours."

If only they knew.

When we got back to the apartment we went to my room, and Dad called Earl. The police had locked Tracie's apartment for the investigation. Earl figured it would be cleaned out in two, maybe three weeks. It was a one-bedroom, identical to Lily's, and usually rented for six hundred dollars. Considering the circumstances, he would rent it to me or Jeff for the remainder of the school year for five hundred dollars a month. Dad thanked him and hung up.

Carol paid fifteen hundred dollars a month for our apartment, but only made Jeff and me pay four hundred each. Mom and Dad said they would give me the extra hundred dollars a month to make up the difference.

Jeff came home from work and took a shower. When we came out of my room, he and Carol were on the couch.

"You've already put in a day's work," Dad said. "Before my Dad died, he was in the nursing home for a few months. The people who took care of him were outstanding."

Jeff smiled. "Some days go better than others."

"Your job must be pretty demanding," Mom said.

"It's not too bad."

"He comes home tired a lot," I said.

"It keeps me out of trouble," Jeff reasoned.

"We'd like to take everyone to pizza," Dad said. "Is there a good pizza place in Evanston?"

"It's a college town, Dad."

"That's what I figured," he said. "Point me in the right direction."

When we arrived at the Pizza Den, Dad ordered the pizzas. We sat at a round table with dark chairs. Faux Tiffany lamps hung above each table as music from the seventies resonated through the room.

"My dad had a bunch of records from the seventies," Jeff remembered.

"That was our era, too," Dad said. "These songs remind me of when we were dating."

"Did your mom keep your dad's records?" Mom asked.

"They survived the first couple moves. Most of them are gone now."

"How many siblings do you have?" Mom asked.

"Two brothers and a sister."

She shook her head. "I can't imagine. It must have been overwhelming for your mother at times."

"What do you think your dad would say about your living situation?" Dad asked.

"He was a strict Catholic," Jeff answered.

"So he wouldn't have approved?"

"Not so much."

"Does that bother you?"

"Since Dad died, everything has been about survival."

"The rent is cheaper, you mean?" Dad ascertained.

Jeff nodded.

"I talked to Earl today. He's willing to rent Tracie's apartment for five hundred dollars a month until the end of the school year. He understands it isn't such an attractive apartment right now. We told Meghan if she moved down there, we'd pay the extra hundred dollars a month so she wouldn't be out any money."

Jeff looked at me.

"We'd offer you the same deal," Dad said.

I looked at Dad. Did he just say that?

"That isn't necessary," Jeff said.

"Maybe not," Dad said, "but it's the right thing to do. If I was gone, I hope there would be other Christian fathers who would be there for my children."

"I see where Meghan gets it," Carol said.

Jeff looked at her and smiled.

"I'll move down there," he resolved.

"Are you sure?" I asked.

"It would make more sense," he said.

The next day, my parents left after brunch. Carol and I were waiting for Jeff when he came home from work.

"What?" he asked, looking from me to Carol and back to me. "Is my zipper down?"

"Are you really going to move into her apartment?" Carol asked.

"I suppose," Jeff said.

"How do you feel about that?" I asked. "Do *you* want to move down there?"

"No way."

"I didn't think so. I'm ready for a bachelor pad."

"Boy, are we fools. We've been feeling sorry for you all day," I said.

"I appreciate that."

"Are you going to walk around naked down there?" Carol asked. "That apartment faces the street. I'm pretty sure people could see you. Maybe some of Tracie's escort friends will stop in now and then."

"I'm not desperate enough to pay for sex. Yet."

"I'm surprised you don't have a girlfriend. You're pretty easy on the eyes."

"Are you coming on to me? Ever since you saw me naked, I'm pretty sure you want me."

"Is it any wonder?" she asked.

"You've got a point."

"Did you want me to leave you two alone?" I asked.

Jeff looked at Carol, then at me. "I'm going to take my shower."

"Do you have feelings for Jeff?" I asked when he left.

"Jeff would never date me. I'm starting to wonder about him, though. I would think he'd have a girlfriend."

"Maybe he does."

"Why wouldn't he talk about her?"

"He's got emotional scars."

"Either that or he's gay."

"Jeff isn't gay," I said.

"I hope not."

The apartment was unmercifully quiet. I waited for the heat to turn on. Each time I looked at the alarm clock, only a few minutes had gone by. It would be hours before anyone started getting ready for the day.

Finally I got up and went to the bathroom. From the hall I heard Carol's deep, rhythmic breaths. Jeff's door was shut. I turned the knob, and he rolled over.

"Did I wake you?" I whispered.

"No. Come in."

"I don't think that's a good idea," I said.

"Fair enough. Give me a minute."

I waited on the couch in the living room. He came in wearing a t-shirt and a pair of jeans.

"Change sucks, doesn't it?"

"I know this is the right thing to do, but now that it's time to for you to go..."

"It's impossible to look at it objectively at three a.m., Meghan."

"This feels final, like it's more than just a move down a flight of stairs."

"You're the one who's always telling me that God works situations out."

"I thought you didn't believe in that."

He sighed. I moved closer. He lifted his arm, and I snuggled into him.

"Why don't we get married?"

He yawned. "No way."

"Don't you love me?"

"Marriage?"

I shrugged.

"You're going to meet a nice Christian man someday."

"Why do you keep saying that?"

"Eventually we're both going to meet someone we're more compatible with. The only question is, who will meet someone else first."

Carol shut the bathroom door. Jeff motioned for me to slide to the opposite side of the couch. When she left the bathroom, Carol stepped into the living room.

"Can't you guys sleep?"

I shook my head.

"What time is it?"

I looked at my watch. "Three-seventeen."

She looked from Jeff to me. "See you in the morning."

"It is morning," Jeff said.

When I opened my eyes, light was sneaking under the shade. My head was cradled by Jeff's chest, his arms were wrapped loosely around me. I slid off the couch. Carol was in the kitchen in her exercise clothes.

"Have you gone yet?" I whispered.

"I'm waiting for you," she said.

"I'll just be a couple minutes."

A few minutes later, we tiptoed through the living room.

"Do you want to let me know what's going on?" she demanded when we were outside the building. "I always knew Jeff liked you, but I never thought he had a chance."

"He's the one who took me on the cruise around Chicago."

"Lovely."

"You made it clear on more than one occasion you wouldn't approve."

"Of course I don't approve. You don't approve. Your parents wouldn't approve. Who would approve?"

"Look, Carol. I get that no one wants us together, but I love him, and he cares about me…"

"Please tell me you're joking. Do you want to wake up next to him five years from now?"

"Yes, I do."

"You two are not even close to right for each other. Have you had sex with him?"

"No."

"Good! You can move on before you do something you'll regret."

"I don't want to move on, and now I don't feel like exercising, either."

She put an arm around me. "Let's work out. When we're done, we'll help Jeff move. Afterward you and I are going out. We'll get to the bottom of this. In the meantime, you are not to be alone with Jeff." She let her arm fall. "You'd think the guy was moving to Siberia."

"It feels like he's moving to Siberia."

"It would be better for you if he was," she muttered.

Bible Study Chapter Eight

Putting death and tragedy into perspective

Read Romans 8:28 and Genesis 50:19–20. When bad things happen to us or to those around us, what do we need to remember?

Read Esther 2:7. What was childhood like for this woman who would later become queen?

Read Daniel 1:3–5. How many times after Daniel was taken captive do you suppose he saw his family?

Joseph, Esther, and Daniel were all people God raised up for His purpose. They all went through a great deal of pain. Does God say that those of us who walk with Him won't experience pain?

Meghan's dad looked at Tracie's death a little differently than Meghan or her mom. How so?

Read Psalm 103:15–16. What is our life compared to?

How long will you be remembered after you're gone?

Read Acts 8:2. How did Stephen's friends feel about his death?

Read 1 Thessalonians 4:13–18. Though we grieve when our loved ones die, Paul tells us not to live like unbelievers. What does he mean?

Homosexuality

The topic of being gay keeps coming up. What does the Bible have to say about being gay? Read Romans 1:26–27. What words were used to describe relationships between two men or two women?

Those are pretty strong words from the apostle Paul. He calls homosexuality shameful, unnatural, indecent and perverse.

Read 1 Corinthians 6:9-10. The Bible doesn't mince words. It tells us homosexuality is a sin. Should it or any sin be glorified or justified?

How do people justify it or glorify it?

It is easy to justify any sin, especially when we know the people involved. A common justification for homosexuality is that gay people can't help it because they are born that way. It is true that we are all born sinful. All of us are born with all sorts of impulses and tendencies; we may be born with a temper and it's our tendency to lash out at people. We may be born being prone to addictive behaviors or being selfish.

We ask why it is wrong for two people who love each other to be happy. You could say the same thing about a person who leaves their spouse for another person. Sometimes we *are* happy enough in the midst of sinning. We can be very happy overeating or when we talk behind someone else's back or breaking our curfew or having sex with whomever we want. But that doesn't mean it is right. As Christians we live by the rules and boundaries God gives us.

Read 1 Corinthians 6:11. Is homosexuality an unforgivable sin?

Are homosexual people worse than you or I? Should we hate them?

Jesus was called a friend of sinners. Over and over we see Him eating with tax collectors and prostitutes. I can't hate a homosexual person without hating myself. I'm equally sinful, but in different ways.

When our plans take the place of God's

When it came time for Jeff to move, Meghan came up with a plan for them to stay together. What was it?

Read Genesis 16:1–4, 15–16, Genesis 21:1–5 and 8–11. God promised Abraham a son. Who came up with a plan to make that happen?

Did God ever give Sarai, whose name was changed to Sarah, a son?

How did Sarah's plan work in the long run? Did it bring Abraham and Sarah joy or grief?

Was Sarah's plan for her husband to sleep with another woman according to God's will? How do we know?

Would Meghan's plan for her and Jeff be a good idea? Why or why not?

Read 1 Corinthians 7:12–16. If Meghan were to get married and five years later tire of Jeff's drinking or perverse language or smoking or lack of respect for God, should she walk out of the marriage and look for a believer?

Who you choose for a spouse, especially in terms of their relationship with God, will make a huge difference in how you live, how you raise your children, etc. The cliché says "love is blind." Pray that God opens your eyes while you are still dating to see if your boy/girlfriend would make a good Christian spouse. If you choose to go ahead and marry an unbeliever, be prepared to persevere, to love, to fight fights with prayer, and to spend many agonizing nights pleading with God for the strength to go on.

If everyone is saying you're going in the wrong direction, perhaps you are

Read Acts 19:29–31. In this account from Scripture, the men of Ephesus were upset with Paul because, as he converted people, the sales of idols were going down. They saw their income in jeopardy so they became a mob. Paul wanted to talk to the mob. Why didn't he?

What two groups of people kept him from appearing before the mob?

Why do you suppose they didn't want Paul to go before an unruly crowd?

In some cases, our friends have a better grasp of the situation than we do. Sometimes our emotions cloud our judgment. How do you know if you should listen to your friends or if you shouldn't?

Chapter Nine: Good-bye for Now

I don't know, Jeff," Carol said. "You don't have much. This apartment is bare."

Jeff shrugged. "I have all I need."

All of Jeff's possessions fit in his bedroom. For the sake of not having an empty living room, we put his desk and beanbag out there.

"We need to get ready," Carol said to me.

"I can't go like this?"

"Where are you guys going?" Jeff asked.

"I'm taking Meghan out tonight."

"What's the occasion?"

"Do we need one?"

"As long as it isn't 'Jeff's gone, let's party.' "

"Just the opposite," she said. "Meghan doesn't seem to think she can function without you. I'm going to show her she can."

"I'm being taken against my will," I explained. "If I had it my way we'd all go out or watch a movie together or..."

"Jeff, will you please tell Meghan she's a big girl and you're a big boy? Didn't you say you were ready for a bachelor pad?"

"That was talk, Carol," I said. "He's just making the most of it. Can't we all go?"

"Carol's right, Meghan. I'm fine down here. I've got homework to do and I work tomorrow, so I should get to bed early. Carol, go ahead. I want to talk to Meghan for a minute."

"I'll get the curling iron plugged in, but if you're not up in five minutes, I'm coming to get you."

Carol shut the door.

"Can I hide in your closet? Will she find me there?"

"What got into her?"

"She saw us on the couch this morning, and I admitted we had been seeing each other."

"Ah," Jeff said. "So she's keeping you away from me."

"If I'm supposed to be a big girl, why can't I make my own decisions? I want to stay with you. I don't want to curl my hair and go out."

"I wish you would."

"You do?"

"Get ready, go have a couple of drinks, then come crawl in bed with me. We'll make your first time something to remember."

"Ha. Ha." I said.

"I'm not joking," he said. "I'll leave the door unlocked."

"Jeff."

"You better go," he said, "or Carol's wrath will come on both of us."

He led me to the door. "Have a good time."

"Do you mean that?"

He smiled. "Of course."

Carol's naturally curly black hair descended halfway down her back. Most days she had it up in a clip or ponytail or a series of barrettes. When she wore it down, it was stunning. She was determined to make my hair look like hers. She started on one side and went all the way around, curling my hair into ringlets. I did as much of my makeup as I could as she curled. When she finished, I put on mascara. She left and came back a minute later with a shirt.

"What's this?"

"My mother sent it to me last year. Apparently she thought I was three sizes smaller than I am because I can barely get it over my head. It will probably fit you."

She perused my face. "Do you have eye liner?"

I shook my head. She retrieved her makeup bag.

"Try this under your eyes," she said, handing me a black pencil. "Then outline your lips with this brown one."

"When have you worn eye or lip liner?"

"Never. I got them with a makeup kit."

I put liner under my eyes and outlined my lips.

She whistled. "You are in fine form tonight."

I went to my room and put on a pair of jeans and the black shirt from Carol. "I can't do it, Carol," I called. "This shirt is too formfitting for me to feel comfortable."

"You look awesome," she said, coming to my door.

"I need a shirt over it."

"I'll see what I have."

She came back with a white shirt, made of the same material, but bigger.

"It might be too big," she said, handing it to me.

I put it over the black shirt. "Definitely better."

"It does look good."

I grabbed my jacket.

"You can't bring that," she said.

"Are you kidding?"

"It's going to be hot in the club and if you dance, no one will be watching it."

"I can't go out in ten-degree weather in this. By the time I get to Chicago, I'll be a popsicle."

"Do you have a sweater you can tie around your waist?"

"Why don't we bring Jeff? He can stay by the coats."

"No Jeff."

Just then he walked into the apartment.

"What's protocol?" he asked. "Do I need to knock now?"

"Yes," Carol said from my bedroom door. "For all you know we may be walking around naked, now that you're not here."

"I won't be," I said, digging through my sweaters for one that was warm but not bulky.

"Can I use the microwave to make popcorn?" Jeff asked.

"Make it quick," Carol said. "We're minutes from leaving."

I found a sweater and some stretchy gloves I could stash in my pockets.

"No purse," Carol said. "Just your ID."

"No money?" I asked.

"I've got it."

I put my license in my back pocket and shut off the light. Jeff was standing against the counter. When he saw me he smiled.

"What do you think?" I asked, spinning around.

"You look like Cindi," he said.

"Is that supposed to be a compliment?"

"It's a compliment," Carol said. "He means you look sexy."

"I definitely want you to stop at my place when you get back," he said, coming toward me.

"Wrong," Carol said, stepping between us. "Her dad was clear about her not being alone in an apartment with a man."

I nodded. "He was."

"I think I need you to stop by."

"Put your stick shift in park," Carol said.

Jeff turned to me. "Did you enlist Carol as your bodyguard?"

"She enlisted herself."

He looked at Carol. "What do you have against me?"

"I'm not going to have Meghan ending up in your bed. There's only one good way for this to end, and that's for it to be over now."

"So you got her all done up to attract a different sort of guy?" Jeff accused. "Any guy she meets tonight will be thinking about one thing."

"Point taken," Carol said. "My bad."

"Is that why you're taking me out? I thought you wanted to spend time with me."

"Why would you need to do your hair and makeup to go out with Carol?"

"That's just what girls do."

"You know you shouldn't be with her, Jeff. It isn't right," Carol said.

"That's not fair, Carol," I said.

"Is this really any of your business?" he responded.

The microwave beeped. He got his popcorn and walked out. I looked at Carol.

"Let's go," she said.

The Excalibur was wall-to-wall people. The music was loud, and the lighting was low. Carol went to the bar, flashed her ID, and ordered drinks. When she turned around, she had two shot glasses.

We moved single file, a few steps at a time, bumping shoulders and elbows with people going in the opposite direction. As we neared the back of the room, three girls stood to leave. We slid into their seats.

Carol handed one of the drinks to me.

"What is it?" I asked.

"A kamikaze."

"If the name is any indicator, I guess I'll crash and burn later," I said. I took a gulp and struggled to catch my breath. "Or I will just burn now."

"I'm only looking out for you."

"By buying me drinks?"

"I can't believe you guys have been dating. You are complete opposites."

"In some ways."

"In most ways."

"He doesn't act like that when it's just the two of us."

"You need to get out while you still can."

I didn't respond. She flagged a waitress and ordered two more drinks.

The waitress left and a man bumped into our table, then looked up and recognized Carol. Apparently the man behind him was his friend, because he stopped, too. Carol introduced me to Dave, and Dave introduced us to Ben. I had already mentally dismissed them, when Carol motioned for them to sit down. When the waitress returned with our drinks, the guys ordered beers. I smiled outwardly while groaning inwardly.

I took a drink. My face must have shown my displeasure.

"That good?" Ben asked.

"Apparently Carol thinks if I'm drunk, I'll break up with my boyfriend."

"What's wrong with him?"

"He's not a Christian."

"And Meghan might as well be Mother Theresa," Carol interjected. "She eats, breathes, and sleeps her faith."

"As you can tell," I said, motioning to the drink.

He smiled.

"It's even worse than it looks," I said, looking around. "I'm under age."

"Don't broadcast it," Carol said, poking me.

I shrugged and pushed the drink away. "I'm not drinking this, Carol."

"You didn't refuse the drinks the professor bought you," she sneered.

My mouth fell open. "I was too intimidated."

Dave smiled. "This sounds like a story."

"It's nothing, really. My professor hired me as his assistant. When he asked me out for drinks I thought it would be one drink…strictly professional."

"And?"

"I got drunk. I think the waitress was in on it, too. Thankfully Carol and Jeff came to the bar and took me home and the only repercussion was feeling crappy the next day."

Dave laughed. Ben's eyes pierced me.

"It's too bad your professor put you in that position," he said.

"Ben, why don't you get Meghan a drink that tastes good?" Dave suggested.

"No," I protested. "I don't care if I drink anything anyway."

When the waitress returned with his beer Ben ordered me a peach daiquiri.

"What are you going to school for?" he asked.

"Graphic design. How about you?"

"I'm finishing my Bachelor's of music degree with a minor in business, and I'm applying for the seminary."

"You're going to be a pastor?"

"Does that make you nervous?"

I shook my head. "You'll be a fine pastor. You're an excellent felon."

"The drink you mean? Is buying for a minor a felony?"

"I doubt it's considered a good work."

The waitress arrived with my daiquiri.

"What's a future pastor doing in a bar?"

He shrugged. "Dave asked, and I didn't have much else to do, so..."

"You came looking for women," I decided. "Why would you be looking when you have, what, four years of school left?"

"A lot of guys are married at sem."

"You *want* to get married?"

He shrugged. "Why do you seem so surprised?"

"I didn't know guys like you existed."

Carol smiled as if to say, "See!"

I kicked her leg under the table. She looked at me.

"I need to use the bathroom."

"I don't know where it is," she said, then reading my stare added, "but I'll help you find it."

Unlike the rest of the bar, the bathroom was bright and busy with women making themselves up, tucking in shirts, and fixing their hair. Once we were in the door, I turned to look her in the eye.

"Is Ben awesome or what?" she asked.

"Did you plan this?" I accused.

"I haven't seen Dave in a year, and until twenty minutes ago I didn't know Ben existed."

"You had nothing to do with these guys being here?"

"No."

"How do you know Dave?"

"We met at a business seminar last year. We were put on the same team."

"And you haven't talked to him since?"

"No."

I still wasn't sure I could trust her.

"It wasn't me," she said making an X over her heart. "Looks to me like divine intervention."

As we approached the table, a slow song started playing. Dave stood and asked Carol to dance.

"Do you mind?" she asked.

"Go ahead."

I sat down and for lack of anything better to do, took a drink.

"How is it?"

"Much better. I'd give you money, but Carol wouldn't let me bring any."

"Forget it."

I looked at the tables around us. Women were putting themselves out there for men. Men were responding, flirting, seducing.

"Do you want to tell me about your boyfriend?" Ben asked.

"Why?"

"I'll tell you if Carol's being unreasonable. Mine is an unbiased opinion."

I considered for a second. "I met Carol when I visited the school last spring. She offered to let me live with her for four hundred dollars a month, which, I'm sure you know, is considerably cheaper than the dorms."

He nodded.

"I knew she was looking for another roommate, but until the day I moved in, I didn't realize it was going to be Jeff."

"You didn't ask?"

"I did. Carol told me she had found someone and we'd get along great."

"Inconspicuously deceptive."

I nodded. "I should have probed deeper, but it never occurred to me she'd let a guy live with us."

"And your parents were ok with it?"

"Oh no. But I was there, school was about to start and I assured them it wouldn't be a problem."

"Jeff is your boyfriend?"

I nodded.

"What do you like about him?"

"Carol's right that he's not my type. I wouldn't have guessed I would like him."

"So why did you start dating?"

"He asked."

"Seems reasonable."

I smiled. "Doesn't it? I was hesitant, but he planned a date that was so romantic..."

"Where did he take you?"

"On a boat tour around the city then to a little Italian restaurant."

"He swept you off your feet?"

"Pretty much. Afterward we decided we weren't going to date because of the obvious differences. Then out of the blue he made me supper, and I fell in love."

"Where do you see the relationship going?"

"Down the toilet, especially now that Carol knows. Jeff is vague about God on his best days, belligerent toward Him on his worst. Marriage isn't an option."

"He would get along well with my ex. She didn't want anything to do with marriage either."

"Most people our age don't."

"You and I made the same mistake. We allowed ourselves to be in a relationship with someone we weren't meant to be with."

"That's your unbiased opinion?"

He leaned toward me. "If you spend enough time with someone, you can fall in love with them whether you should or not. When you add in the physical component, everything gets screwed up. I'm going to assume you and Jeff have at least kissed."

I nodded.

"If you and I, as complete strangers kissed, we could bond, too."

"I can't imagine that being true."

"It's basic biology. Kissing triggers hormones."

I felt my face warm. "I always stunk at science."

"If Jeff isn't what you are looking for in a husband, you shouldn't be dating him, plain and simple. That's why I'm not dating anymore."

"How are you going to find a wife without dating?"

"When I find a woman who's sold out for God, I'll ask her to get married."

"Just walk up to her and ask her to marry you?"

"By the time I figure out how she feels about God, I think I'll know her pretty well."

I sighed. "I'm not sure who I am anymore. Three months ago I thought I knew, but now..."

"If I've learned anything over the past six months, it's that God's grace is bigger than our decisions."

Carol and Dave came back to the table laughing.

"Do you want another drink?" Carol asked.

"I'm done."

"Are you ready to leave?"

"Whenever you are."

"We'll take you home," Dave offered.

"You drove?" Carol asked.

Dave nodded.

"We're in Evanston," I reminded him.

"I don't mind," Dave said.

They had parked several blocks away, and the heater in Dave's car was only slightly warmer than the temperature outside. I determined not wearing a jacket to be my final act of intentional stupidity.

Carol sat in the front with Dave.

"Are you going home for Thanksgiving?" Ben asked.

"My parents are coming to get me Tuesday. When do you leave?"

"Same."

"Where are you from?" I asked.

"Just north of Waunakee, Wisconsin. It's ..."

"A little north of Madison. I'm from Monona," I said.

"Really? My roommate has a car. You should ride home with us," Ben suggested. "It would save your parents the trip."

At the apartment I gave Ben my phone number and told Carol I'd meet her upstairs.

"You are *not* going to see Jeff."

"I need to talk to him."

"Meghan."

"Trust me."

"You've got ten minutes, and then..."

"I know. You're coming down and I better have all my clothes on."

She went upstairs. I knocked on Jeff's door.

"I can't believe you came," he said, letting me in. "Did you have fun?"

"Carol didn't take me out to have fun. She took me out to get me drunk."

"You don't seem drunk."

"I didn't like the way Carol talked to you earlier."

"Is that why you came?"

I shook my head. "Carol's right. If we're not right for each other, we shouldn't be together."

"Last night you wanted to get married."

"And you said you weren't getting married. Has that changed?"

"It needs to be over," Jeff stated matter-of-factly. He tucked my hair behind my ears. "You look beautiful tonight."

I let myself fall against his chest. He put his arms around me.

"You need to go," he said at last, backing away.

The walk from the second to the third floor had never been so lonely.

When I heard Carol, I looked at my watch. Eight a.m. She was talking in her husky whisper, running water, making coffee. Was that Jeff's voice? Why wasn't he at work? My curiosity got the best of me, and I bolted out of bed and into the kitchen. It wasn't Jeff she was talking to but Dave.

"Hey," Carol said when she saw me.

"Hey," I responded.

I trudged toward the bathroom, too surprised to stay in the room. Why was Dave there? He dropped us off last night and drove away. When had he come back?

Once in the bathroom I turned on the water. I had fallen asleep praying, with tears running down my cheeks. I grabbed a washcloth and wiped the mascara from under my eyes.

I felt slow, annoyingly tired. My tongue was sticky. I brushed my teeth and decided to go to the 8:30 service at church.

I went to the kitchen and got a glass of water. After drinking most of it, I put the glass down and looked from Carol to Dave. Neither of them appeared to know what to say.

"What did I miss?" I asked. "Didn't you drive away last night?"

"Their car broke down, so I told them they could crash here and deal with it today."

"What happened to the car?"

"It has a leak in a gasket. I've been meaning to replace it. As long as I keep putting antifreeze in it, it doesn't overheat, but I ran out of antifreeze."

"That's too bad," I said looking at my watch. "I'm going to church."

"Mind if I come?" Ben stood in the doorway to the living room, his hair tousled.

"I don't mind."

"Any chance you have some mouthwash?"

"I'll get it," Carol said.

I grabbed my purse and jacket, wondering what Pastor Jon would think about Ben and I being there wrinkled together.

When Ben was done in the bathroom, we headed out. I couldn't help but feel guilty as we passed the second floor.

"I hate to admit it, but for a minute this morning I thought Dave had returned to spend the night with Carol. I was pleasantly surprised to hear that the car broke down. I don't know how I slept through it. When did you guys come back?"

"It was a while before we called Carol. We thought about walking to a gas station, but didn't know where one was or if it would have antifreeze. The temperature gauge was beyond hot, so we shut it down and walked the mile back to your apartment."

He held the door for me.

"Did you sleep on the couch?" I asked.

He nodded.

"Where did Dave sleep?"

"In Carol's room."

"*What!*"

He shrugged. "She let us in, showed me the couch, told me where the bathroom was, and she and Dave disappeared."

"I can't believe Carol would let him stay with her after what she has put me through."

"I guess we shouldn't assume."

"That's being optimistic."

We walked for a bit in silence.

"I went to see Jeff last night."

"Oh?"

"We agreed not to see each other anymore."

"How's it feel?"

"I know it's the right thing to do."

"Usually that's harder than doing what's wrong."

"In one respect, a weight has been lifted."

"Just be prepared," Ben said. "It's a process."

"I'm not sure I understand."

"You will."

The lighting in the bar was low, but in church Ben's features were noticeable. His light brown hair spiked toward the center of his head in a casual way on top. Jeff could go a day or two without shaving, but Ben had been clean shaven last night and now dark whiskers dotted his chin and upper lip.

When the service was over, we put the hymnals away.

"You've got an incredible voice," I said.

"I'm glad you think so. I get a little carried away when I sing."

"I loved it."

We were almost out the doors when a girl ran up to us.

"What are you doing here?" she asked Ben.

"Hi, Lisa," he said.

I smiled at her and she smiled back.

"The car broke down, so I ended up with a friend in Evanston for the night."

"Crazy," she said. "I couldn't believe it when I looked over and saw you."

She smiled again at me.

"Will you be at Salt and Light on Tuesday?" Ben asked.

She nodded.

"See you then."

"See you Tuesday."

We started down the steps of the church when another girl stopped Ben.

"Hi, Mary," he said.

"It's good to see you," she said. "When do we meet again?"

"I'm pretty sure we're done now until January," he said.

"Are you going home for Thanksgiving?" she asked.

"Yeah. How about you?"

"I leave Tuesday."

"Have a nice break," he said.

"You, too," she said.

"You know more people here than I do," I said. "Girls at least."

"All working relationships," he said.

"Where do you work?"

"Mary and I are on the youth group leadership committee. Lisa and I volunteer at Salt and Light."

"What is Salt and Light?"

"It's a food shelter downtown."

"You weren't looking for women last night, were you? Something tells me you don't have to look too hard."

How different I had planned my year in Evanston to be! I anticipated being like Lisa and Mary, active in youth group and volunteer work. Instead I barely knew the people at my church.

This time of year always seemed dreary. The lawns were brown, the leaves were gone, and the snow had not yet arrived to blanket everything—to turn the ugly and dead into something bright and fresh.

"I think Matt has class until two on Tuesday," Ben said.

"Who's Matt?"

"He's my roommate. He'd be the one driving us home."

"I have to see if my parents will let me go with you guys. They just moved Jeff out of the apartment."

"I'm sure that was a relief."

I looked toward the apartment, and my heart sank. Was that Jeff on the steps smoking? Why wasn't he at work?

"What is it?" Ben asked.

"It's Jeff."

Ben looked at Jeff then back at me. "Do you want me to leave?"

"No, but this doesn't look very good."

"What's wrong?" I asked Jeff as we came up the steps. "Why aren't you at work?"

Jeff put out his cigarette. "I came home on my break."

I had never known Jeff to come home for a break. Had he been waiting for me?

"Jeff, this is Ben. Ben, Jeff."

"Nice to meet you," Ben said, shaking Jeff's hand. "Do you mind if I go up and find Dave?"

"I'll let you in," I said.

I opened the door and came back to Jeff.

"Who's Ben?"

"A friend of Carol's friend Dave. They brought us home last night, but Dave's car broke down a mile away, so they spent the night in the apartment."

"That's convenient. I'll have to remember that one."

"I didn't even know they were there until this morning. I got up for church, and Ben asked to go along."

"Just what you always wanted."

"Why did you come home?"

"My mom had a stroke. My brother called me at work."

I put my hand over my mouth. "How bad is it?"

"I don't know. They're running tests."

"Is she conscious?"

He shook his head. "Ted came to pick her up for church and found her in bed. She couldn't move or talk."

I went to him and hugged him.

The door opened and Dave and Ben came out. I backed away from Jeff.

"Are you guys on your way?" I asked.

"Yeah," Dave said. "Lots to do before break."

"I'll give you a call after I talk to Matt," Ben said.

I nodded.

"Ben lives near my parents," I explained, as they walked off. "He's going home with a friend and offered to give me a ride."

"I'm sure he would give you a ride," Jeff snarled.

"Ben isn't that kind of guy."

"He's a guy, Meghan. And the only way he's seen you is like that."

"What are you going to do?"

"I have a deadline Tuesday. If I work all day, I can turn it in tomorrow and hopefully catch a bus home."

"I'm sorry, Jeff. I'll pray for your mom."

Carol was in her room. I went to my room and knelt beside my bed. When I finished praying, I crawled into bed and fell asleep. I woke a few hours later to my phone ringing.

"Did I wake you?"

"Who is this?"

"It's Ben. I can call back."

"No. I have a lot to do. I have to get up anyway."

"I talked to Matt. His girlfriend Amanda is coming home with him to meet his parents. He said you could come, but you might want to pack light. He's got a Saturn, so by the time we all get in…"

"Got it. I'll call my parents and call you back."

After a lengthy discussion, my parents consented. I called Ben back, and we decided I should be ready around 2:30. When I hung up with Ben, I could hear Carol in the kitchen.

"What's the deal with Dave staying in your room last night?"

"I never said I wouldn't have sex with someone."

"So you did! You barely know him. You aren't even dating."

"In hindsight, I wish it wouldn't have happened this way, but I didn't expect his car to break down or him to show up needing a place to stay."

"He could have slept in the chair."

"Listen, Meghan, we had a great night together at the club and quite honestly, a great time in bed. I don't think he's the type to not call me again, but then again, I don't know."

"After all the fuss you made over Jeff and me."

"That's entirely different."

"I don't see how."

"It just is."

I sighed. "What has changed in the last month, Carol? You're hitting on Jeff, sleeping with a guy you barely know. I don't get it. You didn't seem the type."

"No one has ever paid attention to me."

"This is not the sort of attention you need."

"I could see you and Jeff liked each other from the way you looked at each other."

"Why would you hit on Jeff if you knew we were dating?"

"Who's going to ask me out, Meghan?"

"Why do you think no one will?"

"I'm fat."

"You're a little thick, but you are not fat."

"Call it what you want," Carol said. "No one is asking."

"Since when do you want to date? What happened to 'I've got three years of school after my bachelor's?' Anyway, it's not as if people are lining up to date me."

"If you were to get ready like you did last night, you would have no problem finding a guy. You don't even try."

"Let's at least agree that hopping in the sack with someone after spending a couple hours together is not a good habit to start."

"That may be the only time I have sex."

"That was sex, Carol, not love." I rubbed my face, remembering. "Jeff's mom had a stroke today."

"No!"

I nodded. "He's going to try to go home tomorrow."

"Poor Jeff. She can't die on him."

"I know," I said. "And we broke up last night. Tell me I don't feel like a heel."

"He loves you, Meghan."

"I love him, too."

"As much as I *know* you aren't meant to be together, there is a genuine…"

"Vibe," I offered.

"Yes, between the two of you."

I tapped my fingers on the table.

"You should go see him," she said.

I shook my head. "We broke up. He's got a lot of demons to face, and if we *are* going to be together, some things need to change."

I stood up.

"Do you think Dave will call?"

I looked into her hopeful eyes and my shoulders sank. "Maybe, but honestly, that's not the sort of relationship I'd want to be in."

I went to my room and started working on an assignment, but couldn't concentrate after what Carol said. Jeff loved me. There was something genuine about us. I picked up my phone and put it down twice before I called him.

"Any news?" I asked.

"Nothing's changed," he said.

"How's the assignment coming?"

"It sucks."

"Want me to bring you a sandwich?"

"I'm not hungry."

"If you change your mind…"

"Don't start having second thoughts. We're done. You're free. I'm free."

"Got it," I said.

I hung up wondering why I felt anything but free.

Bible Study Chapter Nine

Peer Pressure

We see a lot of peer pressure in the first part of this chapter. Jeff suggests Meghan come to his apartment for sex once she gets home. She puts a stop to that talk. Carol gets Meghan ready, but Meghan won't agree to wear the shirt that is too tight-fitting. She does get talked into leaving her jacket behind, and she goes along with the first drink Carol gives her. Do you see any change in Meghan from how she acted in earlier chapters?

Read Romans 12:2. During Meghan's first few months at college, did she test anything people suggested before following? Give some examples.

What would Paul's advice about peer pressure be?

Read Matthew 7:13–14. If we believe what Jesus tells us here, most of the things people suggest we do will lead down which road? What does that road lead to?

Read John 10:27–28. Who should you listen to and why?

Sold out for God

Ben said he was looking for a girl who was "sold out for God." Read Deuteronomy 6:5–9 and Matthew 22:34–40. How are we to love God?

From Matthew: With all your _____, and with all your_____, and with all your _____.

What in your life gets in the way of you serving God?

Ben said he wanted a wife who lived this commandment. Sometimes, especially in high school and college, being sold out for God isn't going to make you very popular. How so?

What qualities are you looking for in a spouse? Is *sold out for God* on the list?

If this is right why doesn't it feel good?

When Meghan broke up with Jeff she said it didn't "feel good." Read 2 Corinthians 11:23–29. Did Paul's doing what was right (spreading the Word to the Gentiles) feel good?

Read John 15:18–21. When you obey God's commands and live the way you ought, how is the world going to feel about you?

Read the rest of the account of Potiphar's wife in Genesis 39:13–23. Where did doing what was right put Joseph?

Read verse 21. Does God notice when we do the right thing?

Read Daniel 6:3–23. What kind of man was Daniel? (v. 4)

Where did being sold out for God put Daniel?

What did Daniel do immediately upon hearing about the decree? (v.10)

Did God abandon him in adversity? Why? (v. 23)

Daniel ended up in a pit with lions; Joseph ended up in prison; Paul was beaten and scorned; Jesus was crucified. Doing what is right in God's eyes isn't going to be easy as long as we're in this evil world, but the One you are serving will notice and be with you!

Chapter Ten: A Reason to Give Thanks

My evening class was not meeting, so I was done at noon. I went to SPAC to work out, and then back to the apartment to shower and clean up the few things that could spoil in the fridge. I quickly put on a little foundation and it was time to go.

I knocked on Lily's door.

"I only have a minute, but I wanted to wish you a happy Thanksgiving."

"Happy Thanksgiving to you, too. Are you going home?"

I nodded. "My ride will be here in a couple minutes. What are you doing to celebrate?"

"My daughter Esther and her family from Missouri will be here tomorrow. I can hardly wait. I've been making pies all morning."

"I'll stop to see you when I get back," I said, giving her a hug.

"I look forward to it."

"I do, too."

As I waited in the entry, it occurred to me again how thankful I was that Tracie's murderer had been caught. Jeff and Carol were already gone. Who knew how many other apartments were unattended for the weekend. There was security in knowing some crazy person wasn't lurking in the building, picking locks, and scanning peoples' lives.

Ben hopped out of the car and helped me squeeze my bag in the trunk. When I got in the back seat, I realized how I must look with half-dried hair and minimal makeup, compared to

Amanda, whose reddish-blond hair was straightened and sprayed into obedience. Not only was she wearing mascara but earrings, too. Mom used to say, "when all else fails, wear a smile," so when Ben introduced me, I followed her advice.

"What are you going to school for?" Amanda asked.

"Graphic design. How about you?"

"Elementary ed. I start student teaching in January."

"You're done in May?"

She nodded.

"What then?"

She smiled and lowered her voice to a whisper. "That's up to Matt."

"Does he finish school in May, too?"

She nodded.

"So the job search begins," I said.

"His parents own a lumberyard north of Madison," she said, still in a hushed voice. "It's pretty much a given that he'll work there."

I leaned into her. "So with him having a job and school behind you, you're hoping to get married?"

She smiled and winked.

"What's all the whispering back there?" Matt asked, looking in the rearview mirror.

"She was just telling me what a good catch you are," I said.

Matt puffed out his chest. Amanda smiled.

"How'd you meet Ben?" she asked.

I felt my cheeks warm. "We met Saturday at the Excalibur."

"What were you doing at the Excalibur, Ben?"

"Dave Schubert took me out for a night on the town."

"I know Dave's girlfriend," Amanda said.

"He's got a girlfriend?" I asked, trying to control my surprise.

"A serious one."

"Is it the same Dave Schubert?"

"Business major," Amanda said. "You know him, right Matt?"

"I know Dave," Matt answered.

"His girlfriend Sandy is a sweetie," Amanda continued. "I think he's coming home with her for Thanksgiving. She's hoping for a ring soon."

My dad's words after the murder ran through my head. "Two families destroyed," he said. Carol would be distraught to find out, but when and if Sandy found out, she would be devastated.

"So you've only known Ben four days, and you're going to meet his parents?"

Ben laughed. "Yeah. We're getting married over Christmas break."

"My parents are picking me up at his house," I explained. "I live just outside of Madison."

"Her folks were going to come get her," Ben added. "I wanted to save them the trip."

"I thought that seemed awfully quick, especially for you, Ben."

"Meghan had a boyfriend until Saturday," Ben told her.

"Sounds like a busy weekend," Amanda said.

"It got worse," I said. "Jeff and I broke up Saturday. His mom had a stroke on Sunday."

"Is that why he was waiting for you?" Ben asked, turning to face me.

I nodded. "He left yesterday morning to go home."

"Wow. That stinks," Ben said.

"His dad died when he was twelve," I explained to Amanda.

"Hopefully his mom will recover."

"He hasn't had an easy life, that's for sure."

"Why did you guys break up?" She asked.

"The better question is probably why did we *start* dating. He's a nice guy, but he's not a Christian, and that caused a lot of derision."

"You mean division?"

"Derision…difficult circumstances."

Amanda pulled her Blackberry out of her purse. "How do you spell it?"

"D-E-R...I don't know. I probably made it up. Jeff accused me of that now and then."

"As if the English language doesn't have enough words."

"Shakespeare did it," Ben offered.

"Good luck with that attribute," Amanda said.

"I don't believe in luck."

"I don't either," Ben said.

Amanda plopped her Blackberry back in her purse. "You guys *should* get married."

"Are you free Saturday, Ben?" I asked.

"I'll have to do chores in the morning, but the rest of the day is pretty open."

"There you have it. Two o'clock on Saturday."

"Ooh," he said with a grimace. "I was hoping for an evening wedding."

We laughed.

Once we were on the other side of Milwaukee, Matt stopped at a gas station. When we had been to the restrooms and bought drinks, we returned to the car. Amanda went to the passenger's seat.

"Sorry, Ben, but I get to sit by Matt for awhile."

She looked at me and winked.

"I'll sit behind Matt," I said. "You'll have more leg room behind Amanda."

"Are you going to tell Carol about Dave?" Ben whispered when we were settled and on the road again.

I checked to make sure Matt and Amanda were involved in their own conversation. "Did you know he had a girlfriend?"

He shook his head.

"What a mess," I said. "Carol had just found out about Jeff and me. I think she was feeling...I don't know...unloved."

We rode in silence for a while.

"How long have you known Matt?" I asked.

"We went to grade school together."

"What school?

"Westside."

"We played you in basketball," I said. "I went to Holy Cross."

"Matt played basketball," Ben said. "I played soccer."

"You can't really say Ben played soccer," Matt interjected. "He was on the field, and he ran a lot, but how many goals did you make?"

"I was a defensive player."

"That's what he says anyway."

"You guys room together?"

"We're suitemates," Ben said. "We have our own bedrooms but share the rest of the suite."

"We were roommates our first two years," Matt said. "I never saw Ben. He was somewhere under the pile of laundry and books and papers, but..."

"I don't know that man," Ben said.

Matt laughed. "I know you, all right. He's not as perfect as everyone thinks he is."

Amanda hit Matt's shoulder. "Be nice."

"I am nice. I'm honest, too."

"Where are you from, Amanda?"

"Houghton, Illinois. It's three hours southwest of Chicago."

"How did you and Matt meet?"

"She was hitchhiking and I picked her up."

"Matt!"

He laughed.

"We met over the summer," Amanda said. "Matt stayed to do an internship, and I went to summer school to make up credits after doing a global studies program in Mexico. You don't find many people in the cafeteria during the summer. His internship was during second shift, so more often than not we'd both be in the cafeteria at the same time sitting alone. One day he asked to sit by me, and we've been together ever since."

"That's neat," I said.

Ben's parents farmed north of Waunakee. By the time we arrived, I knew they had two hundred head of beef cows and about three hundred acres. It had been Ben's grandparents' farm, but most of Ben's growing up years were spent there. His younger brother was planning on taking over the farm eventually.

The white two-story farmhouse reminded me of a retired battleship. It seemed anchored to the land. The windbreaks on the north and east sides sheltered what perhaps should have been decrepit for its age. Function, not aesthetics, was the driving force behind its construction.

We said our goodbyes to Matt and Amanda and left our shoes in the enclosed porch before entering the main house. Our first steps brought us into the laundry and wash area.

Ben's mom hurried from the kitchen to greet us.

"Mom, this is Meghan. Meghan, Mildred."

"Call me Millie," she said. "We don't have a proper entryway, so you'll need to hang your coat on a hook."

I handed my coat to Ben, who hung it on one of the several hooks next to the door.

Millie put an arm around Ben for a quick hug then motioned for us to sit at the table.

"I made Amish bread and tea, if you want some."

"I've never had Amish bread," I said.

"It's a favorite of Ben's," Millie explained, cutting several slices and arranging them on a plate. She held it out to me.

"I see why you like it," I said to Ben when I'd taken a bite. "Mom bakes a lot of breads, but mostly to use the produce from the garden...apples, pears, zucchinis..."

"Do you have pear trees?" Millie asked.

"Two pear and two apple."

"And they produce?"

I nodded.

"I don't know why mine never did. Maybe I bought the wrong variety."

"Dad is coming to get me. He's the gardener. You could ask him. Mom stores and prepares all the fruits and vegetables, but he's the one who goes through the seed catalog and chooses everything."

"Mom saves her seeds," Ben said.

"You do? We tried that with salad peppers one year, but they molded."

"That's a shame," Millie said.

"It really was. Dad ordered green peppers, but long, yellow peppers grew instead. He was afraid it was a hot pepper and they would all go to waste, but when we tried them, they were wonderful."

"An unexpected gift," Millie resolved.

The room fell silent.

"Tea," Millie remembered, getting up from her chair. She brought two glasses from the cupboard to the table, grabbed a pitcher from the fridge, and poured tea for Ben and me.

"What will you do while you're home?" Millie asked.

"I work at Cobb's Grocery. I'll be there tomorrow and all day Friday and Saturday."

"It will be busy tomorrow," she said.

"I don't mind the busy days. They go fast."

"What are you going to school for?"

"Graphic design."

"You must be creative," she said.

"On my good days."

"Ben's got a touch of creativity, but the rest of us are pretty cut and dry."

"Oh, Mom," Ben said. "You're always trying new recipes."

"I follow the recipes. I don't create them. That's for people with different brain function than I have."

"At least you appreciate creativity in others," I said.

"I *marvel* at it."

I smiled. "Creativity is time consuming...for me anyway."

"It looks a lot like work," Ben said.

"Sweat and tears included," I added.

Millie stood up. "There's a red van pulling into the yard."

"That's Dad," I said.

I finished my tea and put my glass next to the sink. Ben came with my coat.

"I'll carry your bag."

"We'll all go out," Millie said. "I'd like to meet your dad."

She draped a blue shawl over her shoulders and slipped on her fabric-lined clogs. Dad was starting up the walk when we came out.

"I've been enjoying your daughter's company," Millie said.

"She's been behaving?"

I grimaced and introduced Dad to Ben and Millie.

"You have a beautiful place," he said, scanning the yard. "Are those apple trees?"

"Yes," Millie said. "I have ten apple trees that do wonderfully. It's the pear trees I'm concerned about."

I smiled at Ben. He smiled back.

"Thanks for inviting me," I said. "I wish I would have met you guys a couple months ago."

"Sometimes God's timing is different than ours."

"I wasn't looking in the right places either."

"Like the Excalibur?" he teased.

I smiled. "What time should I be back Sunday?"

"I don't know," Ben said. "We'll go to church and fill up on one last good meal. I'll talk to Matt and give you a call."

"Ready?" Dad asked.

I nodded and thanked Millie.

"Is Ben someone we should be getting to know?" Dad asked, waving to them as we left.

"I only just met him myself," I explained. "He's a friend of a guy Carol sort of knows. Carol took me out Saturday, and as Dave and Ben were taking us home, Ben and I figured out we both lived near Madison. His roommate is from Waunekee and has a car, so there you have it."

Dad nodded. "Where did you go out?"

"The Excalibur. It's a dance club in Chicago."

"Do you go there often?"

"First time," I said, "and probably last."

"Do you think it was a good idea to get in a car with guys you had just met?"

"I guess I never thought of it."

"Something to consider," he said. "How's Jeff doing in his apartment?"

"He's doing fine in his apartment, but his mom had a stroke on Sunday."

"Oh no."

"Unfortunately, yes. I need to call him when I get home."

"Are you and Jeff dating?"

"Why do you ask?"

"When you're old, you pick up on some of these things."

I sighed. "We were, but we broke up and I'm trying to move on."

"Did he break up with you?"

"It was mutual. Our core values are different, and we can't seem to come to a consensus. I'm not going to change for him, and he won't change for me, so it seems best if we quit while we can still be friends."

"Sounds wise."

"I wish, Dad. I rode the whole way back with Ben. He's a good Christian man. He's going to be a pastor. He's what I should be looking for in a guy, but I can't quit thinking about Jeff."

"Some people meet the person they will marry right away in high school or college and never date anyone else. A lot of us fall in love a time or two before we meet our spouse. Maybe you won't end up with either Jeff or Ben."

"Did you fall in love with someone before Mom?"

"Sure," Dad said.

"Did you sleep with her?"

Dad shot me a sideways glance.

"So you did?"

"I wasn't much of a Christian before I met your mother."

"Maybe Jeff *is* the one for me," I said.

"Wait a second. I was ready to settle down by the time I met your mom. When we started dating, I was willing to listen. If Jeff isn't looking to change, you can't force him. And why did you ask if I slept with someone? Did you sleep with Jeff?"

"No."

"Thank God."

"Well it wasn't easy."

"Doing the right thing is never easy, especially when you're in the same apartment. I knew I had to get him out of there."

"It would be just as easy to sleep with him now."

He seemed to mull that over for a minute. "Right now he is all you can think about. I've been there. If you had the ability to look at the future..." he stopped again. "What was important to you during high school?"

"I hated high school. That's why I left."

"Why did you hate it?"

"I didn't fit in."

"So you cared what other people thought?"

"I guess."

"Do you still care about what those people think?"

"The kids from high school? No!"

"But back then your mother and I couldn't convince you of that. It mattered to you, and you couldn't see past those years. This is the same. You only see Jeff. You can't see a future without him, but trust me, two years from now you will be thankful you didn't compromise yourself for him."

"What if Jeff comes to know God because of me?"

"God doesn't need you to save Jeff."

"If I quit hanging out with him, do you think he'll find another Christian to hang out with? That's doubtful."

"You've planted a seed. He may not come back to it for years, but the seed has been planted. Let's say you sleep with Jeff and it doesn't work out. He goes his way, you go yours. Then you find another guy who isn't a Christian and sleep with him. How are you bringing people to know Christ by dating them? If that worked, why wouldn't we be using it as an evangelism tool?"

I laughed and so did Dad.

"I made some mistakes early on," Dad said. "When I met your mom, she was a virgin. Once you give that away, you never get it back. Right now you think Jeff would never hurt you or leave you. I wish that was the truth. If he loved you the way God wanted him to love you, he wouldn't want you to sleep with him unless you married him."

"Ben would get married."

"Don't do that to Ben."

"Do what?"

"Don't use Ben to get over Jeff. Just get over Jeff. Then when and if you find someone, you'll be ready."

"I don't know how to get over Jeff."

"Work on becoming the person God wants you to be. Concentrate on school. Get into a Bible study. Get a job."

"I'm working for a professor at school."

"Then work hard."

"You're probably right."

"I'll take that," Dad said, slowing to take our exit. "Thanks for keeping me in the know. If you can't talk to your mom and me about what's going on, that's a pretty good indicator you shouldn't be doing it."

"That's what Ben said."

"I like Ben."

I looked at Dad and we laughed.

Bible Study Chapter Ten

Living a lie or living in the truth

Read John 8:31–36. Even though Meghan didn't feel great when she and Jeff broke up, she told Ben she felt as if a weight had been lifted from her. At the end of this chapter, we see her confiding in her dad. Jesus said in John 8:34 that we become a slave to our sins. How had Meghan become a slave to her lie of living a double life?

In what ways did telling the truth to herself and then her parents set her free?

Is there a sin in your life that is holding you hostage? Maybe you feel you are only valuable if you look a certain way. Maybe you gossip about other people to make you feel better about yourself. Maybe it's an addiction. Wouldn't if feel good to bring it into the light and get out of its grip?

Read John 8:44. Where do lies and half-truths come from?

Read Proverbs 12:22. Why would we want to be detestable to God when we can be His delight?

Work

Ben and Meghan's conversation with Millie included a discussion about being creative. Ben and Meghan both agreed it amounted to work. Read Exodus 23:12. How many days were the people of Israel to work?

Read 1 Thessalonians 5:12–14. What attributes does Paul tell us to respect (verse 12)?

Who puts people (like bosses) over us?

What does the word "admonish" mean?

Verse fourteen tells us to warn what kind of people?

Read 2 Thessalonians 3:6–13. Paul gives us at least two good reasons for us to work. What are they (verses 8 and 11)?

Read Colossians 3:22–24 and Ecclesiastes 5:18. What should our attitude about work be, whether it is homework, chores at home, or a job?

Solomon used the word "toilsome." Paul speaks to slaves. Is our attitude supposed to be positive toward our work only if we have a great job where we make lots of money?

Understanding the Great Commission

Read Matthew 28:19–20. How do you reconcile this passage with the statement that Meghan's father made that God didn't need Meghan to save Jeff?

Read Matthew 10:5–7, 14. What is our job?

Read 2 Corinthians 1:21-22. Who is at work when a person comes to faith?

God took all the pressure off of us. We cannot make anyone believe. Our job is strictly to share the message. The Holy Spirit is at work in the hearts of those who come to faith, and those who reject the Word have been given the free will to do so.

Chapter Eleven: The Road Trip

The first snowstorm of the season arrived the day we were going home for Christmas break. Giant flakes came down furiously, coating the walks and the windshields. Matt pulled the car up to my apartment, and I took my place next to Amanda. As Matt, Amanda and Ben stared at me it occurred to me I hadn't worn makeup in a week. I had showered and brushed my teeth that morning, but I couldn't remember if I had combed my hair.

"Are you sick?" Amanda asked.

I shoved my stocking cap further down onto my face. "I just haven't eaten or slept in a week."

"What's going on?"

Matt started down the road.

"Carol and Jeff are dating," I said.

"Jeff is your ex-boyfriend. Who is Carol again?" she asked.

"My roommate and best friend until a week ago."

"Oh," Amanda moaned.

"When did that start?" Ben asked.

"Carol came back the Sunday after Thanksgiving and decided to give Dave Schubert a call." I turned to Amanda. "Dave had a one night stand with my roommate. I wasn't going to say anything, but now I know what it's like to be on the other end of this, and I think Sandy should know."

Amanda covered her mouth with her hand.

"I'm sorry, but it's true."

Amanda groaned and waved her hand for me to continue.

"When Carol called, Dave told her he had a girlfriend, so Carol went to see Jeff, who had just gotten back from a week of dealing with his dysfunctional family and his mother's stroke. They comforted each other by having sex. Then they decided to pursue a relationship, but there was just one problem."

"You," Amanda whispered.

I nodded. "Carol couldn't get over the guilt every time she saw me, so last week she got it off her chest."

"What did you say?"

"I walked out of the room. I haven't talked to either of them since."

"What are you going to do?"

"I've considered moving to Africa. At least then I wouldn't have to see them together."

"Do you see them much now?"

"I hear Carol moving around the apartment, but I've stayed away from her. I assume she goes to his place when they're together."

Ben peered around the seat. "Carol slept with Dave. I'm not at all shocked she'd sleep with Jeff."

"That was different. This is with the guy I dated and liked for three months, who, not to mention, was only single for one week."

Amanda shoved Ben's head back into the front seat. "Thank you, Ben, for that deep expression of sympathy."

She turned to me. "God has a plan."

I covered my face to yawn, and then looked at her. "I hope He clues me in."

"You look tired."

"I'm exhausted."

She pulled her iPod from her purse.

"Here," she said, programming it, and handing it to me. "Listen to Bebo Norman and go to sleep."

"Bebo?"

"Trust me."

I put the ear buds in.

God my God, I cry out. Your beloved needs you now. God right here calm my fears, your kindness is what pulls me up and your love is all that draws me in.[6]

I shut my eyes and let the tears fall as I leaned against the window and fell asleep.

Amanda tapped my knee to wake me. "We stopped at a gas station."

Ben and Matt were waiting outside the car when we came out. "Do you want to switch again?" Ben asked Amanda.

She looked at me. "What do you want?"

"It doesn't matter to me."

Amanda sat next to Matt while Ben and I settled into the backseat.

"You should have called," Ben said.

"So you could hear me blubbering like a fool?"

"I would have been praying for you."

"I don't know why I didn't see it coming."

"At least you know it's over. Half the difficulty of a breakup is wondering if there's a chance to get back together."

"What happened with your girlfriend?"

He ran his hand across his chin.

"We dated most of last year," he began. "When she moved home for the summer, she thought she might be pregnant. Her mom found the pregnancy test in the garbage, and her parents put an end to the relationship."

"Pregnant with your baby?"

He nodded.

Even Ben? Was I the only virgin left?

"What did your parents say when they found out?"

He shook his head. "To say they were disappointed would be an understatement of gigantic proportion. The talk that ensued was the worst hour of my life."

"Did they want you to get married?"

"Her parents were adamant that she wasn't getting married. My parents said to respect her parents."

"So that was it? You haven't seen or talked to her?"

"I was told not to e-mail, text or call, and she didn't come back to Wheaton."

"So for all you know she might be seven months pregnant right now?"

Amanda whipped around in her seat.

"There's a thought to blow your mind," Matt said.

"She said it was negative, and I believed her. Don't you think someone would have told me?"

"Her parents might think if you knew then you'd want to see the baby and that would mean they wouldn't have control of the situation," Amanda proposed. "Legally, you'd have a right to see it."

"I can't see someone doing that," he said.

"I can't either," I said. "But Jeff always said it's foolish to assume everyone thinks like I do. Where does she live?"

"Minnesota."

"Could you go see her?" Amanda asked.

"Just show up on her doorstep?"

"Maybe you wouldn't have to," I said. "I can't imagine she could hide it, could she?"

"You hear of girls who have a baby in the bathroom at school and no one knew," Amanda said.

"I'd go with you," I volunteered.

"My parents would be thrilled to hear I was taking off with you...or any girl for that matter," Ben said.

"What if we all went?" Amanda suggested. She shifted further in her seat to face him. "We've got to go to Minnesota, Ben."

We came home on Wednesday. On Friday we got back on Interstate 94 and headed north. A few hours later, we crossed the border into Minnesota.

Our parents knew only that we were going to the Casting Crowns concert. Amanda found the event online, and since it was in Minneapolis it seemed the perfect alibi for going to Minnesota to spy on Becky.

Becky's family lived in Oronoco—one of those places almost too small to be called a town. Ben hadn't been to her house, so we stopped at the one restaurant on the highway. We ordered soft drinks and Ben looked up her address on his phone.

"What are we going to do?" Amanda asked. "We can't just park across the street from her house. In a place this small, there'd be an officer there in no time."

"We could ask someone here if they know her family," I offered.

"And if they say yes then ask if they know if Becky's pregnant?" Matt asked.

"That would start the rumor mill," I said.

"We don't even know if she still lives at home." Matt pointed out.

"Even if she went to a different school, everyone's out by now," I said. "It's a week before Christmas."

"It wouldn't do us a lot of good to see her with her winter coat on," Amanda said. "We may or may not be able to tell."

Ben excused himself to the restroom.

"Oh, my..." Matt said.

"What?" Amanda asked.

"She's here."

"Who? Becky?" I whispered.

He nodded. "She's right there...the waitress talking to the bartender."

"How come you didn't see her before?" I challenged.

"I don't know. Maybe she was in the back or we were too busy figuring out what to do, but that's her," he said.

"You better go tell Ben," Amanda said.

Matt headed for the bathroom, while Amanda and I checked her out. She had a slender build and looked young in her jeans and Tilly's Tavern T-shirt and black apron. Her hair was long and dark and pulled back in a ponytail. She had side-swept bangs tucked behind her ear and she wore dark-framed glasses. The bartender finished making the drinks and handed them to her. She delivered them to the table and turned around just as Matt and Ben came down the hall from the bathroom. She saw Ben at the same time he saw her. She put her hand over her mouth and headed for him. When she reached him she fell into his arms.

Amanda and I looked at each other.

"Romeo and Juliet," she sighed.

Matt came back to the table, scooted his chair closer to Amanda, and put his arm around her.

"As you can see, she's not pregnant."

"I wonder if they would have stayed together if her parents hadn't broke it off," I said.

He shrugged. "There's definitely some emotion over there."

"Maybe they'll end up getting married after all," I proposed.

"Then again, maybe not," Matt said, seeing Ben approaching the table.

"Ready to go?" Ben asked.

"If you are," Amanda said.

"I'm ready," he said.

We paid for our soft drinks and went to the car. Ben sat in the front with Matt. Once we were on the way to Minneapolis, Amanda tapped his shoulder.

"So?"

"She's got a boyfriend. She didn't like the way our relationship ended, but she knew she didn't want to get married to me or anyone else anytime soon. And as you saw, she is not pregnant."

"What did you say to her?" Amanda asked.

"I said I was sorry about what happened and wished her the best."

"That was nice of you," I said.

Ben didn't talk the rest of the way. Amanda chatted for a bit, but Ben's mood affected us all. She finally gave up and put on her iPod.

We were in Minneapolis by three. Unbeknownst to Ben and me, Amanda and Matt had decided we'd stay at a hotel with an indoor water park.

"Merry Christmas," Amanda sang when she told us.

"I didn't bring a swimming suit," I said.

"Who doesn't bring a suit when you go to a hotel?" she asked.

"I thought we were going to a concert. Typical I wouldn't have one."

"What's typical about not packing a swimming suit?"

"Not having a swimming suit has gotten me into my share of trouble."

"Why don't you have a suit?"

"Oh, I have one."

"So?"

"My first weeks at NU, Jeff, Carol, and I went to the beach every night. Usually we didn't get there until dark. For some reason, the water being cold was never a deterrent."

"You swam at night?"

I nodded. "The lights of Chicago glowed on the water in the distance. It was really beautiful."

"Sounds fun. Why haven't I ever done that?"

"Maybe because you obey the signs. Beaches close at dusk. I never saw anyone else in the water. It's definitely not the safest thing I've ever done."

"So why didn't you wear a suit?"

"Sometimes we did, but as often as not we didn't plan to go in the water. We'd be walking and get our feet wet and the next thing you knew, we wanted to swim."

"So you swam in your clothes?"

"A few times."

"How did that get you into trouble?"

I lowered my voice to a whisper. "It wasn't the times I swam with my clothes on that got me into trouble. It was the times I took them off."

"You went skinny dipping?!" she cried.

"Total lapse of judgment," I said.

Matt cleared his throat. "We'll have to stop someplace to get Meghan a suit. Help me look for a mall."

"A week before Christmas...this should be fun," Ben grumbled.

"I'm sorry."

"Don't worry about it," Amanda said. "I love Christmas shopping!"

"We don't do it in my family," I declared.

"I want to be part of your family," Ben resolved.

"Me, too," Matt said.

"No presents at all?" Amanda asked.

I shook my head. "We go somewhere for a day trip as a family instead. We came up here to the Mall of America a couple years ago."

"So you didn't shop before Christmas, but then went to the biggest mall in the Midwest after Christmas? That makes sense," Matt teased.

"They have an amusement park and an aquarium. We didn't spend much time shopping."

"There's a Target over there, Matt," Amanda pointed out.

Once the car was off, Matt turned around to face me. "I'm not going to fight with you if you're a conscientious objector, but I'm pretty sure the hotel has a policy about wearing...something."

"Matt!" Amanda cried.

He laughed. "We'll wait in the car."

"This should be humiliating," I said when we were inside, shuffling through the few suits they had.

"Here's a tankini," Amanda said, holding up a maroon two-piece.

"Does it have padding in the bust?"

"A little."

"I'll take what I can get."

Amanda had booked a suite thinking there would be two separate sleeping areas; one for the guys and one for the girls. Upon arrival we found the suite to be one large room with a king-size bed and a pull-out couch.

We stood looking at the room, and then at each other.

"Sorry, guys," Amanda said. "I envisioned this being a little different."

"Let's go to the front desk," Ben suggested to Matt. "Maybe we can get two rooms."

The guys left their bags and returned about ten minutes later.

"The hotel is full," Matt explained. "It's this or a smaller room with two queen beds. They'll upgrade someone to the suite, but we'll still have to pay for it."

"What a deal," Amanda muttered. "What are we going to do?"

"Could we make it work?" Matt asked. "Amanda and Meghan can take the bed, and we'll take the pull-out. We can leave while you guys are changing and vice versa."

I looked from Matt to Ben. Ben shook his head. He walked first to the window, then to the bedside table and grabbed the phone book. When he found what he was looking for, he dialed.

"Do you have any rooms available tonight...either...how much...I'll take the non-smoking double." After he gave his credit card information he ended the call.

"That's where we're sleeping tonight," he told Matt, pointing down the street to a smaller hotel.

"You guys might as well stay here until after the concert," Amanda suggested. "Otherwise we won't have any time to enjoy the water park. Meghan and I will step out and let you guys get ready first."

A few minutes later the guys emerged in suits.

"See you down there," Matt said.

I put my suit on, but couldn't shake the sick feeling in my gut. I had put my body out for Jeff to see without hesitation, but as I looked in the mirror, I couldn't help but cringe.

"What?" Amanda asked, standing next to me.

"I hate my body," I said.

"Are you kidding me? People go to great lengths to look like you. There's not an ounce of fat on you. Look at my thighs. Look at my gut."

"Look at your boobs."

"You're perfectly proportioned," Amanda said. "We didn't bring you here to bum you out. We were hoping to put a few smiles on your face. It's not about having a perfect body. None of us could go swimming if that were the case."

"You're right," I said. "It is what it is."

"Let's go."

We walked into the swimming area and found a place to put our shoes and room key. When I saw the guys, I leaned over and whispered to Amanda.

"I'd say Ben comes pretty close to a perfect body,"

She nodded. "Farm boy."

"What are you whispering about now?" Matt asked as they walked up to us.

"How hot you guys are," Amanda said.

Matt flexed his muscles.

"And humble, too," I said. "What more could you want in a man?"

"Nothing," Amanda said, taking Matt's arm and heading toward the pool.

I couldn't tell if Ben was annoyed at being left with me, or at life in general. I grabbed a tube and followed him to the top of the slide. Once at the bottom, we got out and started back up.

"So Ben, are you okay after today, or shouldn't I ask?"

"At least I know it's over. Now I just deal with the demons and move on."

"That's where I'm at," I said. "Maybe we could find a support group."

"Or start one," he said.

"The DLD group," I suggested.

"DLD?"

"Dating like dummies."

"How about IEPL?"

"Let's hear it."

"Ignore everything previously learned."

"Or CAP. Christians acting pagan-like," I offered.

166

"That's good," he said. "Is there anyway we could get an R in there?"

"Sure. Christians really acting pagan-like."

"I like that," he said.

"I think I could make a logo for that."

"I don't want to know what it would look like."

"I'm thinking of a person crying and wearing a hat with 'C.R.A.P.' on it, and the words, 'If you've been dumped, join C.R.A.P.'"

Ben laughed so hard he didn't get his tube in the slide properly. I followed him down. When I got through the tunnel, I saw him fall into the water. He was on his belly behind his tube, still holding onto it with one hand.

When we got out of the water, he showed me the burn on his side, where he had rubbed against the slide.

"I was saying crap the whole way down!" he said.

I wiped the tears from my eyes. "It's good to cry from laughing for once."

"I agree," he said, ushering me up the steps. "When we left Tilly's, I was wishing we would turn around and go home."

"When I got in the car Wednesday, it was the last place I wanted to be."

"Speaking of the car, what's the deal with you skinny-dipping with Jeff?"

"Just more crap," I said. "It was dark. I didn't think anyone could see me. Turns out Jeff could and did, which was a long-standing issue between us. I thought he should have had enough integrity to not look...like I didn't."

"Put a guy on a beach with a naked woman...I don't think I'd bet on that."

"My bad. I thought it was a no brainer."

He smirked and gave me a push, then hopped on his tube and followed me down.

"Didn't the guilt overwhelm you?" I asked on our way back up.

"You mean from having sex?"

I nodded.

"It was a progression of pushing the limits on how far we'd go. When we actually had sex, I told myself it would be fine because we'd get married. Most of the guilt came after my parents found out."

"I always felt guilty when Jeff and I were..." I didn't want to say intimate and make it sound like we had sex. Making out sounded dumb. Ben didn't wait for me to figure it out.

"That's good."

"It wore on Jeff. He wanted to be with someone who didn't think about it as much."

"And now he is."

"I guess he is," I realized.

We went down the slide a few more times then stayed in the water, floating with the current.

Matt and Amanda came carrying tubes. Amanda put hers in the water. When Ben and I came around, she hopped on. Matt was right behind her.

"Where have you guys been?" I asked.

"You'll find out. You and Ben should go up and start getting ready. We're going to hang out down here for a bit, and then we'll come up. We need to leave in about forty-five minutes."

Ben and I looked at each other. Why would they be sending us up instead of Amanda and I going up together? We followed the current to the side of the pool, then got out and put our tubes away.

"This is uncomfortable," I said, as we made our way to the room, wrapped in towels.

"I thought it was just me," Ben said.

A smorgasbord of finger food was waiting on the table in the room.

"I think I love Matt and Amanda," I said.

"I do, too," Ben said. "Mostly because there is nothing in here trying to get the two of us together."

I nodded and took a cluster of grapes. "I'm going to take a shower."

When I got out of the bathroom, Ben went in. I had my makeup on and hair mostly dried by the time he got out. I had just sat down next to the food when Matt and Amanda came in.

"I can't believe you guys did all this," I said.

"Matt's mom gave us the idea," Amanda said. "Saves a little money."

"Healthier, too," I said.

Amanda got in the shower. Ben finished shaving and announced he was going to the vending machines.

"You guys want anything?"

"Yes," I said. "Something with caffeine."

"Mountain dew?"

"Dr. Pepper would be my first choice, but since they probably won't have that, I'll take a Pepsi or Coke."

"How about you, Matt?"

"I'll stick with water," he said.

Ben left and for lack of anything better to do I curled my hair. When Amanda came out and Matt went in the bathroom, I moved into the living area so Amanda could dry her hair and get ready. I was just finishing with hairspray when Ben came in.

"How far away are the vending machines?" Matt asked emerging from the bathroom, dressed, but drying his hair with a towel.

"I went to a gas station a couple blocks away," Ben said, handing me a Dr. Pepper.

"For this?"

He nodded.

"You shouldn't have done that. You must be frozen. You didn't have a jacket."

"I ran."

"Do you like to run?"

"Not so much in the gym, but when the weather is decent I enjoy it."

"I think I like you."

He wrinkled his forehead. "Cause I run?"

"Cause you're nothing like Jeff."

"Good theory," he said.

"Oh my!" Amanda said, coming up to me. "I love your hair. Why don't you wear it like that more often?"

"It's her bar do," Ben said.

I grimaced but couldn't keep from smiling.

Ben smiled too. "I didn't know. That's the only time I've seen you like that. It caught my attention."

"No more than your bod at the water park today," Amanda said.

"Were girls looking? Why didn't you tell me?" Ben asked.

"Congratulations. You're both beautiful," Matt said. "Now if you can get over yourselves, we've got a concert to attend."

"Thanks for putting the food away, Matt," Amanda said.

"No problem," he said, hitting the lights and shutting the door behind us.

I had never heard of Tenth Avenue North, but their songs couldn't have penetrated my heart more. By the time Casting Crowns took the stage, my soul was laid bare before the Lord. I was soaking up the truth and loving it when they stopped playing and Mark Hall announced they had spent the afternoon praying over each of the seats and for everyone who would be sitting in them. Their next song was "At Your Feet."

When they got to the part that said, "Here at your feet I lay my past down, all my mistakes I give to you now," I broke. At first I wiped the tears, but finally I let them run.

When the lights came on at intermission, I headed for the restroom. I grabbed a paper towel and stood over the sink washing the mascara from under my eyes.

"Kind of emotional, huh?" Amanda asked, coming to my side.

"I've been in an ugly place. It's hard to believe how low you can sink in such a short time."

"The prodigal son," Amanda said.

I nodded.

"Well the angels in heaven are rejoicing tonight."

"Yes, the little broken lamb is back."

"God will put you back together."

Outside the Excel Energy Center, a gentle snow fell on trees lit with white lights. Jeff had told me to forget about fairy tales, and I had, but walking through the park with all those lights, it seemed maybe I was outside of a palace after all.

When we got back to the hotel, Matt and Amanda asked if we wanted to go for a walk with them.

"I'm beat," Ben said.

They looked at me.

"I'm tired, too, and I'd like to read my Bible before I crash."

"Ben, can you get our stuff together?" Matt asked. "Give us ten minutes. We'll just walk up the street and back," he said, taking Amanda's hand and walking away.

I took out my Bible and sat on the couch while Ben got the guy's bags in order. When he finished he came and sat on the other end of the couch.

"What are you reading?"

"Lamentations three. It must be something with the binding of this Bible. It's where it naturally opens up."

He nodded.

When I finished the chapter I shut my Bible.

"I don't think Becky saw what we did as a moral failure," he said.

"It is odd that she's dating if she doesn't want to get married, and that her parents are okay with it."

"That's what I thought."

Matt opened the door and held it for Amanda.

"You guys missed a beautiful walk," she said. "There are lights everywhere. I love Christmas!"

Ben shot me a paradoxical glance, neither totally forlorn, nor altogether hopeful, before he stood to leave. I thought of how I used to love Christmas, too, and nights with my family, and all sorts of simple pleasures. Now I mostly felt an ache and a void that seemed almost too big to fill.

"Ben will be driving us home today," Matt announced when he and Ben returned around nine the next morning. "I barely slept. Ben snores like a bear."

Ben dropped his bag on the floor. "Sorry."

Amanda gave Matt a hug. "How did you share a room with him for two years?"

"I slept with a pillow over my head."

"I'd put a pillow over *his* head."

"Did you hear that Ben?" Matt asked. "My girlfriend wants to suffocate you. Do you have anything to say about that?"

"Meatballs," Ben replied.

"Meatballs. Very enlightening," Matt said.

"Mom makes meatballs for Christmas every year. My mouth is watering just thinking of them."

We laughed.

"It's a good thing you're so lovable," Amanda said.

"I'm glad you think so."

I flipped the pull-out bed up and put the cushions on so I could sit on the couch. "It's hard to believe Christmas is almost here. I've barely thought about it."

"Don't remind me," Matt said.

"Quit worrying," Amanda reprimanded. "They'll love you."

Ben smirked and took a seat on the couch. "Meeting the in-laws?"

Matt pulled his collar away from his neck. "It's going to be a long week if they don't like me."

"Are you there for Christmas?" I asked.

"No," Amanda answered. "We're with his folks for Christmas. We're going to my parents on the twenty-seventh and staying there till we go back to school. Ben will have to take you back to school for us."

"You mean Ben and whichever parent drives us back," I corrected.

Ben turned to me. "I'm taking my car to school this semester. I've got an internship at Salt and Light."

I felt warmth creeping up my neck. "Oh."
Amanda looked at Matt and smiled. Matt smiled back then straightened his face and shrugged when he looked at me.

Bible Study Chapter Eleven

How can I be a good friend?

Read Romans 12:15. What can this passage teach us about being a good friend?

How does Amanda show us in this chapter that she is a good friend to Meghan?

Read James 5:16. What is one of the most loving things you can do for another person?

Why did Ben say Meghan should have told him about Carol and Jeff?

Do you pray for your friends? Do you ask your friends to pray for you?

Read 1 Samuel 18:1 and 1 Samuel 23:16. This last verse takes place when Jonathan's father Saul was trying to take David's life. In the midst of David's distress, what did Jonathan do for David?

If you don't have a friend who can help you find strength in God in your most distressing days, start praying now for the Lord to give you that kind of friend. Start figuring out how you can be that kind of friend to others. Those friends are worth more than gold.

Gossip

Read Deuteronomy 5:20. What are we told not to do?

Martin Luther's explanation of this commandment says, "We should fear and love God that we do not tell lies about our neighbor, betray him, or give him a bad name, but defend him, speak well of him, and take his words and actions in the kindest possible way." [7]

Someone once asked Jesus who his neighbor was. Jesus responded in Luke 10:29–37. Who is your neighbor?

Is it okay to speak badly about anyone?

In this chapter of our book, whose good name was put in question?

Do you see how quickly rumors start? Meghan questioned Becky's honesty, and Amanda questioned Becky's parents' motives for keeping a nonexistent pregnancy secret. Read the following passages from Proverbs and write down what each passage says about gossip.

Proverbs 11:13—

Proverbs 16:28—

Proverbs 26:20—

Read James 3:3–6. You will either be a good friend, a good spouse, a good child, and a good neighbor—or you will curse, gossip, lie, and use your mouth for profanity. The rudder may control the ship, but the person steering the ship can move the rudder. Your mouth and the way you use it are a clear indication of what controls you, namely the condition of your heart. If your mouth needs a change of course, then so does your heart. Pray God would help you to do that.

More than just a pretty face

When it came time to go swimming, Meghan lamented that she didn't have the perfect body. Read Genesis 29:16–17. Who was the pretty sister?

Read Genesis 29:31–35. Whom did God bless with children?

Who gave birth to Judah, through whom the ancestry of Christ would come?

Read Genesis 30:1. What characteristic is used to describe Rachel? Is that a beautiful trait to have?

Read Psalm 139:13–16. Who determined what you would look like?

Do you think He knew what He was doing when He made you? (He also made the trees, the ocean, the stars, the planets, etc.)

Read Romans 8:20–23. Why aren't we perfect?

Sin took the perfection out of all of us. It's why we don't all look like Barbie. When will our bodies be perfect?

If I've noticed one thing throughout my life it is that God rarely, if ever, gives a person everything. I've known people who have beautiful children that struggle with health issues. I've known families that are loving and kind and peaceful that barely have money to make it through each month. I've known beautiful people with terrible attitudes. I've known not so good-looking people with terrible attitudes. Some good-looking acquaintances have been the last to get married. I've come to find that some of the things I don't like about my body are the very things my husband loves. The most healthy attitude I've found to have regarding my body is that it houses my soul, and when my soul shines with God's love, few people care about my physical shortcomings.

Chapter Twelve: A New Start

It was 9:15 p.m. I hopped out of bed and went to the kitchen.

Mom was rolling out sugar cookies. "Did you have a good nap?"

"It's nice to be home. I wish I didn't have to go back to school."

"Why?"

"Jeff and Carol are pretty much living together."

"So you're upstairs in the big apartment by yourself?"

"More or less."

"Your name isn't on either lease, is it?"

"No."

"Then you could find a different place to live, right?"

"I guess."

"Why don't you call Pastor Jon and see if anyone in the congregation has an extra room?"

"I don't have a car. Unless they live close to campus, I'd have a long walk."

"Could you get into the dorms?"

"Too expensive."

"Call Pastor and go from there." She put a pan of cookies in the oven. "Where'd you go this afternoon?"

"I helped Ben with his Christmas shopping. Afterwards he took me to eat."

"Where did you eat?"

"TGI Fridays. He likes their jerk chicken. I told him it was an appropriate choice for him."

"I thought Ben was nice."

"He is, but he doesn't have any empathy about my situation with Jeff and Carol."

"Oh?"

"He says it's stupid to think they're going to act like Christians when they aren't Christians."

"He's got a point."

"Jeff said that was a major flaw of mine. I assume everyone thinks like I do."

"I guess you should take that into consideration."

"I hate admitting either of them is right."

"Humble yourself."

"I've been humbled."

"Being humbled and humbling yourself are two different things. Given the choice, I'd rather be humble."

I sighed. "I think I'll take a shower. I have to be at work at six tomorrow morning."

"I'll take you to work," Dad said coming into the kitchen. "It's starting to snow. We're supposed to get almost a foot overnight."

Mom moaned. "Mom and Dad are coming tomorrow."

"We'll see what the morning brings," Dad said.

Dad was up before five Christmas Eve morning, shoveling the driveway so I could get to work. The main roads were plowed, but snow was still falling. We slid around turns, and the van groaned when taking off from a stop.

Except for the occasional customer who came for donuts or bagels, the grocery store was lifeless until shoppers began trickling in after it quit snowing. I was scheduled to work until two, but because the last-minute shoppers arrived later than normal, I worked until the store closed at four. By the time I counted my drawer, it was almost five.

Grandpa and Grandma decided not to come. They lived further east where it was still snowing. For the overnight trip, it wasn't worth the risk. Mom agreed with the decision, but couldn't hide her disappointment.

It hardly seemed like Christmas. The church was decorated and full of people. We sang "Silent Night" and "Joy to the World," but my heart was neither joyful nor silent.

After the service I saw high school friends also home from college. I had seen them at Thanksgiving when Jeff and I had just broken up, but it wasn't real then. It still seemed he would miss me so much he'd come back and tell me he couldn't live without me.

I gave Amy and Clair hugs. Clair asked first. "Is there someone new in your life?"

"I'm very single."

"It's only been a little while," Amy reminded me.

"I don't think I'm relationship material right now."

"There's a plan," Claire said.

"I keep hearing that. I'm just hoping it's not the same plan as Sarah."

"Sarah who?" they asked.

"Abraham's wife. She was ninety when she had a baby."

They laughed.

"You've got a lot of years before you're ninety," Clair said.

Dad walked past and gave me the 'wrap-it-up' look, so I said my good-byes and followed him to the car. The roads were sloppy on the way home.

"It's a good thing your parents didn't come," Dad said to Mom.

"I know," she said.

We passed Winnequah Park and the Youth Dream Play Area. How many days had I played under the words MAKE YOUR OPTIMISM COME TRUE? Jeff was right. My optimism was no match for reality.

While the soup was warming, we called Grandpa and Grandma and wished them a merry Christmas. When we hung up, Dad said a special Christmas prayer, and we grabbed our plates.

"What's in the Crock-Pot?" I asked.

"Meatballs," Mom answered.

"Meatballs?"

"Yeah, why?"

"We don't usually have meatballs."

"I started craving them the other day," she said.

It was our tradition to watch the "Swiss Family Robinson" series sometime over Christmas break. We knew the theme song and all the episodes. As unrealistic as it was that they would have such an elaborate makeshift house on a deserted island, there was something powerful about risking it all to go on a voyage and being shipwrecked, only to start over and find they didn't miss all they had lost.

It was late when we turned off the TV and brought our dishes into the kitchen.

"I almost forgot," Dad said, handing me a package. "Ben brought this over today and asked me to give it to you."

"Really?"

"Seems like a nice boy," Dad said.

"At least I don't need to do any evangelizing," I said.

Dad smiled. "I'm thankful for that."

I shut my bedroom door, sat on my bed and opened the package. It was Third Day's *Revelation* CD. Taped to the CD was a note that said, "I read Lamentations chapter three. I don't think it's coincidence your Bible keeps opening there. Where else is there such a clear picture of how our sin leads to brokenness, but God is there, offering restoration?"

I waited until late the next afternoon to call.

"Have you had your fill of meatballs?" I asked.

"For today," he answered.

"Did they live up to your expectations?"

"Mom's cooking rarely lets me down."

"Well, I think I'm in love," I announced.

"With?"

"My new CD. I feel indebted to you now. First the drink and now a CD."

"I'm glad you like it, but let's forget about the drink and anything else illegal I might have done."

I laughed.

The next evening I called Pastor Jon. He agreed with Mom and thought it best I get out of the apartment entirely. He told me he'd do a little checking and get back to me in a few days.

He called back on New Year's Eve day.

"There's an elderly couple, the Harbachs. They'd be happy to let you stay in one of their bedrooms. They don't want any money. Evelyn suggested maybe you could help her clean once a week. It's getting hard for her to vacuum and bend down to wash the floors."

"I'd be glad to do that!"

"She said they don't eat much for meals anymore, but you are welcome to use their kitchen."

"Where do they live?"

"Just a couple blocks from church."

"Perfect."

"When will you be coming?"

"I'm not sure yet."

"I'll give you their number. You can let them know."

"Thank you."

"Happy New Year."

It just might be, I thought.

Ben offered to help me move. We decided to go back on Saturday. We'd still have Sunday to finish moving if we needed before classes resumed on Monday.

I put off calling Carol until Friday, when I knew I couldn't wait any longer. She sounded happy to hear from me.

"Are you back in Evanston?" I asked.

"I just got in. When are you coming?"

"Tomorrow. How's Jeff's mom?"

"She's still in rehab. Sounds like it's going to be a long recovery."

"That's too bad."

"At least she's still alive."

"Right."

"How are you doing?" she asked.

"I've decided to move out."

"Really?"

"I need a new start."

"Where are you going to live?"

"A couple from church have an extra room. Ben's driving me back tomorrow. He'll help me move."

"This isn't what I wanted," Carol said.

"It's not the way I hoped things would go either."

"Let's talk about it tomorrow. What time will you get here?"

"We're leaving at nine."

"We'll be here."

Mom and Dad were unyielding. I would not live in the same apartment as Jeff or Carol. It was time to move on. It would be unfair to the Harbachs to accept their invitation then decline it.

It was a mostly sleepless night. By the time I finally dozed off, it was only a few hours until the alarm went off. I showered, got my things together, and Dad gave me a ride to Ben's.

"Don't let them talk you into staying," Dad said. "When you came home two-and-a-half weeks ago, you looked like you had one foot in the grave. You shouldn't have lived with Jeff. It's time to start over. God's provided a way for you to do that."

"I know."

"I know you know. I just don't want you to give in once you're in front of Jeff and Carol."

"Ben will be there. He'll help me."

"I don't want to be part of any meeting with Carol and Jeff," Ben said once we were on the road and I explained the situation. "I agree with your dad. It's time you got out. There is no need for you to sit with them and be talked out of what's best for you. Of course Carol wants you to stay. She wants your rent money. If you're ready to start over, start over. If you stay with Jeff and Carol, you'll just continue on the same path you've been on for the last four months, and that's brought nothing but chaos and pain in your life."

I hadn't expected such a strong answer from him. I didn't know how to reply, so I didn't. I turned toward the window and fell asleep.

When I woke up, we were in Chicago.

"Where are we going?" I asked.

"We're meeting Matt and Amanda for lunch," he said.

I sat up and lowered the visor to fix my hair and put on some makeup.

Amanda and Matt were waiting for us at Jung Kim's Chinese Restaurant.

I hugged Amanda when I saw her.

"You're looking better," she said.

"Looks are deceiving. I barely slept last night."

Ben and I slid into the booth across from them.

"What's going on?"

"My pastor found an older couple from the church for me to live with."

"That's great!"

"When I told Carol last night, she said she wants me to sit down with her and Jeff today to discuss it."

I saw Amanda and Matt's eyes flash to Ben, then back to me. Ben rubbed his face with his hands. He couldn't wipe away the look of disgust.

"I don't know why you're so mad at me. I never said I wanted to stay there."

"Why did you agree to meet with them?" he demanded.

"They were my best friends."

"Were," he said.

"Have you heard the saying 'Fool me once, shame on you. Fool me twice, shame on me?'" Amanda asked. "I think Ben just doesn't want to see you get devoured by the situation again."

"I don't want that either."

"Thank God," Ben said.

"Getting together might help get through the hurt," I said.

"Some things are better to avoid," he said.

"Seeing Becky brought you closure," I said. "How is this different?"

"Again, that was your idea. Not mine."

After we ordered, Amanda and I went to the bathroom. I washed my hands and was fussing with my hair in the mirror.

"I think you should reconsider," she warned.

"Why?"

"You've got a chance with Ben, but you're pushing him away."

"If you and Matt broke up, how long do you think it would take to get over him?"

"I don't know if I ever would."

"I loved Jeff. My mind gets that the whole experience was wrong, but my heart isn't cooperating. I've only known about Jeff and Carol for three weeks. Why does everyone think I should be able to walk away from this unscathed?"

"I think it's because we see how wrong Jeff was for you, and how right Ben could be."

"I have to deal with this before I can date anyone else. I'm nauseated thinking about seeing Jeff today. I don't know what I'm going to feel."

"That's why Ben doesn't want you around him."

"His being kept from Becky left him in limbo for months."

She folded her hands across her chest.

"I know Ben is a nice Christian man. Right now I just need friends."

"I just hope he's still around when you're ready."

"If he isn't, it wasn't meant to be."

She went to the mirror and straightened her hair.

"What is that on your hand?"

She smiled. "Matt asked me to marry him."

I grabbed her hand to look at the ring more closely. "Congratulations! When's the wedding?"

"Next December."

I let her hand fall. "You should have shut me up. This is so much bigger than my issues. How'd he propose?"

She opened the door with a huge grin. "I'll let him tell you all about it."

It was a quiet ride to the apartment. Ben found a parking spot and turned off the car.

"Were you planning on me participating in this discussion?"

"I don't know. We'll just have to see how it goes."

When I opened the door to the building, it occurred to me that this would be one of my last times here. I climbed the stairs that Jeff, Carol and I had run up and down so many times.

Carol and Jeff were on the couch. They both stood when they saw me. The tears started before I even got through the door. Carol came and wrapped her arms around me. When she let go, Jeff pulled me to himself and held me.

He cleared his throat. "We're both sorry we've hurt you so bad."

I shook my head. "I know you and I were not meant to be together, Jeff."

Jeff let me go and left the room, returning with a roll of toilet paper. "As usual, my job is to supply snot rags."

I stepped in to make room for Ben. "Carol, Jeff, you remember Ben. He has been nice enough to listen to me mope."

Jeff shook Ben's hand. "That was good of you."

I wiped my eyes and nose and gained my composure. "I don't want to drag this out. I think it would be better for all of us if I wasn't living here...for my sanity and your relationship."

"I agree," Jeff said.

I looked at Ben, then back at Jeff. "You do?"

"I can't be in a good relationship with Carol while you're around," Jeff said.

Carol nodded.

"Phew. That was easy," I said. "Let's hope the moving goes as well."

"We'll help," Carol said.

Ben brought his bag and guitar from the trunk, so he and Jeff could put the drawers from my desk in. They took my clothes, still on the hangers, out while Carol and I packed my toiletries and sweaters in bags. Once the bags were on their way to the car, Carol and I were left in an empty closet.

"So much for this," I said.

"Are you and Ben seeing each other?"

I shook my head. "I don't have anything to give right now."

She nodded. "I hope down the line we can do things together again."

"This is a start."

Ben and Jeff came back up.

"That's all we can take this trip," Ben announced.

"We'll be back," I said to Carol.

"We'll be here," she said.

"I was wrong," Ben said when we were in the car. "I'm sorry I was so hard on you."

"Forget it. You're helping me now," I said.

The Harbachs' house was a 1950s three-bedroom ranch. Evelyn answered the door and quickly invited us in. Herbert was right behind her. I would have the room across from the bathroom. It had a futon against one wall and a small chest of drawers empty and ready for my use next to the closet.

We unloaded the car and headed back to the apartment.

"Let's leave the bed for today," I told Ben as we scanned the contents of the room. "I can sleep on the futon."

"I don't mind making another trip," Ben said. "It's still early."

To get the bed to the Harbachs', we drove with the mattress on the roof of the car and the windows partially open to accommodate the rope holding the mattress in place.

"This day has taken some strange turns," I said, rubbing my hands together in an effort to ignore the breeze. "In the bathroom today, Amanda insinuated I was letting you slip away because I wasn't over Jeff."

"You're kidding!"

I shook my head. "I was thinking Amanda would be my new best friend, but she didn't have much compassion…"

"Nor did I," Ben added.

"While Jeff and Carol, who I had all but crossed off as friends, understood where I'm at and didn't try to pooh-pooh my feelings."

"It's unfortunate," Ben said. "It's knocked me down a notch or two."

"You have been good to me this afternoon. I couldn't have done it alone. My parents would have had to…oh, I need to let them know what's going on. Remind me to call them."

By the time we returned to the apartment, it was already dark. Jeff and Carol were eating.

"Are you hungry?" Carol asked.

I looked at Ben.

Jeff handed Ben a plate with a sloppy joe on it and returned with another plate for me. He offered me a chair, but I refused, eating instead by the counter. When I finished I slipped into the room to gather the last of my belongings.

"I found a few more odd and ends in the kitchen," Carol said, putting down a bag of groceries.

"You don't realize how much you have until you move it," I said.

"That's for sure."

"Oh, here's the key."

She went to the window and looked out, before turning back to me. "Your love runs deep. When it's stepped on, you break harder. We weren't prepared for that. We want you to get back to your bubbly, trusting self."

"I don't know if that's going to happen," I said.

"If I had a quarter for every time you said nothing was impossible with God…"

"You're preaching, Carol."

She smiled.

"I'll see if Ben's ready."

Ben stood when I came out. "Are you waiting for me?"

"I'm ready when you are."

"I'm ready." He turned to Jeff. "Thanks for the food."

Jeff stood up. "I'll help with the desk."

With Carol and Jeff's help, we took the last of my stuff and Ben's items to the car. I thanked and hugged them both. Ben shook their hands.

"Don't forget to call your parents," Ben said when we were in the car.

I watched Carol and Jeff go into the apartment, wondering why I hurt so much. I willed myself not to cry, but my will was no match for a day's worth of tears. My nose didn't cooperate either, and soon I was sniffing.

Ben opened the glove box and handed me some napkins.

"I learned that from Jeff today."

I wiped my nose. I learned a lot from Jeff, too, most of which I'd need to forget. "I've been trying to keep it together. I don't want to cry all the time."

"You won't. This is your time to cry." Ben rubbed his forehead. "This day *has* been strange."

"Can you not go to the Harbachs' yet? I don't want them to see me like this."

He turned off the car. I wiped my eyes and nose again before grabbing my phone.

Mom answered.

"We're just taking the last load to the Harbachs'," I managed.

"How'd it go?"

"Jeff agreed I should move out. He and Carol helped."

"Really?"

"Yeah."

"How are you doing?"

Tears wet my face. "I'm hanging on."

"We're praying."

I wiped my eyes again and put my phone back in my purse. Ben leaned against the window.

"Are you okay?" I asked.

"Praying."

I prayed, too, for God to comfort and strengthen me. When I finished, I lowered the visor and fanned my red eyes.

"Ready?" he asked, yawning.

"I suppose."

Herbert helped Ben unload the desk. It barely fit inside the room with the bed still in pieces on the floor.

"You've been driving and moving all day," I said, noticing how tired Ben looked.

"You can stay the night," Evelyn offered. "We've got a bed in the other room."

"I *am* tired," he said, "now that I've eaten."

"I'll make up the bed," Evelyn said.

"Do you want us to get your bed together for you?" Herbert asked me.

"If it's all right, I'll sleep on the futon. We can put it together tomorrow."

The next morning we took turns showering. Evelyn told us to help ourselves to toast in the kitchen. Once we were home from church, Herbert and Ben put my bed together. When they finished, Ben asked if I needed him to take me to the grocery store. Evelyn said she could take me, so Ben left and I unpacked, settling into my new home.

Bible Study Chapter Twelve

Humility

Meghan's mom told Meghan to humble herself or be humbled. What does the word *humble* mean, and what is the fundamental difference between humbling yourself and being humble?

Read Psalm 25:9. Why is it important for us to be humble before the Lord?

Read 1 Peter 5:5–6. How does God feel about pride? Have you ever considered that when you pat yourself on the back and think you are really wonderful and you're full of pride, whether after playing great in a basketball game or getting your grades or performing well in a play, you are setting yourself in opposition (as an opponent) of the Lord?

Who gave you your talent, whatever it may be?

Who should get the credit when you do well?

Read Luke 14:7–11. If we are continually boasting about ourselves, exalting ourselves, we're getting all we're going to get. But if we walk humbly with the Lord we leave room for what?

Read Ephesians 4:1–3. Paul is talking about living a life worthy of bearing Christ's name. How humble does Paul tell us to be?

How does being humble lead to the peace Paul is talking about in verse three?

Read Isaiah 66:2. What three qualities is God looking for in us?

Giving thanks in all circumstances

For Meghan and her mother Christmas didn't seem like Christmas. Read Job 1:18–22 and 2:9–10. What was Job's response to his children dying? What did Job say we should accept?

Read 2 Samuel 12:15–23. What was David's response to his baby dying?

Read 1 Thessalonians 5:16–18. When should we be joyful? For what should we give thanks?

My father-in-law died unexpectedly six days before Christmas. In the years following his death, I came to appreciate that what we celebrate at Christmas is not dependent on our circumstances. Our joyfulness and thankfulness don't need to be, either.

Forgiving

Read Matthew 18:15. What course of action should we take with people who mistreat us?

While Meghan didn't go to Jeff and Carol to show them their sin (neither of them professed Christianity and as such don't live by the same rules), she did take the stance that talking to them may get her to a point of being able to deal with the issue. Ephesians 4:26 says not to let the sun go down on your anger. I've found the same is true for any tough situation. It is better to deal with it than to let it fester and lose sleep over it.

To forgive means not to hold something against someone. Do you think Meghan forgave Jeff and Carol? How do you know?

Read Matthew 6:14–15. Why should we forgive others?

Read Luke 23:34. If Jesus was willing to forgive those who mocked and beat Him and hung Him on a cross, shouldn't we be able to forgive those who have hurt us?

Read Matthew 12:31. The unforgivable sin is failing to recognize that Jesus' blood atoned for our sins. It's a blatant disregard for Christ's sacrifice by someone who either believes their own merit covers their sin or that sin doesn't exist in the first place. Is there a sin too horrid for you to forgive?

How do humility and forgiveness go hand in hand?

Chapter Thirteen: Deal or No Deal

I took Dad's advice and dove into my classes and into my work as Mark's assistant. When he asked me out for drinks, I told him I had quit drinking.

"You're too young to quit drinking."

"I'm not into temporary fixes anymore. I'm after something that lasts."

"Nothing lasts forever."

"A few things do," I replied.

That was the last time he asked.

I hadn't gone to youth group at church but decided to give it a try. I was barely in the door when Lisa gave my arm a squeeze.

"Good to see you!"

"You, too," I said. "Have you seen Ben lately?"

"We had supper together. He brought me here."

"He's here?"

"Right over there."

He waved and came over and gave me a hug.

"How are you?"

"I'm getting there," I said. "I'm here."

"I'm glad."

"Do you always come to this group?"

"No," he said. "I brought Lisa tonight."

Amanda's words went through my head: *I hope Ben's still around when you're ready.*

I sat through the meeting taking it all in. Afterwards Ben offered to take me home.

"Thanks anyway," I said, "but I'll run."

"It's dark," Ben reminded me.

"I get my exercise these days running to and from campus."

"You're sure?"

I nodded.

Temps were below zero. The cold air burned my lungs as I ran, but the pain felt good.

I couldn't go back to youth group and risk seeing Lisa and Ben. Instead I began my own Bible study, starting with Genesis 1:1. I brought my Bible to campus and read between classes. I read into the night and early in the morning.

Every Saturday morning, Evelyn and I cleaned. She dusted while I vacuumed. She scrubbed the sinks and counters while I washed the tub and floors. When we finished cleaning, we went to the grocery store. One Saturday I saw Earl.

"Any chance you'll be seeing Lily later?" I asked.

"I'm taking these groceries to her."

"Can I give you a note for her?"

"Sure."

"For whom?" Evelyn asked.

"Lily Menteen. She lived downstairs in the apartment building where I used to live."

"You aren't living there anymore?" Earl asked.

"I moved in with Evelyn and her husband when I came back from Christmas break."

"Can I ask why?"

"Jeff and Carol started seeing each other, and it didn't work for us to live together."

"I know Lily Menteen," Evelyn said. "I went to school with her."

"You're joking," I said.

"I'm not. I used to see her out and about every now and then."

"She doesn't go out much anymore. Church or holidays are about all," Earl said.

"Is she able to get around?" Evelyn asked.

"Oh yes," I said.

"We should invite her for tea," Evelyn suggested.

"That's a great idea!"

"She'd like that," Earl agreed.

The following Saturday after our chores, we went to the grocery store. On the way home, we picked up Lily. Evelyn and Lily hugged when they saw each other.

"Good to see you, Lily," Evelyn said.

"And you," Lily replied.

Back at the Harbachs', we served tea and scones and fruit salad.

"I don't care much for winter anymore," Lily said.

"Poor Meghan probably roasts over here, but I have a hard time staying warm," Evelyn said.

"I do, too. Other than my hands, I don't move enough."

"Lily makes hats and scarves and mittens for the homeless shelters," I told Evelyn.

"That doesn't surprise me in the least," Evelyn said. "I have never forgotten the year Dad was out of work, and your mother showed up on the steps with a hundred dollar bill for us. Back then it probably put food on the table for a month. Mom was overwhelmed by your mother's generosity."

"Mother never told me that, but she was always helping where she could."

"I wish I could find a way to help," Evelyn lamented. "The older I get, the less I do. I feel more like a burden than a help."

"Your hospitality is a blessing to me. I'm saving four hundred dollars a month."

"You are doing something I can't," Lily said. "I don't have the room, but I would like the company."

"You'll have to come over every Saturday," Evelyn offered.

Herbert came up from his office downstairs. "Are you ladies having a tea party?"

"A very informal one," Evelyn said. "You remember Lily Menteen, don't you? She used to be Lily Schroeder."

"Of course I remember Lily Schroeder. Are you still around these parts?" Herbert asked.

"Just down the street," Evelyn said. "She lives in Meghan's old apartment building."

"You don't say."

Lily smiled. "Imagine my surprise when there was a knock on the door one day, and I opened it to find Meghan."

"I thought you might like the company," I said. "From our apartment we could see you in the window."

"She's a special girl," Lily told Evelyn.

"Don't we know!"

"You bring lots of life to the house again," Herbert added.

"I'm glad you all like me so much. I don't fit in with people my age."

"Only because you're so mature," Lily said.

If only she knew. Naïve was my middle name.

"Did you want to sit down?" Evelyn asked Herbert. "We've got plenty of scones."

"I was hoping I was invited."

February came and went, and we waited for the thaw. The hours of daylight were getting longer, but temps lingered in the teens and snow still came often.

When we picked up Lily the last Saturday of February, she seemed troubled.

"Is something wrong, Lily?" Evelyn asked.

Lily pulled her jacket collar closed. "I heard a scream in the building this morning. Earl checked the stairwells and hall, but he didn't feel he could knock on apartment doors at five o'clock."

"Oh dear," Evelyn said.

"I just hope it's not another incident like the one last fall."

"Have you heard screaming in the building before?" I asked.

Lily shook her head. "Not like this."

Once we were at the Harbachs', I excused myself.

Carol answered on the second ring.

"I wanted to make sure you're okay." I said.

"Why wouldn't I be?"

"Lily heard a scream in the apartment building this morning."

"Lily?"

"The old woman downstairs."

"When did you talk to her?"

"She comes over every Saturday."

"Oh, well, I didn't hear anything, and we're good."

"Were you in your apartment or Jeff's?"

"We were in mine. Why?"

"Just wondering."

"How are you doing?" Carol asked.

"I'm getting there."

"Glad to hear it."

I went out and sat with Lily, but the mood was somber. I was as troubled as she was about the scream.

Jeff found me at Norris on Monday. I was at a table reading my Bible between classes.

"Did you hear about the murder?" he asked, sitting down.

"Are you referring to the screamer?" I asked, shutting my Bible.

"Yep. Second floor again."

"Thank God I didn't take that apartment."

"I think it's Earl."

"It's not Earl."

"It could be."

"It could be you."

"You know me better than that."

"I thought I did."

"Ah yes. The bitterness has arrived," Jeff murmured.

"I'm really not," I said.

"Good."

"I'm surprised you found me here."

"I've seen you here every week, but figured I was the last person you'd want to see," Jeff said.

"Who was she?"

"I'll be watching the news like everyone else to find out."

"This can't be related to Tracie's murder."

Jeff shrugged. "Unless it's Earl."

"It stunk living there during all of that. I'm sure you guys could stay at the Harbachs' if you want. There's a futon in my room and a bed in the other room."

"That would be uncomfortable."

"Just offering."

"Maybe I should buy a gun."

I cringed. "Wouldn't it be easier to move?"

"Where?"

"I don't know."

"You're getting pretty serious about that," Jeff said pointing to my Bible. "Every time I see you, you're reading."

"I'm trying to live it now."

"You've always done that."

"Never more so than when I was skinny-dipping, and drinking with Professor Hollis, and in your bedroom."

Jeff waved his hand as if to dismiss those things. "You're a good person."

"None of us are, Jeff. That's the point. That's why we need Jesus."

"Good luck with that."

"You know how I feel about luck."

He shrugged.

"How's it going with Carol?"

"Between the two of us, we almost make one whole person. I cook and clean, and she pays for everything."

"Have you managed to clean her room?"

"I don't set foot in her room."

I grinned.

"Is Ben the one for you?"

"I'm not dating Ben."

"I didn't know."

"He's dating someone else, and I'm waiting for someone who wants to wake up next to this every morning."

"If you'd start doing something with yourself, you'd have no problem finding a...husband."

"You nearly choked to death getting *husband* out."

"Care to bet?"

"Bet what?"

"Do your hair, clothes, and makeup the way you did the night you and Carol went out, and I bet in one week's time at least two guys ask you out."

"What do I get if they do?"

He thought for a minute. "I'll make you lunch for a week."

"I have to come to the apartment?"

"I'll bring it to you."

"And if I lose?"

"You won't."

"Sounds like a lot of work to prove a point."

"You don't have to go out with them."

He held his hand across the table. "Every day for one week. No hats, no running pants, hair curled, makeup on. Deal?"

"I don't know."

"What do you have to lose?"

"I guess nothing," I said, shaking his hand.

"Good," he said. "You start tomorrow."

Professor Hollis was the first person to notice.

"On the prowl again?" he asked.

"Not so much. Just living out a bet."

"What's that?"

"My ex-boyfriend said if I did this every day for a week, at least two guys would ask me out."

"What's the prize?"

"Lunch for a week."

"With him?"

"Made by him, brought to my house."

He raised his eyebrows. "What's in it for him?"

"Just the chance to say he was right."

Mark seemed to ponder the idea.

"I'm not taking it too seriously. I don't want to date."

"Why not?"

"It's too painful."

"Who says you'll get hurt?" he asked.

"Who says I won't?"

"Not ever going out again is a sure way to not get hurt. I'd think it would get old, but it's safe, that's for sure. Just remember, you only have a few months left of school. There are lots of single guys here."

I decided to go back to youth group. I recognized a few people from the last time, but I hadn't tried to get to know them then. I took a deep breath and got busy introducing myself.

Two seniors, Elly and Tim, led the group. They opened with an icebreaker. We wrote down three facts about ourselves; two true, one false. It was up to the group to decide which two were true.

I put down that I was from Wisconsin, that I would finish school in May, and that I had a tattoo of Jesus on my back.

Everyone grappled a bit while sizing me up. Finally they decided I wasn't done with school in May.

"No tattoo," I said, smiling. "Although He is tattooed on my heart."

"That's the best place," Tim said.

After the meeting Tim thanked me for coming.

"I enjoyed it," I said.

"Are you on campus?"

I shook my head. "I live with the Harbachs."

"Now that you say that I have seen you in church with them." He paused. "Do you need to get home right away?"

"I guess not."

"Do you want to go to Mel's?"

One point for Jeff. "Why not?"

"What are you going to do when you're done with school?" Tim asked as we walked.

"No clue. I feel stupid saying it, but I didn't realize how fast it was coming until a professor pointed it out yesterday. What about you?"

"I'm applying for jobs and grad school. Whichever pans out is the direction I guess I'm supposed to go."

"What is your dream job?"

"I'd love to start or work at a nonprofit."

"What kind of nonprofit?"

"I'm not sure."

"Have you heard of Salt and Light?"

"I know some of the people who volunteer there."

"I know someone interning there this semester. I can give him a call and see if you guys could get together. He might be able to give you some insight."

"That would be great."

I looked at my watch. "It's not too late. I'll call him now."

Tim opened the door and we went into Mel's and found a booth. Once we were seated, I dialed Ben.

"How are you doing?" he asked.

"I think I'm going to make it."

"I've been praying for you."

"You have?"

"Of course."

"I appreciate that." I looked at Tim and got back to business. "I went to youth group tonight and started talking to one of the leaders. He's a business major finishing up in May."

"I know Tim," Ben said.

"He mentioned he'd like to work at or start a nonprofit. I thought maybe since you're interning at Salt and Light, you could show him around, maybe help him out."

"Can he come tomorrow?" Ben asked. "I'm there all morning."

"Hold on. I'll see."

"Can you meet him tomorrow morning?"

"I have class at one," Tim said.

"He's got class at one," I repeated.

"See if he wants to meet me at nine."

"Could you meet him at nine?"

He nodded.

"You've got a date," I said, "figuratively speaking of course."

"How about you meet me for lunch," Ben said. "Then I will have a date."

"What about Lisa?"

"What about her?"

"I have class till noon."

"Meet me downtown at 12:30."

"Where?"

"Give me a call when you're on the train, and I'll let you know."

"Hopefully there's something in this to show me if this is right or not," Tim said as I put my phone away.

The waitress walked up. I ordered hot chocolate and Tim ordered coffee.

"You mean like a sign?" I asked when the waitress left. "Don't you have to be careful about looking for signs?"

"I would go down a lot of wrong paths if I didn't ask God for direction. He always shows me which way I should go. Sometimes it's nothing more than everything falling into place."

The waitress delivered our drinks.

"Look at the children of Israel. When they didn't ask for His direction, it usually led to trouble."

I stirred my hot chocolate. "What do you do when you ask God for direction?"

"I pray, immerse myself in His Word, and keep my eyes and ears open."

"Do you pray for a sign?" I asked.

"Have you heard of the David Crowder band?"

I shook my head.

"They have a song called 'shine'. The lyrics start, 'send me a sign, a hint, a whisper. Throw me a line, 'cause I am listening.'"

"I'll have to look it up when I get home."

"The gist of the song is that Jesus was the sign and He's done everything that needs to be done."

"So you don't ask for a sign?"

He shook his head. "I pray God opens my eyes to see what He's trying to show me and to make the situation clear. Sometimes He does that in a sermon, or a conversation, or through what I read in the Bible. Sometimes He just gives me all the information I need so I can figure it out."

"So you don't go around looking at license plates or checking clouds," I joked.

He laughed. "No, but I don't believe in coincidence, either."

"Neither do I."

"Coincidence. You coming to youth group and arranging a meeting with Ben."

"You might not feel so good about that coincidence this time tomorrow," I said.

"Either way I'm glad you came. You've never been there before, have you?"

"Once. In January."

"I don't remember you."

"Glad I made such an impression on you."

He cringed. "I'm sorry."

"It's ok. I was in recovery mode. I probably looked like the pathetic forlorn girl."

"Now that you say that, I think I do remember you. What were you recovering from?"

"A breakup."

"How long had you been dating?"

"Three months."

"Not so long."

"Just long enough to fall in love."

"He broke up with you?"

"It was mutual."

He gave me a puzzled look.

"He started dating my roommate a week later."

"Ouch."

"I'm working through it. I moved out of the apartment and into the Harbachs'. Now my ex is pushing me to move on."

"That's odd."

"Odd or God. I'm not sure which."

He smiled and nodded. "You'll figure it out."

"I'm sure I will."

"Let's hear the stats," Jeff said. It was the first time he'd called since we broke up.

"Technically, I've been asked out twice."

"Ha. I've already won!"

"But, Ben asked me to lunch over the phone, so it had nothing to do with the way I look."

"I thought he had a girlfriend."

"I did, too."

"Well, we're only on day three. Who was the other guy? Anyone interesting?"

"He's a youth group leader at church."

"Is he cute?"

"Remember the guy who sold us tickets to the cruise, the way his hair hung across his face?"

"I remember."

"Tim reminds me of him."

"Trendy type of guy, huh?"

"He's got a tattoo, too."

"Where?"

"Around his wrist."

"What is it?"

"A watch."

"Shut up!"

I laughed. "Just kidding. It kind of looks like barbed wire. I think it's the crown of thorns."

"He sounds a little on the wild side."

"Maybe."

"That could be fun."

"I don't know."

"Are you on the El?"

"Yep."

"Where are you going?"

"I'm not sure. I have to call Ben."

"Meghan."

"What?"

"It's good to talk to you."

I nodded my agreement. "It's good to have the past behind us."

"Meghan?"

"What?"

"The past will always be behind us."

I laughed and hung up to call Ben.

Ben was waiting at the El stop.

"It's good to see you," he said as we started off the platform.

"You, too."

"You're looking cheerful."

"I just got off the phone with Jeff."

"Is he still with Carol?"

"Happily with Carol."

"What did he want?"

"He wants me to get on with my life."

Ben opened the car door and motioned for me to get in. "For once Jeff and I agree." He shut the door and walked to his side of the car.

"How'd it go with Tim this morning?"

He pulled out of the parking space. "I don't remember the last time I met someone with his enthusiasm. I'm a little worried about him though."

"Why?"

"He's interested in you."

"Does that bother you?"

Ben turned to face me for a second before looking back at the road. "I've liked you since the night we met. I've been waiting patiently at times and not so patiently at others for Jeff to get out of the way."

"Jeff's out of the way."

"I see that."

"I thought you were with Lisa."

"What made you think that?"

"She said you two had supper before coming to youth group together."

"I gave her a ride from Salt and Light. We picked burgers up on the way. I came hoping I'd see you. After you blew me off, I decided I'd wait until you called me."

"It's good that I went out with Tim then 'cause I wouldn't have called. I thought you were off limits."

"I'd like to be off limits."

"I'm still trying to figure out if I want to stick my neck out again."

"Are you interested in Tim?"

"Tim's not my type. He doesn't realize it, but I'm not his either. He's only seen me like this. He doesn't get that this isn't my status quo. I like his tattoo, though. It works for him."

"I'm glad."

I laughed. "If that wasn't sarcasm I don't know what is."

He smiled and pulled into a parking spot outside of Rosie's BBQ. Once we were inside, the hostess took us to a table and left us with menus.

"So what do you think?"

"About?"

"You and me."

"I may be interested. In two months I'm on my way home. I haven't looked for a job. I don't know what I'm going to do. I've got to start thinking about my future."

The waitress came and we ordered soft drinks.

I picked up my menu. Ben picked his menu up, too, then peered around it. "Do you think you'd be ready to get married by September?"

"This September?"

"I'm going to seminary."

"Don't you think our families would think we were crazy?"

"I think my family would be thrilled if I married you."

"In September?"

"Yeah."

"I don't know what my family would think."

I hid my face in my menu. March. April. May. June. July. August. Six months. Married, in six months? I thought I was going to lunch, not planning a wedding.

The waitress returned and we ordered.

"Why don't we take a week and pray about it," Ben suggested when she left. "Even better, let's fast and pray about it."

"I've never fasted," I said. "I don't think I could make it a week."

"You don't have to fast the whole week. Skip a meal or two each day and focus on praying. Ask God to make it clear."

"To help us hear the whispers," I said.

"What?"

"Tim and I were talking about asking God for direction last night."

Ben smiled wistfully. "If God has a different plan for either of us, I'll be the first one to support it."

"I will, too."

"Then after today, we won't talk for a week. We'll wait on the Lord to show us if we should be planning a future together or not. Deal?" he asked, reaching across the table.

"I'm not sure if I'm thrilled or scared to death," I said, shaking his hand and making my second agreement of the week.

Bible Study Chapter Thirteen

Where do you turn when it all falls apart?

What was Meghan's response to her assumption that Ben was dating Lisa? What did she start doing?

What do we sometimes turn to when life or relationships aren't going as we hoped?

Meghan's choice was the best. What else can we do in the interim of waiting for God to work things out for us?

I've realized that helping others is a good distraction from my own problems. God helps me to see others are going through difficult times, too, that I'm not alone, and that some people have much more serious issues to deal with than I do.

What was Jeff's plan to find someone for Meghan?

Was it a godly plan?

Did it ultimately have anything to do with her being with Ben?

Using your gifts

In this chapter, we see Evelyn lamenting she doesn't do much compared to Lily (who makes hats and scarves for the poor), but Meghan reminds Evelyn how Evelyn is helping her. Read Romans 12:4–8. Paul uses the body as an example. The different parts—eyes, ears, hands, feet—all work together to make the body function. The same is true of the gifts God gives each of us. Why doesn't He give us all the same gifts?

Do you know what your gifts/talents are?

Notice as Paul goes along, he not only tells us to use our gifts, he tells us *how* to use them. What words does he use? (v. 8)

That seems like a pretty good motto for our lives: Let us use whatever God has given us generously, diligently, and cheerfully.

Fasting

Ben and Meghan decided to pray and fast before pursuing a relationship. Let's explore what the Bible says about fasting.

Look up these passages and fill in the blanks.

Psalm 35:13. Fasting can be an act of _____.

Acts 13:2. Fasting can be an act of _____.

Read Matthew 6:16–18. Why fast? Who sees what you are doing?

Read Daniel 10:2–3. Daniel fasted by abstaining from what things and for how long?

Read Esther 4:15–16. Describe Esther's fast. How many people fasted and for how long?

Read 2 Samuel 12:15–20. How long did David fast? What had taken place just prior to this section of the Bible? Did fasting change the outcome of the situation?

Read Matthew 4:2. How long did Jesus fast?

Fasting can take on many forms. You can fast from sweets, from your favorite beverage, from using the computer. It can be an act of humility and worship between you and the Lord. Why might it be a good idea to fast from your favorite things once in a while? (Hint: What is the first commandment?)

Let's say you usually give ten percent of your money to church, but every now and then you put extra money in the offering plate.

Fasting is the same sort of thing. Most of us pray often, several times throughout the day. Fasting is giving up something for a time in order to focus on God. It's a reminder that He, more than our food, or our computer, or whatever we are giving up, fills us up and provides our answers.

Chapter Fourteen: The Best and Worst of Times

"Who won?" Jeff asked, sitting down at my table in Norris.

"Just Ben and Tim," I said, shutting my Bible.

"We'll call it a tie."

"It served its purpose."

He wrinkled his face. "What's that mean?"

"What's the latest on the murder?"

"What have you heard?"

"I haven't heard anything," I said. "Lily was sick on Saturday."

"Don't you read the paper?" he reprimanded. "This is old news."

"I've got bigger things on my plate."

His eyes widened. "Like what?"

"Are you going to tell me or not?"

"Vicki Henderson: forty-five-year-old wife and mother of one thirteen-year-old girl. Husband was taken in for questioning, once again leaving Earl on the loose."

"Where's the thirteen-year-old?"

He shrugged. "Are you going to keep up with the hair and makeup?"

"Not for classes. Special occasions maybe."

"You look nice when you put a little time into yourself."

I grimaced. "You think I should do this everyday?"

"What's the big thing on your plate?"

"None of your business."

"So it has to do with a guy? It's Ben, isn't it? When are you going to realize he's perfect for you?"

I twirled my earring, wondering if I should care about Jeff's opinion.

He leaned closer to me. "What can I do to make you move on?"

"Help me understand how you went from telling me you loved me to having sex with Carol in one week's time."

"Once you've had sex, it's very easy to have sex again. Not having sex is the hard part, and since you deprived me for months…"

I rolled my eyes.

"You got hurt because you fell in love with the wrong person."

"Why didn't it hurt you?"

"It hurt seeing how badly you were hurting."

"Feeling sorry for me isn't the same as having a broken heart."

"I wasn't lying when I said I loved you, but there was no sense mourning what shouldn't have been."

"Why are you so sure Ben's the one for me?"

"Carol told me."

"I should base my future on Carol's opinion?"

"Future? As in marriage?" He shrugged. "If God didn't put Ben in your life, I don't know who did."

"If you believed He existed, that might mean something."

"Okay. It was a *huge* coincidence that the night I moved out of the apartment, you went to a bar where you've never been before or since, a bar I doubt Ben frequents, sat down, and a good-looking, crazy-for-Christ Christian just happened to sit at your table. I'm fine with that."

"You think Ben's good-looking?"

"You're so shallow. Of all I've said, you focus on that."

I laughed.

Jeff shook his head. "I don't know how many Bens there are. If you pass up an opportunity to be with him, you'll regret it."

On the way home I considered Jeff's words. *You got hurt because you fell in love with the wrong person. Why mourn what wasn't meant to be? Once you've had sex, it's easy to have sex again. Not having sex is the hard part.*

Ben called Tuesday afternoon. "Where are you?"

"At the Harbachs'."

"I'll be there in ten minutes."

I touched up my makeup, put on a necklace, and changed into a blouse and jeans. When I heard a knock, I went to the door.

"Do you mind if we go into Chicago?" Ben asked when we got to the car.

"I don't mind."

Neither of us spoke. The last time I was this nervous was the day I went to see Carol and Jeff about moving out.

Ben took an exit before downtown. He went through the side streets, stopped, looked at the street signs, and took a few more turns before finding the street he was looking for. He pulled into the parking lot of a church and circled the building. Behind the church was a hill, and on top of the hill stood three crosses.

There was still snow on the ground, so Ben had me wait while he cleared a path. When he came back to the car, he held out his hand. I took it and followed him up the hill to the center cross.

He let go of my hand and turned to face me. "I was attracted to you the first night I met you, and I'm even more attracted to the person you've become since. You've got a heart for God. That's what I'm looking for. I just need to know how you feel about me."

I smiled with trepidation. "I can't think of a better person to start over with than you."

"Well, then." He shoved his hands in his pockets. "I called your dad today."

"My dad?"

He nodded. "I told him what we had been doing for the last week and what direction seemed right to me."

"What did he say?"

"He told me to do whatever the Lord showed us."

"Really?"

"I want you to go with me when I move to Mequon in the fall."

"You've mentioned that."

He brought his hand out of his pocket and opened it to reveal a solitaire diamond ring. "Would you consider it?"

I stared at the ring. Ben took my hand and slipped the ring on my finger.

"It seems like a good fit," he said. "What do you think?"

I bit my lip. "I think it's crazy to say yes, but even crazier to say no."

He smiled. "So you're sure?"

"If you're willing to step out in faith, I will too."

He leaned in to deliver his first kiss, but stopped short of my face.

"Did you have sex with Jeff?"

"Not quite."

"Can you forgive me for being with Becky?"

"If you'll forgive me for what I did with Jeff."

"I can beat him up."

I grinned. "I believe you could."

When we turned to leave, the sun was setting in an orange, red, and pink sky.

Ben held my hand, at times feeling the ring, as he drove to a little restaurant on the western edge of Chicago.

"What would you have done if I said no?" I asked.

"I would have told you to fast for another week, 'cause you heard the wrong answer."

I smiled. "What made you so sure you were getting the green light?"

"The apostle Paul said if you could be single, you should be single. I don't want to be single."

"I don't either."

"I have never felt so sure of knowing where someone stood in regard to their faith as I do with you."

"Aren't you worried I might have traits that annoy you?"

"I saw what I needed to know on our trip to Minneapolis. You're the same whether you have makeup on or not, whether your hair is wet or curled. Your heart is tender and open to God's Word."

"I had no idea I was under such scrutiny."

"That's what I was attracted to most. You weren't trying to impress me."

Ha! Who knew?

"What made you decide to move forward?" Ben asked.

"Mostly Jeff."

"Really?"

"He helped me put what happened between him and me in perspective and to understand why you would want to get married sooner rather than later. I sifted through all the times you and I spent together looking for red flags and I found two; your snoring and your supposed messiness, but I decided those weren't deal breakers. I had been willing to be with Jeff and he'd had sex before, too, so I couldn't hold that against you. Besides, if Jeff wouldn't have been so good about not pushing it, I probably would have ended up having sex with him."

"You know," Ben said. "I'm really starting to like Jeff."

"I'm happy for you."

He turned into the Applewood Supper Club parking lot.

Matt and Amanda waved as we drove up.

"You invited them?" I asked, waving back.

"Yep."

"But I haven't told my parents."

"Your parents know."

I gave Amanda a hug before Ben took my hand and led me inside.

"I guess this means you're together?" Amanda asked once we were sitting at a table.

"We're together," Ben said.

"We knew you were perfect for each other," Matt said.

"It's about time, Ben," Amanda chided.

Ben put his hands up. "Don't look at me."

When they looked at me, I smiled. "How are the wedding plans?"

"We've got the church, the photographer, and the florist. Everything else will get done this summer," Amanda reported.

"Are you moving home in May?"

She nodded. "It's going to be a bummer being six hours from Matt, but I'll apply for jobs and get my teaching license and work on wedding stuff, so it should go fast. What about you? What will you do when you're done with school?"

"I'll be planning a wedding."

"For who?"

Ben lifted my hand onto the table to show the ring.

"Whoa!" Matt cried.

Amanda grabbed my hand. "Are you serious?"

"I'll take that as congratulations from both of you," Ben said.

"When's the wedding?" Amanda asked.

"Sometime before September so I can move to Mequon with Ben. Or at least, that's the plan now. I guess we'll see when it comes to making arrangements."

"I'm okay with a simple wedding," Ben said. "I don't need much."

"Did you hear that, Amanda?" Matt asked.

"I'm only getting married once."

"We can all be grateful for that," he teased.

"So it's going to be fancy," I ascertained.

"Right down to the white gloves the guys get to wear," Matt said.

"That will be pretty, especially at Christmas."

"Finally, someone who appreciates good taste," Amanda said. "Just for that, I'm not going to hate you for getting married before us."

"You can have a baby first," Ben said. "Just as long as you wait until after the wedding."

Amanda perked up. "Deal!"

"Wait a minute," Matt grumbled. "Who said anything about having a baby right away?"

"It's probably better you get married sooner rather than later. Ben needs a wife. He will be a great pastor, don't get me wrong, but the guy needs someone to take care of him."

"Don't scare Meghan," Matt scolded.

"I wasn't trying to."

"Are you talking about him being messy or is there something else I should know?"

"Messy isn't a strong enough word," Amanda said. "You know the cartoon character from Peanuts who walks around in a cloud of dust? That's Ben."

"Hey!" Ben cried.

We laughed.

The waiter came and set down four champagne glasses.

"I'm not drinking anymore," I whispered to Ben.

"It's cider."

"Really?"

"I'm not much of a drinker, and you're underage."

"To long and happy marriages," Matt said, raising his glass.

We tapped our glasses and took a drink.

"Now," Matt said, opening his menu. "What are we going to eat tonight?"

"I'm in the mood for jerk chicken," I said.

"That a girl," Ben said, giving me a nod.

Matt and Amanda looked at each other and laughed.

"Once again irony bites me," I told Ben on the way back to the Harbachs'. "Now that I should plan a wedding, I just want time to enjoy being with you. I don't want every waking moment to be about the wedding."

"I don't either, although we probably need to get a few things done right away."

"What kind of wedding do you want?" I asked.

"I'd like it in a church."

"I would, too."

"I'd like our friends and family to be there," Ben said. "Other than that, I don't care. Whatever you want is fine with me."

"I'll work on making the wedding happen in six months," I said. "You find us a place to live."

"And work."

"Deal."

Ben tapped my knee. "That wasn't so hard, was it?"

"I had no idea this is the direction my life would take today."

"Are you glad it did?"

"I'm getting more excited by the minute."

"I knew I could love you right away."

How was it I ignored Ben so long? At the Harbachs', he walked me to the door.

"I'm glad I have this ring or I might think this was a dream."

"You're not going to call tomorrow and tell me you've changed your mind, are you?"

"I scrutinized you over the last week, and what I saw was a very handsome answer to my prayers. I don't think I could find anyone better."

He smiled and kissed me. "Good-night."

"Great night," I corrected.

When Evelyn and I picked up Lily that Saturday, she looked frail.

"What's the matter, Lily?" Evelyn asked when Lily got into the car.

"This murder has me worried," she said.

"About what?" I asked.

She shook her head.

"What?" Evelyn prodded.

"Let's wait till we get to the house," Lily said.

At the Harbachs', I hung Lily's coat in the closet while Evelyn put water on the stove for tea. She put out a plate of muffins, got the tea bags in the cups, and settled into her chair.

"Now what's wrong, Lily?" she asked.

"I told you about the night of the murder," she said. "I heard the scream."

"Yes, I remember," Evelyn said.

"And I told you I called Earl."

We nodded.

"What I didn't tell you is that when I called him, I heard his phone ring."

"He was in the building!" I cried.

She nodded. "Not just in the building. He was upstairs. I was so startled to hear his phone, I hung up. A few minutes later, he called back and asked if I had called. I told him I heard a scream. He said he was checking it out."

"You don't suppose he was involved in the murder?" Evelyn asked.

"I'm starting to wonder. The day the other girl died, he came to my apartment early in the afternoon. He never stops unless I've called and asked him to come."

"What did he want?" I asked.

"I'm beginning to think he wanted an alibi."

"But why would he murder either of these women?"

"That's what I don't understand. He won't be able to find anyone to rent the place soon."

"It's a college town, Lily," I said. "When I came, I didn't know anything of the goings on of Evanston. Each fall he gets a fresh batch of students, who, for the most part, don't care about what happened the year before."

"If he is the murderer, you'd think they'd figure it out before long. Two might be a strange coincidence, but if there's a third people will know something's going on," Evelyn said.

"Unless it's an old lady who dies 'peacefully' in her sleep," Lily said.

"You don't think...?"

"I don't know anymore," Lily said.

"You need to talk to the police," Evelyn said.

I nodded. "You need to get out of that building."

"He might even be happy to get rid of you," Evelyn said, then quickly added, "I mean, if you were to go somewhere for a week or two."

"First, I want to see Margaret," Lily said. "If Earl is behind this, she needs to know."

Lily called her granddaughter Margaret and asked her to come over. She joined us at the table a half hour later.

Evelyn set a glass of tea in front of her.

"I don't want to upset you, Margaret, but I have to talk to you about Earl," Lily began. "Have you noticed a change in him since the murders?"

Margaret's brown hair hung in loose curls just past the collar of her button down sweater. "What sort of change?"

Lily wrung her hands, and then set them down matter-of-factly. "The morning the second murder took place I heard a scream. I called Earl to report it and I heard his phone ring...upstairs."

"I see."

"I'm not pointing fingers. There may be a perfectly logical explanation, but I'm nervous. He knows I know he was there."

"Have you told the police?"

"Not yet," Lily said. "I wanted to talk to you first."

Margaret nodded. "I don't know if he had anything to do with the murders or not, but you should report what you know. We'll let the pieces fall where they fall."

"You didn't notice him gone that morning?" Evelyn asked.

"My husband and I have led separate lives for many years," Margaret confessed. "My schedule as a nurse rotates between day and night shifts, and even when I'm home he rarely sleeps in my bed, so I'm afraid I wouldn't know if he was there or not."

"You don't think he's capable of this, though?" Lily asked.

Margaret smiled softly and shook her head. "Twenty years ago I would have given everything I had to defend his innocence, but he's not the same man he was twenty years ago. He's insolent, demanding, and as often as not he's drunk."

"I never would have guessed that," Lily stammered.

"I kept it to myself, at first for the sake of our children. Now that they're grown, I just haven't rocked the boat."

"Have you tried to get him help?" Evelyn asked.

"He doesn't want help. We used to fight about it. I'd dump and throw bottles of whiskey, leave notes, try to love him out of drinking. In these last years I've gone on with my life instead of trying to change his."

"I wish you would have told me," Lily said.

"What could you have done?"

Lily put her hand on Margaret's. "I would have prayed and I would have been there for you."

A detective in an unmarked car came, and Lily and Margaret told him everything they knew. He asked if either knew of a romantic connection between Earl and Tracie.

Margaret shook her head.

"I never knew which apartment he went to. I didn't see the two of them together," Lily answered.

The detective thought, too, it would be good for both to get out of their living situations. We decided Lily would move into the spare bedroom. Margaret would tell Earl she was going out of town for a week and would stay with a friend. Earl was used to her coming and going and Margaret didn't think he would suspect anything.

When the detective left, we prayed for God to protect us, for the truth to be revealed soon, and for Earl, if he was the murderer and a threat, to be kept from doing harm to anyone else.

"I don't like Lily moving into the Harbachs'," Ben said. "If it is Earl, he's already killed two women. I don't want you to be next."

"She has to go somewhere."

"Doesn't she have other relatives?"

"Earl knows where her relatives live. He is a relative."

"It wouldn't be too hard to figure out where Herbert and Evelyn live."

"I don't know what to do."

"Can't the police put her in a safe house?"

"Where she knows no one?"

"Isn't that the point?"

I considered that option.

"If Earl is concerned about her suspecting him, don't you think he'll watch to see who she goes with? He's probably got cameras."

"If there were cameras in the building they would have captured the murderer's activity."

"I don't like it."

I had mixed feelings about leaving that Thursday to go home. On the one hand I was excited to spend time with Ben and do some wedding planning; on the other I didn't know when Earl would realize Lily was gone and how he would react.

Jeff and Carol were going to see Jeff's mom for Easter. I called and told him to be on his guard when they got back.

"I knew it was him," Jeff said.

"Well, you can know all you want. As of right now, there's no proof."

"What's the motive?"

"The detective asked about Earl being romantic with Tracie."

"Ah ha! The other woman knew so he killed her."

"Who knows?"

"Her apartment was across from Tracie's. She probably heard them...or saw them."

"Let's see what pans out. In the meantime, keep your eyes open."

When Ben and I got to Ben's parents' house just after five on the Thursday before Easter, the driveway was full of cars.

"What's going on?" I asked.

"Isn't that your parents' van?"

"You don't suppose they've gotten together to talk us out of getting married, do you?"

"I guess we'll find out," Ben said.

We walked into a house decorated with white streamers and wedding bells. Both our extended families were there.

Ben's nervousness was replaced with an easy smile. "We didn't expect this."

Ben's dad, Ed, was next to Millie. "We thought it was pretty special the way you two went about this. We want to make sure you know when you're walking with the Lord, you can count on us to support your plans."

My dad was on the other side of the kitchen. He nodded in agreement.

I looked at Ben and smiled.

"We appreciate it," Ben said.

"Good," Millie said. "Now let's eat. There's lots of food, and we've got church in a couple hours."

We decided to attend my church since it was the one we'd get married in.

"Why don't we talk to the pastor," Ben suggested after the service. "Maybe we could set a date."

Pastor Glubke looked at the calendar. "What month are you looking at?"

I looked at Ben. "When do you have to be at school?"

"I'm not certain. Sometime in September."

"Will we go on a honeymoon?"

"What's open in August?" Ben asked.

"August twenty-third and thirtieth are both open."

"I'd rather have an extra week to get settled than be rushing to get you to school."

"Should we plan on the twenty-third?" Ben asked.

"Sounds good to me."

And so it was set. In five-and-a-half months, I would be Mrs. Ben Martin.

"I hope everything else falls into place that easily," I said as we walked away.

"Keep praying," Ben said.

He gave me a hug, and I went home with my parents.

Mom and I were up early. Dad worked with a man who did wedding photography part-time. His wife showed us his wedding albums, and we booked him.

Next on the agenda was finding a place for the reception. By our fourth call, I was convinced that was not the route to go.

"Okay, Lord, if all the banquet centers are booked, where can we have our reception?"

"What about Ben's parents'?" Mom suggested.

"If it rains, it would be a mess."

"Church?"

"How many people fit in the fellowship hall?"

"I'd guess three hundred."

I cringed. "It's kind of drab with folding chairs and tables."

"We could hang white sheers on the walls and over the doorways and string white Christmas lights around the room. I'm sure Betty Loftus would help. She's the one who puts on the Mother's Day teas."

"I suppose we could rent a punch bowl and some plates."

"Real plates? Who would wash them all?"

"Wouldn't your sisters? Ben's got a couple aunts."

"That's asking a lot. Three hundred main course plates. Three hundred dessert plates. Do you want real silverware, too?"

"I don't know, Mom. I just don't want it to look like a picnic."

"Maybe we could have real plates for the main course and paper for cake. Let's think about it," Mom said. "We don't have to decide everything today."

Ben thought having the reception at church was a great idea. He was sure his aunts and cousins would chip in with dishes.

"Who are we going to have in the wedding?" I asked.

"I'd like my brother to be the best man," Ben said.

"And my brother and sister and your sister should be in it."

"What about Matt? We've been friends since grade school."

"Fine with me. But we need another girl."

"Amanda?"

I cringed. "She's planning the wedding of the century. I'm not sure she'd want to be in our little thing."

"Amanda's not like that."

I shrugged. "I don't have a problem with her."

"Okay. She's in."

"It's all cut and dry with you, isn't it?"

Ben put his arm around my neck and squeezed me into him. "It's all good," he said.

"It sure is," I said, wrapping my arms around him.

The Good Friday service had barely begun when I started to cry. I went out and got a couple tissues and sat back down next to Ben. When they showed a video in place of the reading, I wept again.

Ben leaned over. "What's wrong?"

I shook my head.

After the last hymn, Ben asked again what was wrong.

"It's so overwhelming," I whispered.

"The wedding?" he asked.

"No. Grace."

He smiled, and put his arm around me. "I love you," he whispered.

I wiped my nose and tried to dry the tears that wouldn't stop.

After church Easter morning, we headed to Ben's car to go to his parents' house for brunch. Two sheets of paper were on my seat.

One was a full-time job posting for advertising layouts for the *Milwaukee Journal*. The second was a part-time job as a church secretary at Salem Lutheran Church in Milwaukee. The hours were flexible and some work could be done from home.

"I was thinking I'd apply for the part-time job," he said.

"What experience do you have with office work?"

"I did some with Salt and Light."

"It would be nice if we got both these jobs. We might have enough money for school and an apartment."

"Maybe even food," Ben said.

"It would be good to get out of school without a lot of debt," I said.

"I have loans," Ben said.

"You do?"

"There's no way I could pay my way through Wheaton."

"Didn't your parents help?"

"They paid for the first year," Ben said.

"So you took out loans for the other three?"

"Every summer I've made enough to pay for my lodging."

"What do you owe?"

"I don't know. Maybe fifty thousand."

"That's probably more than your yearly salary as a pastor."

"Don't you have loans?"

"Thanks to the Harbachs letting me live there, I'll only owe a couple thousand, but I don't have a four-year degree. I'll have an associate's degree and a graphic design certificate."

"Hopefully that's enough to land you a job," Ben said.

Or two, I thought.

We were near Milwaukee when my phone rang.

"Earl's been across the street all afternoon. I think he's waiting for you to come home so he can ask about Lily," Evelyn warned.

"Did he come to the door?"

"He did, but we didn't answer. We left the curtains closed and the lights off, so it looks like no one's home."

"Do the police know?"

"They're a block away watching him."

"Oh, Evelyn."

"It will be okay. Just stay at Ben's tonight."

"What about tomorrow?"

"Call tomorrow after class, and we'll go from there."

"I'll be praying," I said.

"We are, too."

Despite my objections, Ben insisted I sleep in his bed and he'd stay on the couch. That would require a bit of tidying in his room, so I waited in the living room. I tried to concentrate on praying, but between the debris on the floor and the dust looking like a layer of fur on the lamp shade, I couldn't sit still. I went to Ben's closed door and asked where the vacuum might be. He told me to check the entry closet. It must have been a hand-me-down from someone's mom, because it showed wear which it obviously hadn't gotten there. I vacuumed the floor, the lampshade, the couch. When I couldn't find anything else, I used a sock from the floor to dust.

"I am going to like being married to you," Ben said when he emerged from his room.

"I'm not sure I share your sentiment at the moment."

"I'll make it up to you in other ways."

"If that's a sexual innuendo, I don't want to hear it."

"I was referring to the fact that I can change oil and fix motors and hang curtains and do hundreds of other tasks to help out."

"Sorry."

He shook his head.

"Right. You aren't Jeff."

"Matt is going to faint when he gets home."

"He can't be such a neat freak if this is how he keeps house."

"His room is picked up."

"When is the last time anyone vacuumed or dusted or," I looked down, "scrubbed the kitchen floor?"

Ben shrugged. "Give me that sock. I'll dust my room."

"Get your own sock. I'm keeping this one. I went through the pile on the floor, and this is the best of the bunch."

He smirked and picked out a sock before returning to his room.

I couldn't find a bucket, so I ran water in the kitchen sink and used another sock to wipe down the cupboards and wash the floor.

"Do me a favor and drain that," I said to Ben when he came out. "I'm afraid of what's in there."

He laughed and drained the water.

"I'll be back in a couple minutes. I'm going to throw my sheets and blankets in the washer."

"That bad?"

"I don't think so, but I'm guessing you might."

"Because it's been a couple weeks since you've washed them, right?"

"Give or take," he said.

"Um hm."

"You probably don't want to go in the bathroom."

"I've figured as much."

"If you have to go, just keep the light off."

"I think there was a gas station a couple blocks away."

He smiled. "I didn't know you were coming."

"I'm thankful you're letting me stay."

"Good."

He left and I put socks on both of my hands, grabbed the dish soap, and headed for the bathroom.

I called my parents to let them know what was going on. When I couldn't wait anymore I called Evelyn. Earl had finally left.

"Do you think this guy is crazy enough to show up on campus with a gun?" Ben asked after I hung up.

"How would he know where to find me?"

"This is exactly what I was afraid of."

"We couldn't just leave Lily there."

"It's not worth it if you all die."

"Don't talk like that."

"What a mess."

I yawned. "Do you think the sheets are dry?"

"I'll check."

"I hope I can sleep."

"If you can't, then come out here."

"So we can worry together?"

He stood up. "At some point, you'll learn to listen to me."

"You forget how it turned out with Carol and Jeff. Clearly I was right that time."

"For your sake, I hope you are this time, too."

I shivered feeling the cool evening air as the door closed.

Bible Study Chapter Fourteen

Dealing with heartbreak

Would it have been good for Meghan to marry Jeff?

Jeff told Meghan he didn't mourn their breakup because there was no sense mourning what wasn't meant to be. Read 1 Samuel 15:10–11 and 15:35–16:1. What was Samuel doing?

How did God respond to Saul's mourning?

Read Jeremiah 29:11. If God has a plan and a future for us, what should we do when we don't see things working out in our lives?

Read Psalm 40:1–5. When we get ourselves in a slimy pit of trouble, what is the first course of action we should take (v. 1)?

Once we have turned to the Lord, what must we do (v. 4)?

When you are at your lowest and you wonder if God sees you or has anything or anyone for you, go back and read Jeremiah 29:11 and Psalm 40:5.

Often our heartaches come when we make our own plans and they go wrong. Read Psalm 25:4–5. What is the cure?

Repentance

What are some of the things Ben and Meghan are doing differently now versus in their previous relationships?

Contrition and repentance are two concepts that are closely related. Contrition is sorrow over sin; repentance is the resulting change of heart and mind which leads the sorrowful sinner to resolve to change his ways. Read Matthew 3:8 and Acts 26:20. What always accompanies true repentance?

Repentance does not mean we will never sin again. Because we have a sinful nature, we will struggle with sin our whole life, but turning from our sin is an honest effort to live differently than we did in the past.

Read Ephesians 4:14. This verse sounds a lot like Meghan's life in the first chapters of the book. What is the term used in this verse to describe someone who gets talked into doing things and is tossed around instead of holding ground and standing firm in the faith?

Read Ephesians 4:15. Once we've matured out of infancy, what will we be able to do?

True repentance is followed by spiritual maturity. Not only will we not go back down that road of sin, we will warn and speak the truth in love to others.

Encouragement

Read 1 Thessalonians 5:11 and Hebrews 3:13. Why is it so important to encourage people who are living the way God would have them live?

Do you suppose most people at school would encourage Meghan and Ben or criticize them?

Do you think it was a good idea for their parents to throw a party for them? Why or why not?

Read 1 Corinthians 4:10–13, and 2 Corinthians 11:24–26. What is standing firm in the faith going to get you in this world?

Read Revelation 2:10. What is standing firm in the faith going to get you in heaven?

Are you willing to risk persecution? Are you willing to be called hurtful names? Are you willing to endure loneliness so as not to partake in sinful activities? Are you willing to stand firm for Christ in your school, on the internet, in your neighborhood? I hope you are, but be prepared. It will come at a price, just as it came at a price for Jesus and Paul and Martin Luther and multitudes of others. It turns out that the price you pay is not even worth comparing to the reward you will receive, so *stand firm*!

Chapter Fifteen: Out with the Old

When I called Evelyn after class the next day, she told me to come home and we would decide what to do. I called Ben and he said he'd come to the Harbachs', too.

The day reminded me why we endured winters in the Midwest. As I walked home, the cacophony of drips was drowned out only by the rush of melted snow running into the sewers. Unfortunately, upon arriving at the Harbachs', I found the curtains closed and the air inside stale.

"We have a daughter an hour south of Chicago," Herbert told me when we were seated around the table. "She said we could stay as long as we wanted. Lily, too."

"Do you want to leave?"

"I think we should."

"What about Margaret and the rest of your family, Lily?" I asked.

"We told Margaret Earl had been here. This is her busy week at work. She went home today as planned, but it will only be a few hours before she goes into work tonight," Lily answered.

"We're concerned with how this affects you," Evelyn said. "Maybe you could stay with Pastor Jon."

"I could see."

"I don't know if you should walk home after your evening class," Herbert advised.

The doorbell rang.

"Ben," I said, getting up.

When I opened the door it wasn't Ben, but Earl standing on the step.

"Oh, hello," I managed.

"Your dad sent me a check for six hundred dollars, a hundred dollars for each month Jeff will be in the apartment. I cashed it in December before I knew you had moved out. I came to return his money."

He handed me a check made out to my dad. Herbert came and stood beside me.

"Thank you," I said.

He turned to leave and I shut and locked the door.

"Maybe it's not him," I said handing the check to Herbert and wiping my palms on my jeans.

"This *is* puzzling," Herbert agreed, studying the check. "How can he have a conscience about something so small when two lives may have met their demise at his hands?"

Evelyn shook her head. "I'm sure I don't know."

"Good thing he didn't see you," I said taking my seat next to Lily.

"He's always seemed reliable. I never would have suspected him if I hadn't heard his phone."

Ben's knock cut her off.

Herbert answered the door and brought Ben to the table.

"Do you think it's possible he was involved with Tracie?" Herbert asked.

Lily shrugged. "She was a beautiful woman."

"Let's not forget she seduced for a living," Herbert added. "Maybe she was with him in exchange for something…like reduced rent."

"But why would he kill her?" Evelyn asked.

"What if he had been in the apartment with her at the time she was called down to meet that girl's father?" Herbert asked. "Is it possible he didn't know she was an escort?"

"I didn't know," Lily said, "and I watched her go to work every night."

"That would do it," Ben said. "If he fell in love with her, only to find he was just one of many."

"The other man was a good smoke screen," I said. "He was belligerent and had motive."

"But what did he use to kill her?" Evelyn asked.

"He had to have used more than just his hands," Herbert said. "Maybe he used a rock or fire extinguisher or..."

"Smoke screen," Lily whispered, nodding. "That's why he came to my apartment. He asked for the broom, and it smelled like cigarettes when he brought it back."

"What are you talking about?" Evelyn asked.

"The container for cigarette butts," Lily explained.

"That would be heavy enough," I deduced. "If he hit her with that, it could kill her."

"Why would he kill Vicki?" Ben asked.

"Did she know Tracie?" I wondered.

"I wouldn't know," Lily said.

"Maybe she knew Earl and Tracie had been together and blackmailed him," Ben suggested.

"And having just been seduced and taken advantage of by one woman, he wasn't about to be made a fool of by another," Herbert concluded.

"Herbert, I think we've watched too many Agatha Christie movies."

"We'll let the detective figure it out," Herbert said. "I'll give him a call."

"I didn't think he was dangerous," Lily murmured. "Maybe he'll turn himself in," she added, nodding thoughtfully.

The detective arrived and sat at the table. The cigarette container was not the weapon used to kill Tracie. It had been tipped over, but it was heavy and awkward enough that it would be hard to hit someone without the person moving away.

"Why would he sweep the cigarettes up if he was the murderer?" Herbert asked.

"To make it look like he wasn't," the detective said. "When he called 911 he said he was cleaning up the mess when he noticed Tracie's body."

"He knew she was dead when he returned the broom," Lily realized, shaking her head.

"What was the weapon then?" Evelyn asked.

"Likely it was an everyday object from Tracie's apartment; a flashlight or screwdriver even, picked up in a fit of rage," the detective answered. "It appears Tracie got out of the apartment and ran down the steps, but slowed to hit the security latch, giving her assailant time to catch her. She was hit on the back of the head, probably just as she reached the outer door, causing her to lose her balance, knock over the cigarette container, and fall down the steps where she died. The killer probably never set foot out the door."

"Why do you think she came from her apartment instead of being in the entry talking to the father of the girl she recruited?" Herbert asked.

"Alex Carter said Tracie didn't let him in or meet him downstairs, and I think that's pretty realistic. He said they exchanged all their words over the intercom."

"The argument I heard," Lily deduced.

He nodded. "Tracie didn't have shoes on and her shirt was only partially buttoned. Once she figured out she was in danger, she fled quickly."

"Did Alex Carter trigger the assault?" Herbert asked.

"I would suspect," the detective said. "Carter's statement said Tracie explained the escort position as very profitable as long as you were able to overlook the clients, most of whom were moronic baboons, I think she called them."

"Ouch," Ben said.

The detective nodded. "There was a sapphire necklace still in the box on Tracie's nightstand. The jeweler is reviewing the register tape to find the credit card information, but the description he gave of the buyer matches Earl's."

"He had feelings for her," Lily resolved.

"Unreciprocated feelings," Herbert clarified.

"What about Vicki?" Herbert asked.

"Vicki was strangled in her apartment."

"I still don't understand how Vicki's scream woke Lily, but it didn't wake anyone else," I said.

"I wasn't sleeping," Lily said. "I'm always up and down. I'll read for a bit, crochet maybe, then go back to sleep."

"Vicki was alone in the apartment," the detective added. "Her daughter was at a friend's house, and her husband worked nights."

"Still, you'd think the neighbors or someone would have heard and come or called…" I said.

"You are that type of person," Lily said. "But there aren't a lot of people like you. In all my years at Candlewood, many people have seen me in the window, but none have stopped. Only you."

"How did Earl know the daughter and husband were gone?" Evelyn asked.

"It would be easy enough to find out Mr. Henderson worked the night shift. As for the daughter, who knows if he knew she'd be gone, or if it just worked out that way," the detective answered. "Hopefully we'll get answers to some of these questions once we bring Earl in for questioning and get his DNA. I'm confident these cases will be put to rest."

"It seemed much cheerier when Agatha Christie's murders were solved," Evelyn muttered.

"Because they were just fiction," Herbert reminded her.

"Do you think we're in danger here?" Lily asked the detective.

"Typically people in Earl's position do one of two things. Either he'll be on his best behavior or he'll try to take everyone down with him. The fact that he dropped off the check makes me think he's the type to be on his best behavior. If that's the case, you don't have anything to fear."

A few days later Margaret came to see Lily.

"I'll leave you two alone," I heard Evelyn say.

"No. I'd like all of you to hear this."

Evelyn called Herbert and me and we took our seats around the table.

"Earl gave his DNA voluntarily," Margaret began. "It didn't match the DNA found on either woman."

We looked at each other in disbelief.

"He also showed me the facility room on the second floor. It's been his refuge for the past I don't know how many years."

"A home away from home?" Herbert anticipated.

She nodded. "With all the comforts ... a couch, TV, and fridge among the cleaning and painting supplies."

"But why?" Herbert asked.

"He doesn't have to worry about anyone pouring out his whiskey there."

"That explains why I heard his phone," Lily realized.

Margaret nodded again. "He heard the scream and was contemplating what to do about it when you called."

"How did you not know about this room?" Evelyn asked.

"How did *I* not know?" Lily gasped.

"How would you? If you saw him come in and didn't see him go out, you probably thought he'd gone out the back door or you had missed him," Margaret said.

"And you never go up to the second floor," I added.

"My work schedule is so random," Margaret explained. "I'm sound asleep by ten if I've worked all day and gone by six if I'm on a night shift. I'm starting to see it hasn't been the best for our marriage."

"So he's not a murderer," Lily determined, "which is good, but he certainly has a problem."

"Hopefully this will be the impetus of change," Margaret said pensively.

"If he's telling the truth, isn't that the first step?" Herbert asked.

"I hope," Margaret repeated. "Which is more than I've done in a long time."

"Then one question remains," Herbert said. "Who *is* the murderer?"

"Well…"

"Do you know?" Lily asked.

"After you called him about the scream, Earl stepped out of the facility room and saw someone going down the steps."

"Did he recognize the person?" I asked.

Margaret nodded. "It was Vicki's husband."

"Wasn't he at work?" Evelyn asked.

"He was supposed to be," Margaret said.

"Why didn't Earl tell the detective?" Herbert asked.

"Because he was drunk," she answered.

"Vicki was killed by her own husband?" I whispered.

"DNA doesn't lie," Margaret said.

"They've run his DNA?" Evelyn asked.

Margaret nodded. "He was taken in for questioning before Earl. His DNA was under her nails."

"Funny the detective didn't mention that," Herbert muttered. "Why would he kill his wife?"

"Maybe he was in love with Tracie," I suggested.

"Now I'm confused," Evelyn said. "Did *he* kill Tracie?"

"What about the necklace and description of Earl?" Lily asked.

Margaret shrugged. "I don't mean to sound callous, but I'm not sure I care. My husband has been cleared, and I hope we can start rebuilding our lives."

"Of course, dear," Evelyn said.

When Margaret left I saw in Herbert an unspoken uneasiness.

"I suppose I can move back home now," Lily said.

"No hurry," Herbert assured. "You can stay as long as you want."

I had just come in from youth group, and was in my room changing when I heard a knock at the door followed by the muffled voice of a woman. I finished putting my pajamas on and went to see what was going on.

It was Margaret. Lily went into the living room, but I stayed in the hall.

"What's the matter?" Lily asked.

"They've taken Earl."

"Who's taken Earl?"

"The police."

"What did they say when they took him?" Herbert inquired.

"That he was under arrest for murder."

"Whose murder?" Herbert asked.

"Vicki's."

"I thought you said the DNA…" Lily started.

"It *was* her husband's DNA under her nails."

Herbert looked at his watch. "It's quarter to ten. I'll call the detective and see if he can fill us in."

When Herbert put down the phone he sighed. "He didn't answer. We're likely not going to find anything out tonight."

I retreated to my room. It was several hours later when they stopped talking, determined Margaret would spend the night and turned off the lights.

Herbert and Lily took Margaret to the police station in the morning. I stayed in my room working on my final portfolio. At 11:30 Evelyn knocked and I joined her in the dining room for tomato soup and grilled cheese sandwiches.

We were clearing the table when Herbert came home.

"Where are Margaret and Lily?" Evelyn asked.

"I dropped them off at Margaret's house," he answered.

"Did you find out anything?"

"No. The police are putting together a case against Earl, so they won't talk to us. Earl's hired a lawyer. We may find out more from him."

I hadn't been back to the apartment since the day I moved out. Jeff and I sat on the couch. Carol sat between us on the floor.

"You were half right about Earl," I said to Jeff.

"And half right is mostly wrong," Carol touted.

"Unbelievable," Jeff said. "We had our own soap opera going on one floor below us. Who knew?"

"I'm glad I didn't," I said. "In this case ignorance was bliss."

Carol nodded. "Imagine if you had been in that apartment, Meghan. You'd have gone out when you heard Vicki scream and probably would have run into Earl leaving the scene of the crime. He'd have had to kill you, too."

I shivered. "You're probably right."

"Can you imagine killing someone's wife because they killed your mistress?" Carol asked.

"Perfect plan, really, going in after they'd just had sex," Jeff said. "Earl hears the husband leaving, the husband leaves the door unlocked, his DNA is all over his wife."

"What did he use to strangle her?" I asked.

"The paper said an extension cord."

"Really?"

Carol nodded.

"So Earl loved Tracie. He must have known what she did for a living and that Vicki's husband was a customer," I supposed.

"How could he not?" Jeff asked. "He practically lived across the hall, probably monitoring her every move."

"But why wasn't his DNA on her?" I asked.

"Who knows how long it had been since their last rendezvous," Carol reasoned.

I cringed. "It was Henderson's DNA on Tracie, which they couldn't match until his wife was killed and his DNA was collected."

"Earl set him up," Jeff said. "He knew Henderson had been with Tracie the day she was killed. He probably heard him knock on her door."

"Tracie let him in," Carol narrated. "They did their business and were getting dressed when the other guy beeped in on the intercom."

I nodded. "Alex Carter spouted off about Tracie, and called her a few choice names. She defended herself saying she wasn't any of those things. Then she made the fatal error of saying her customers were the moronic baboons...all she did is take their money...or something like that."

"Carter huffed away..." Carol continued.

"And Henderson picked up the stainless steel candleholder, thinking how this moronic baboon would show her a thing or two," Jeff added. "He chased her down the steps, and ..." he pretended to hit her.

"Apparently he lived in the delusion that she cared about him," Carol said.

"They all did," I surmised.

"Do you think the detectives sit around a game of Clue?" Jeff asked. "Earl with the knife in the hall. No. Earl with the rope in the bedroom. Henderson with the knife in the entry. No...the candlestick."

"I doubt it, Jeff. It's ironic that Earl thought telling everyone about the facility room would clear him. Instead it put all the pieces in place," I said.

"If they hadn't found that extension cord in his man cave he'd probably have gotten away with it," Carol said.

"Why would he keep it there?" I asked.

"He must have felt pretty confident that they were buying his story," Jeff said. "And Henderson's DNA was on both women."

"I wonder if either will plead guilty or if these cases will go to trial," Carol pondered.

"Either way I'd guess you won't see either of those men again," I said. "You probably won't see much of Lily, either. She's moving in with her granddaughter."

"It won't even be like living in Candlewood with Lily and Earl gone," Carol said.

"Hopefully some young pup who likes to dress in front of the window gets Lily's apartment," Jeff stated.

I looked at Carol and shook my head.

"That's quite a ring," she said, grabbing my hand. "Ben went all out."

"I'll be paying for it," I said, "like everything else for the next several years."

"How do you feel about that?" she asked.

"I don't mind. I'll work the first four years and he can work the forty after that."

"That's a pretty good deal," Jeff decided.

"Don't even think about it," Carol said.

"Lawyers make a whole lot more than journalists."

"Lawyers also know how to get what they want out of a divorce."

"Do you think you'll get married?"

"Hard to say," Carol said.

"We're surprised we've made it this long," Jeff added.

"When do you move home?" Carol asked.

"I move home in a week and to Milwaukee a couple days later. Ben found us an apartment."

Jeff gasped. "He's moving in with you?"

I nodded. "Right after we get home from the honeymoon."

"You had me worried for a minute."

"No need for that. You've still seen more of me than he has."

He shook his head. "Poor guy."

"It's amazing I'm still friends with you," I said.

"Oh, we're going to stay friends. Once I'm done with school, you can get me a job at the paper. Not everyone gets hired that quickly and in such a big market."

"Were you planning on moving to Milwaukee?" Carol asked him.

"Maybe he'll let you move to Milwaukee, too, Carol."

"I was wondering."

"Well, he's not moving in with Ben and me," I assured her.

"I *am* hard to resist," Jeff touted, "so I can see how you wouldn't want me around you."

"I don't think that would be a problem. Have you seen Ben without a shirt on?"

"Can't say I have."

"I'd like to," Carol offered.

I shook my head. "I'm keeping him all to myself."

"Sounds pretty selfish…for a Christian girl."

"Add it to the list," I said. "Arrogant, flippant, selfish."

"In the end you did win," Jeff said with chagrin. "At least this time."

I smiled. "I agree."

May sixteenth was sunny, and the forecast called for a high of sixty-seven degrees. Ben finished school the day before, packed his car, and spent the night in the spare bedroom at the Harbachs'. Herbert, Ben, and I carried my boxes to the living room. When Mom and Dad arrived just after nine, Ben and Dad carried things out while Mom and I loaded and sometimes reloaded the van. Once the mattress was in, Dad told Mom not to sneeze or the van would explode. Ben's car was equally laden.

By ten we were ready to leave. The Harbachs gave us coffee and muffins for the road.

"We sure will miss you," Evelyn said as I hugged her.

"I'll miss you, too. You were such a blessing to me."

"The house is going to be awfully lonely," Herbert added.

"I'm sure Pastor Jon could find you another student," I suggested.

"Maybe," Herbert said, looking at Evelyn.

"The chapter closes," I said as we drove out of Evanston.

Ben smiled. "And another chapter begins."

"I wonder if we'll end up anywhere near Chicago."

"Only God knows the answer to that."

I let my mind drift. Where would Ben's ministry take us?

"I'd like to plan the wedding service," Ben said.

"Alone, you mean?"

"Is that okay?"

"Are you going to do something bizarre?"

"I'm going to be planning church services the rest of my life. I'd like to start with our wedding."

"I thought we'd do that together, but if it's that important to you, I'll let you."

"Good. I've got a couple ideas already. And I doubt you will have time to do much any more."

"I know."

"I don't think I'm going to like you working two jobs, and I'm still sore Salem hired you over me."

"I knew I was more qualified. Anyway, what else am I going to do? We won't have a yard. I won't know anyone. You're going to have to study."

"How about we get to know each other? I don't want to have to schedule an appointment to see you."

"I don't foresee that being an issue. If you get a part-time job, maybe between the two of us we could pay down your student loans. It would be nice not to have to worry about that when we're ready to start a family."

His tone softened. "We'll see."

My phone rang.

"We heard on the radio that David's Bridal in Milwaukee is having a ninety-nine dollar sale. Should we stop?" Mom asked.

"Do you think there will be anything left?"

"We'd be there by noon."

When we arrived at David's Bridal the parking lot was full of activity. Mom and I got out across the street, and Dad and Ben drove off to find parking spots.

There were several women involved in a commotion in front of the store. We were about to walk past when one woman yelled, "Are you looking for a dress?"

She was looking at me.

"Yes."

"Do you want this one?"

"What's wrong with it?"

"It's not my size. It was a madhouse in there, and my mom grabbed the wrong one."

"What size is it?" I asked.

"Eight."

Mom looked at me. We went closer and others took the opportunity to walk away. It was slightly off-white with one inch straps and a seam under the bust. It hung straight until it scalloped down to the train.

"It's pretty," I said, "but I'd want to try it on."

"There's about a two-hour wait for a dressing room in there," the mother said.

"Just take off your shirt," Mom said. "You have a tank top on. Once the dress is on, you can take off your shorts."

"Try it on out here? Won't it get dirty?"

"We'll help," the daughter said.

I took off my shirt, and the moms helped me into the dress while the other woman held the train.

"Take off your shorts," Mom said.

I handed them to her.

"Well?" I asked.

"It's beautiful," Mom said.

"I wish I could see the back."

"Do you have a camera on your phone?"

Mom got my phone out of my purse and took a picture.

"Can you hold out the train?" I asked.

Mom snapped several pictures and handed the phone to me. "Is this what you had in mind?"

"I hadn't given it much thought," I said. "It's beautiful."

"It's like it was made for you," Mom marveled.

"You're right. It doesn't get any easier than this. The dress came to us."

She smiled.

"You'll take it then?" the woman asked.

"I guess," I said.

"It looks nice on you," she said.

"Now we get to go back into that mob," her mom said.

Mom made out the check. "We'll pray you find something."

I got dressed and we called the guys to pick us up. Mom took the dress in the van. I asked Ben if he wanted to see the pictures.

He considered. "I think I want to wait."

"You're sure?"

"I want to surprise you with the service. You surprise me with the dress."

I chuckled. "It was a surprise to me, too."

When he looked at me his face quickly changed to show concern. "Are you okay? You're shaking."

"All those years of wrapping up in sheets and walking down a pretend aisle...and now it's for real."

He smiled and grabbed my hand. "You'll make a beautiful bride. Should we have a candlelight wedding?"

"No lights?"

"There will still be daylight coming in the windows. We can put candleholders at the ends of the pews."

"How do you know about candleholders?"

"Amanda."

"I can't imagine what she will talk about once the wedding is over."

"She'll move right from weddings to babies."

I grinned. "I think you're right."

"She'll keep Matt on his toes," Ben said.

"A year ago I was pretty uptight about my life being just so."

"I like you now."

"It's a good thing."

"It sure is."

Once we were home, Ben went to help Dad. Mom took the dress in the house.

"What do you want me to do?" I asked, approaching the van.

"Go inside," Dad answered. "We'll bring the boxes that far, then you figure out which ones you'll be taking with you and which ones will stay till after the wedding."

I nodded.

"Oh, Meghan," Dad called.

I turned around.

"The dress is beautiful."

When the van was empty, Ben and Dad came in.

"So much for this move," Dad said.

"I'd better get going," Ben said. "My car is still full."

"Thanks for helping," Dad said, shaking his hand.

"Yes, thanks," Mom added. She and Dad walked out, leaving us in the room.

"I want to go with you," I said.

"Are you sure? Don't you have a lot to do here?"

"I have two days until I'm over an hour away and working sixty hours a week."

"Okay," he said. "Let's go."

I helped Ben carry his things to his room. The floors creaked as we walked up the steps.

"Do you wake everyone up if you go to the bathroom at night?" I asked.

"I don't notice it anymore."

I helped Ben put his clothes in his closet and his socks in his drawer.

"Just put that box of papers on the desk," he said. "I have to go through it."

"Have you gone through last year's papers?"

"Nope."

"The year before?"

"Uh..."

"Didn't think so," I said, leafing through the stack of papers already there. I stopped to read one.

Ben came behind me and looked over my shoulder. He pulled the sheet from my hand, crumpled it, and threw it on the floor. "I'm sorry you saw that. There's a lot of Becky in there."

"It's like she's living here."

He apologized again on the way home. "That was probably the worst thing you could have seen."

"That's going to be hard to get out of my head."

"I journaled after our breakup to work through things. I never imagined anyone would read it."

"Do you still think about her body?"

"No."

Once Ben was in my parents' drive, I reached for the door, but he stopped me.

"I love you."

"What if you don't like sex with me as much as sex with Becky?"

"I want a wife who wants to have sex with me. We'll work the rest out."

"I need you to get rid of everything from her or about her. I don't ever want to come across anything like that again."

"I will."

I started out of the car.

"Call me when you get up."

The next morning I was walking back to my room after taking a shower when Mom stopped me.

"Ben called."

"Thanks."

She followed me to my room, walked to the desk, and looked down at my ring.

"Something wrong?"

I took the towel off my head and brushed my hair. "Why do you ask?"

She picked up my ring. "This is the first time I've seen you take it off."

"I saw something in his room last night that hurt."

"Don't you think you should talk to him about it? Maybe he doesn't even know what he's done."

"He knows."

She put the ring back and sat on the bed. "How are you going to react when he hurts you after you're married? Are you going to ignore him, or are you going to go to him and tell him how he's hurt you so he can do something different the next time."

"There better not be a next time." I turned to face her. "I found a note he wrote to his last girlfriend. He told her how much she meant to him, how he loved her body, loved being with her."

"It wasn't that long ago that you felt that way about Jeff."

"I know, but Jeff and I didn't…"

Mom walked out and returned with her Bible. She sat on my bed and began reading.

"The Lord is compassionate and gracious, slow to anger, abounding in love. He will not always accuse, nor will he harbor his anger forever; he does not treat us as our sins deserve or repay us according to our iniquities. For as high as the heavens are above the earth, so great is his love for those who fear him; as far as the east is from the west, so far has he removed our transgressions from us. As a father has compassion on his children, so the Lord has compassion on those who fear him; for he knows how we are formed, he remembers that we are dust."

She shut her Bible. "Twenty-three years ago, your grandmother read Psalm 103 to me and advised me to learn to live it if I wanted a happy marriage. I had to learn to forgive, too."

She stood up. "Throughout the course of your marriage, you are going to go to Ben lots of times and ask to be forgiven, and when you do, you'll be praying he has the grace to be merciful."

She shut the door as she left. I found my Bible in a box near the door and opened it to Psalm 103.

When I called Ben, he sounded morose.

"I'm sorry I didn't call right away. I needed time."

"I'm sorry about last night."

"I told you I would forgive you and I do. I just wasn't prepared for…"

"You shouldn't have to be. It won't happen again."

"Perfect."

"What do you want to do today?"

"We have lots to get done."

"Dad could use my help for a bit. We've got calves coming."

"I'll come out. When you're ready, we'll get busy."

Mom dropped me off an hour later.

"Come in," Millie said. "Ben's in the barn with Ed. They shouldn't be much longer."

"Do you need help in here? I can do the dishes."

"You don't have to do dishes."

"I might as well do something."

"I guess if you're willing, I'll take the help."

"I'm willing," I said, going to the sink. She grabbed a towel and as I washed, she rinsed and dried.

"I'm sorry about what happened last night," Millie said. "I feel partially responsible. I encouraged Ben to work through his feelings by writing. Neither of us considered what a landmine his room was for you. We felt terrible last night."

"I'm just glad it happened now so he can get rid of it before August."

"That's gracious of you."

She leaned against the counter and waited until I looked at her. "Ed and I are thankful he's marrying you."

"My parents are equally grateful I'm marrying Ben."

She started rinsing dishes again. "Some people need to stumble a time or two to figure out how big God is."

The outside porch door slammed, then the inside door opened. Ben peered around the corner.

"The twins are out."

"Good!" Millie cried.

"I'm going to get cleaned up," he said to me.

"Okay," I said, wringing the dish cloth and draping it over the sink.

Millie hung her towel over the chair. "That didn't take long."

"What else can I do?"

"Do you want to fold socks?"

"Sure."

"There are lots to fold. Before Ben got home, I was helping with the calves."

We sat on the living room floor and spread the socks in front of us. Ed, Ben, and Ben's brother Aaron all wore the same style white socks. Between the two of us, we managed to get all the matches together.

Ben came through the kitchen wearing only a towel wrapped around his waist.

"Sorry," he said. "I'll be down in a minute."

I had a hard time not smiling when Millie looked at me. She shook her head.

"Soon enough," she said.

We put the folded socks back in the basket, and she took them upstairs to put them away.

I heard Ben bouncing down the steps before I saw him bolt through the door.

"Thanks for coming," he said wrapping his arms around me.

"I need more than that today."

I pulled his face toward me for a kiss. When we heard Millie on the steps, Ben backed away. Millie stepped around us with the laundry basket and went into the kitchen.

"What's on the agenda?" Ben asked.

"First I'd like you to take your shirt off. I could look at you all day," I whispered.

He smiled. "Soon enough."

"That's what your mom said."

He winked.

"Invitations and bulletins," I said.

"Where do we do that?"

"Let's look online."

"I'll grab my laptop."

He brought it down and put it on the roll-top desk in the living room and connected it to the modem. I pulled up a rocking chair and sat next to him. His screen saver was a picture of three crosses with a setting sun.

"It looks like the hill where you proposed to me," I said.

"That's why it's there."

He typed "Christian wedding invitations." After a few sites, we realized they were all about the same.

"What do you want to use for a Bible verse?" I asked.

Ben ran upstairs and returned with his Bible. He flipped it open, turned a couple pages, and stopped. "The Lord is good to those whose hope is in Him."

"Lamentations three."

He smiled. "Meatballs."

"Did I tell you Mom made meatballs for Christmas, too?"

"Maybe we should have meatballs at the wedding," Ben said.

"That would be different."

Once we had our information on the invitations, we saved it and Ben typed in "Christian bulletin covers." Several websites later we landed at Marna's Wedding Boutique. Halfway down the page was a bulletin with white roses and the words "God bless our wedding day," followed by Jeremiah 33:10–11. "There will be heard once more the sounds of joy and gladness, the voices of bride and groom...saying, "Give thanks to the Lord Almighty, for the Lord is good; his love endures forever."

"Looks good to me," I said.

He bookmarked the page. "What's next?"

"We need to make a list of friends to invite."

He typed as I named my friends.

"Should we invite Jeff and Carol?"

He tapped his fingers on the desk.

"Sure. Anyone else?"

"That's it for me," I said.

He put his friends on the list and attached it to an email to me titled "These people will know how much I love you."

"Should we take off?" he asked. "I want to take you somewhere."

"Bring your laptop, and we'll show Mom the invitations."

I followed him out of the house. Birds were busy in the yard and the mama cows were mooing. I was grateful for a mom who wasn't afraid to put me in my place. My day would have been considerably different if I was still at home, pouting.

Bible Study Chapter Fifteen

The Adulteress

Herbert made the point that Tracie seduced for a living. Read Proverbs 5:3–9 and Proverbs 6:23–28. What kind of traits does this type of woman have?

The Bible warns men to stay away from that type of woman. What do these passages say will happen if you don't?

Read Proverbs 7:21–23. What is the man who allows himself to be seduced compared to?

Ladies, look at this from the other perspective. How do you talk? How do you dress? Are you trying to seduce a man with your sexuality? Consider the words used in the Proverbs to describe this type of woman.

God's gifts

Ben said over and over that everything would fall into place. Read John 6:14–15. What did the people want from Jesus?

Why were the people going to make Jesus king "by force"?

Do you ever try to make God your genie? How do you know Meghan and Ben weren't looking at God in that way, but instead, Ben's words were words of trust?

God knows our needs. Often we aren't willing to take what God makes available to us, because we want something different. Meghan could have spent a lot of time and a whole lot more money looking for a wedding dress. I saved tons of money raising my kids by using hand-me-downs. Some of the clothes weren't the style or color I would have chosen, but I thanked the Lord for providing all the clothes my children needed and didn't worry about getting different ones.

Read Mark 2:1–12. When his friends lowered the paralytic before Jesus, what were they looking for?

What did Jesus give the man first?

Isn't it interesting that Jesus healed the man's soul first? What good is a whole body with a broken soul? How often are we content with the spiritual gifts God gives us, if they are not accompanied by physical gifts?

As Ben and Meghan plan their wedding, where is their focus? Is it on the spiritual or the physical?

In chapter four, Meghan told Jeff God supplies daily bread, not steak and lobster. The world's idea of prosperity is expensive food, lavish clothes, a nice car, a huge house with expensive trimmings. God's gifts are so much more valuable, and they're gifts no one but He can give. They are things like faith, health, wisdom, protection, and children. Make sure you appreciate what's important!

Reminders of our sins

When Meghan went up to Ben's room, she found "a whole lot of Becky up there." Read 1 Corinthians 5:6–8. Was she right to insist he not bring that stuff into their marriage?

Do you have souvenirs from previous sins or a time when you weren't acting so Christian?

Read Proverbs 3:3–4 and Psalm 77:11–12. What do we want to keep in front of us? What reminders do we want to have?

Chapter Sixteen: I Do

"I don't get Ben sometimes."

Amanda put her lemonade down. "He is stitched from different cloth, that's for sure. What did he do now?"

"Millie and I were in the living room when he got out of the shower and came through wearing a towel around his waist."

"Just a towel?"

I nodded. "Once he was dressed, I told him the first item on the agenda was for him to take off his shirt because I could look at his bare chest all day."

Amanda laughed. "Matt would have said, 'you first.' "

"Not Ben. He drove twenty minutes away and took me for a hike up a hill. He said it was the first time I'd talked about his body and he was glad to know I was attracted to him."

"Who isn't attracted to Ben?"

"Thank you! He's always had girls interested in him. I should be the one needing to be told he's attracted to me. Why does he take me twenty minutes away to climb a hill when I make a comment about him being hot?"

"We may be physically weaker than men, but in my experience, they need a lot more reassurance. Matt does, anyway. He's always second-guessing himself."

"That shocks me."

"They hide it well in front of other people, but deep down they seem to have a lot of insecurities."

"I don't know what Ben's deal is. All I know is that we have this bizarre talk up on the hill, he gives me a quick kiss, and off he goes back down. Sometimes he is so strange."

"I have a little insight as to the quick exit."

"You do?"

"There's too much temptation on a hill twenty minutes from nowhere."

"Is that what he told Matt?"

She nodded. "He knew you were attracted to him…there was no one around…makes a guy start thinking."

"I wish he would have told me. Sometimes I'm afraid I'm getting into a cold marriage."

"He's not affectionate?"

"He holds my hand and gives me hugs and pecks on the lips, but nothing to knock my socks off. Jeff made it clear when he was thinking about sex and how interested he was in being with me."

"It wouldn't hurt to let each other know you're waiting with anticipation."

"Communication. Sex. Misunderstandings. We've got three months till the wedding, and we already stink at marriage."

She laughed. "At least you're figuring it out. It's gotta be good to know Ben's not a lunatic."

We took our trays to the garbage and went to the one major store in the mall we hadn't been to.

"Do you like this?" Amanda asked, holding up a pale pink dress.

"I like the style, not the pink."

"What about this?"

She held up a bright blue tank dress with black trim. It came with a matching jacket.

"That's not bad. How much is it?"

"Seventy-five."

"I like the color."

"I'll try it on. You keep looking."

She called me to the fitting room a few minutes later. "What do you think?"

"I love it. Try this red one on, too. It's a bit longer."

She put it on and twirled around.

"Which do you like better?" I asked.

"The red one is pretty, but honestly I'd probably never wear it again."

"I agree. The blue is more usable."

"I could wear it to my rehearsal. With the jacket on, you wouldn't even know it was a tank dress. We wouldn't wear the jacket for the wedding, would we?"

I shook my head. "Just the dress. It's pretty similar in style to mine."

"So, is this the one?"

"You tell me. You've seen all the options."

"I'd say it's between this one and the black one at Macy's."

"I'd rather have blue for our color."

"This blue would be pretty."

"I hope Ben likes it."

"He will."

"Let's see if we can find a shirt and tie to match."

An hour later we were holding a blue shirt and a black and blue swirled tie to complement the dresses.

"That seals the deal for me," I said. "Now I just need to get everyone down here to get the right sizes."

"It will be amazing. I'm going to get blond highlights so everything about me is bright."

"Just don't wear blue eye shadow."

She laughed. "No blue mascara either?"

I cringed and shook my head. "Thanks for taking time away from Matt to help me."

"It was fun."

I gave her a hug.

"Not long now," she said.

The church required that we have six premarital counseling classes before we got married. Ben picked me up in Milwaukee on Saturday mornings. Starting in July we went to our classes Saturday afternoons.

Our last class was two weeks before the wedding and focused on how to cope when things weren't going as we hoped they would. Pastor Glubke reminded us to go to our families for encouragement, support, and prayers.

"That won't happen if you keep everything to yourselves," he said. "I sometimes wonder how many people in the pew are suffering but unwilling to ask for guidance and support."

Just like that Ben started spewing. He told Pastor he'd had sex with Becky and I had lived with Jeff. He told him about being scared to show me affection for fear of it leading to sex and my tendency to shut down and quit eating and sleeping when things went wrong. Never had I wanted to disappear more than when Ben was telling the pastor who baptized and confirmed me about "the compromising situations" that came from my living with Jeff. Pastor listened without showing any sign of shock or disappointment. Sometimes he nodded knowingly.

"As much as we try to keep our young people active in the church, they go away to college where temptation is everywhere. No experience is lost in ministry. If you let Him, God can and will use this."

"I'm not sure that's something you'd like me sharing," Ben said, looking at me.

My immediate thought was that he might have considered that a few minutes prior.

"I hadn't thought about it," I said.

Pastor Glubke smiled. "You'll figure it out."

He said a prayer and we stood to leave.

"Give me a call this week, Ben. We need to get together."

"What's that about?" I asked as we got into the car.

"We're going through the service."

"Oh."

"If you hate the service than either we shouldn't be getting married or I shouldn't be a pastor or both, so trust me, I'm putting my best into it."

"You'll have the bulletins made?"

"As soon as Pastor and I nail everything down."

"Could you e-mail me the page with attendants? I'll make sure you spelled everyone's name right."

"Good idea."

"What about a note from us?" I asked.

"A thank-you-for-coming type of thing?"

"Yeah."

"We can work on that together."

"I don't mind if you write it, but I wouldn't mind seeing that, too, before it goes in the bulletin."

"What do you want to say?"

"Something like, thank you for coming. Our new address is blah, blah, blah...and if you're ever in Milwaukee, call and see if Ben won't pick up the apartment so you can come over."

He laughed.

I sighed. "You've done as much if not more of the wedding planning than I have."

"You sound like you're not okay with that."

"I trust you."

"Was that supposed to convince me or you?"

"Are you *sure* you're remembering everything? We're only getting married once."

"I don't intend to disappoint you."

My phone woke me. "Good morning," I said.

"It's our wedding day."

"How's the weather?"

"It's about seventy-five degrees right now with a gentle breeze and a whole lot of humidity."

"I'll take it," I said.

"Mom wants to know if you got the decorating done, or if you need help."

I yawned. "It's done. I couldn't leave till I had it just so or I knew I wouldn't sleep."

"Nothing until pictures then?"

"I guess I'm ready. Are you?"

"I'm ready."

I wandered into the kitchen. Beth and Troy, Mom and Dad were at the table.

"What's everyone doing?" I asked.

"Reminiscing," Dad said.

"It all changes today," Mom added.

"We were so busy last night, I didn't even think about it being my last night as a Shanahan," I said, sitting down. "I guess things *will* change now."

"It's a strange transition," Dad said. "It's the end of your childhood."

"That's sad."

Mom nodded, wiping a tear. We started reliving memories, at times laughing and crying simultaneously. When I looked at my watch, it was after ten.

"We've got to get going."

Dad stood and gave me a hug.

"I don't want to cry tonight, Dad."

"Nothing but happy," he said.

We showered and got dressed and had a sandwich before leaving for the salon. The ladies at the salon started on my nails while some of the girls got hair done and some had makeup done. We rotated through until Millie, Mom, my bridesmaids, and I looked more glamorous than we had ever looked before.

It was after one when we left. The moms went home to get dressed and get the men to church on time while the rest of us went straight to the church. Pastor was there and a few of Ben's relatives. We went to the nursery and put our dresses on.

"This seems unreal," I told Amanda as I put my earrings in. "I walk in as Meghan Shanahan, and I'll walk out as Ben's wife."

"I can't wait for December," she said. "Now that I'm here and have a job, I'd rather just be married."

"I was not thrilled about Ben wanting to get married so quickly, but in hindsight, it's a blessing."

At 1:45, the photographer knocked.

"We'll be out in a minute," I said.

"I'm going to start with the guys," he said. "They're ready."

I looked around the room. "What am I forgetting?"

"Did you put your garter on?" Ben's sister, Katie, asked.

"Thanks," I said, pulling it out of my bag and sliding it up to my thigh. "Ben probably won't even see it. I'm going to change before we leave the church. I don't want to sit in the car for two hours on a bustled train."

She shrugged. "It's your something borrowed and blue."

"And old," I added.

"By tonight, I doubt Ben will care if you have a garter on," Amanda said.

We laughed as I straightened my dress and slipped on my shoes.

"Have some water," Beth said, handing me a bottle.

I took a sip and handed it back to her. "How do I look?"

"I can only hope to look as good on my wedding day," she said.

"I won't," Amanda said, "but then, Matt knew that going in."

I shook my head. "You'll be gorgeous."

As we walked into the narthex, the florist handed us our bouquets. The bridesmaids carried a mix of white roses and light blue daisies. My bouquet was twelve long-stemmed white roses tied with ribbon.

When we walked into the sanctuary, Ben smiled.

"You're stunning," he said as I got to the front of the church.

"So are you."

Ben's aunts came in, dinging forks on glasses.

I laughed and gave Ben a kiss on his cheek, then rubbed my lipstick off his face.

The next two hours were spent posing and smiling and kissing and gazing. At four o'clock, we went to have snacks. People began arriving at four-thirty, so we were put in a Sunday school room to wait.

I don't know if my stomach or my hands were shaking more. I tried not to pace. The bridesmaids and groomsmen were laughing and having fun, but Ben was quiet, too.

Pastor came in at 4:45 with the marriage certificate. Ben signed it, then I did, then Beth and Aaron.

"Where do you want it?" Pastor asked.

"My stuff is all in the car," I said.

"I'll take it out," Ben said. "I have to be at the front of the church when the service starts anyway."

Pastor and Ben left. At five o'clock, we got the knock.

"Here we go," I said.

"Are you nervous?" Amanda asked.

"I just hope I like the service he planned."

She shrugged. "You'll be married either way."

"I know, but I don't want to be disappointed. Ben kept telling me to trust him."

"How many women have fallen at the hands of a man who's told them that?"

"My point exactly."

From the narthex we watched Ben and Pastor go in the side door.

A violin and piano played the processional. I recognized the melody right away. I learned the lyrics in grade school. I went through the words in my head, trying to piece Ben's story together.

Let us ever walk with Jesus,
Follow His example pure.
Flee the world, which would deceive us
And to sin our souls allure.
Ever in His footsteps treading,
Body here, yet soul above,

Full of faith and hope and love.
Let us do the Father's bidding.
Faithful Lord, abide with me.
Savior, lead; I follow thee.[8]

Dad stood beside me. "The way I see it, I'm not losing a daughter. I'm gaining Ben as a son."

I smiled. "I like that."

"Good," he said pulling me into him for a hug.

"I'd give you a kiss, but I don't want to leave my lipstick on you."

"You'd better get over that," Dad said taking my arm and leading me to the door. "Once the service is over, I don't think Ben's going to go for that."

We chuckled and started down the aisle. I could see the faces of our friends and relatives, but my eyes stayed on Ben. When we stopped next to him, Dad let go of my arm and took my flowers while Ben held his arm for me. Once I had Ben's arm, Dad placed my flowers on my other arm, gave me a kiss on the cheek, and took his seat next to Mom.

Several people had told me the wedding would go by in a blink, so I determined to hear and take it all in. When Pastor finished the first reading from 1 John 4, I was still meditating on those words and focused on Pastor when Ben let go of my arm and whispered, "Stay here. I'll be right back," and walked behind me. I glanced at the groomsmen. Aaron, Troy, and Matt met my puzzled look with smiles not unlike the Cheshire cat in *Alice in Wonderland*.

When I heard the music, I turned to find Ben on the other side of our bridesmaids next to a microphone, playing guitar. It was his sweet tenor voice singing words too lovely to miss.

"Love is not proud, love does not boast
Love, after all, matters the most
Love does not run, love does not hide
Love does not keep locked inside..."[9]

When he returned, his eyes searched mine. I smiled my delight and linked my arm in his. The Cheshire cats tried to go back to poker faces, but none of them could, so they smiled their way through Pastor Glubke's reading of Lamentations 3:22–26.

I always knew when Pastor Glubke was ending a sermon. He tended to use several "wrap up" sentences. By the time he got around to it, I was as eager as he was to say "Amen."

Pastor motioned for me to give my flowers to Beth. Then I turned and gave Ben my hand and looked into his eyes. Ben didn't repeat his vow. He recited it.

"I, Benjamin David Martin, promise God, these witnesses, and you, Meghan, that I will be faithful to you in whatever circumstances God deems right for our life. From this day on, I will take care of you, love you, and pray for you to the best of my ability until God takes one or both of us to be with Him."

"Meghan," Pastor Glubke said. "Repeat after me."

"I, Meghan Mabel Shanahan...promise to be faithful to you, Benjamin, in every way.... As God gives me strength...I will take care of you and nurture you...pray for you and with you...and follow you wherever God takes you...from today until God takes one or both of us to be with Him."

When I took my flowers back from Lisa, Ben left again. This time I knew where to look. The violin player joined him and Aaron, too, with a set of bongos. I was familiar with "A Page is Turned" thanks to Amanda introducing me to Bebo Norman.

There wasn't any smiling from the boys this time. As Ben and Aaron came back, we all stood in hushed reverence.

After the prayer and blessing Pastor Glubke smiled and motioned for us to turn around as he presented us as Mr. and Mrs. Ben Martin.

Once we were out of the church, I threw my arms around Ben.

"That was awesome!"

"You liked it?"

"More than I can begin..."

He kissed me with the kiss I had been waiting for, the kiss that told me he knew it was okay to give himself totally to me. The groomsmen and bridesmaids who were making their way out of the sanctuary huddled around us, clapping and patting us.

"Should we bustle your train so you can usher everyone out?" Beth asked.

"Not yet," I said, kissing him again, then whispering, "I'll give you a better thank-you later" in his ear.

He backed away from me, grinning. The guys took turns hugging him and congratulating him, while the girls worked on bustling my train. Our parents didn't wait for us to usher them out. The photographer snapped pictures as Mom, Dad, Millie, and Ed took turns hugging and congratulating us.

When I was bustled, Ben took my hand and led me to the front of the church.

"What was that music playing as we ushered everyone out?" I asked when the last guests were out of the church.

"It's a CD I made."

"That was you singing, wasn't it?"

He smiled.

I followed him to the front of the church and watched as he put his guitar in the case.

"I knew you could sing and I knew you played guitar, but I had no idea how good you are. Why didn't you show me?"

"I gave away part of my intimacy before its time. I was determined to save something to give to you today."

"Not quite the farm boy I thought I was getting."

He set his guitar on the front pew. "Way hotter, right?"

I nodded. "Way hotter."

"I didn't want you to know how hot I was until we could do something about it."

I laughed.

He smiled and put his forehead on mine, and his hands under my chin to kiss me.

Matt cleared his throat from the back of the church. "Your guests are waiting."

"You always have been a killjoy," Ben muttered as we walked out of the church.

"And your timing has always sucked. That was probably your problem with soccer."

"My timing doesn't suck. I have a degree in music."

Matt laughed and patted Ben's shoulder. We entered the fellowship hall to applause, cheers, and whistles. When we sat down, Amanda leaned forward.

"Do you trust him now?"

"Yes. And I'm three-hundred-percent positive I'm not in for a cold marriage, either."

She laughed. "That service was unbelievable."

"That's quite a compliment coming from you."

"Ben *will* be singing at our wedding."

I looked at Ben as he laughed with Aaron and Matt. He was like a gigantic gift with only a corner of the wrapping paper peeled back. Each time I took off a strip of paper, I was more amazed at what I found.

Pastor Glubke said a prayer and each table took turns getting food. When most people were seated and eating, Matt stood and turned on the microphone.

"If I can have your attention," he began. "I've been friends with Ben since kindergarten and in case you didn't know, he stinks at soccer."

Ben shook his head and smiled.

"I lived with Ben all during college. One Saturday night last November he went out, and when he came home, he told me he'd met the girl he wanted to marry. I didn't think too much of it at the time, but that girl was Meghan. He talked me into giving her a ride home with us for Thanksgiving. She came out of her apartment building with wet hair and a smile that lit up the car. Within a few minutes, Ben was giving me a look that said, 'What did I tell you?'

"Little did we know how hard Meghan would make Ben work to get a date with her. I had honestly given up on the idea of the two of them, but not Ben.

"When I got a call last March inviting my fiancée and me to dinner, I had no idea that when we got to the restaurant Meghan would be next to Ben. A few minutes later, they were showing us her ring. So apparently he does something better than he plays soccer."

He waited for the laughing to stop.

"I didn't write a toast for the two of you. If you don't mind…I wrote a prayer."

The room fell silent.

"Heavenly Father, bless Ben and Meghan. Bring them happiness and health all the days of their lives and let their marriage be long in years, but short in troubles. In Jesus' name. Amen."

Beth and Katie stood next to read a poem they'd written. When they finished, the glass-chinking began. We kissed several times before Ben took the microphone.

"The night we met, I told Meghan I was looking for a wife who was 'sold out for God.' When I put the engagement ring on her finger, I knew that's what she was. I'm feeling pretty blessed right now to be standing here looking at the woman I'll be sharing my life with.

"Our aunts are going to start clearing dishes. Don't take that as a sign that we want you to leave. Take it as a sign our aunts want to get the dishes done so they can enjoy the rest of the evening."

As the plates were cleared, people stood and moved around the room to talk. I asked Amanda and Beth to help me go to the restroom before they wandered off. We were just coming out when I saw Jeff heading my way. I told Amanda and Beth to go ahead.

He gave me a hug. "Did you wait?"

"I'm a married woman. You can't ask me about sex."

"So you jumped the gun."

"No. We didn't."

"Wow. Tonight will be special for you."

"Thanks to you."

"I *should* get some of the credit for that."

"As long as you take the blame for corrupting me."

He smiled. "Speaking of that, I was just thinking it was about this time last year you moved in with us."

"It was."

"Perfect temperature for a little late-night swimming. Milwaukee has plenty of Lake Michigan."

"Wouldn't that be perfect? Ben's first week of seminary he's skinny-dipping with his wife."

"That's the kind of pastor I want."

"I think you and Ben would get along pretty well, actually."

"Can't you see Carol and me in the front row?"

"He'd make you get married."

"If we're still together in four years, he can marry us."

"I'll hold you to that."

Jeff smiled. "I'm happy for you."

"I'm happy, too."

"I'm starting to wonder if I've ever been wrong. I knew you'd find a Christian. I knew Ben was the one. I pegged Earl all along."

"Even before he had murdered anyone," I reminded him. "Hands down, I stink at figuring people out."

"You're right. You do stink at figuring people out. Let's hope Ben's better at it than you."

Ben came and slid his arm behind my back. "Better at what?"

"Figuring people out," I said.

He shook his head and cringed. "Not so much."

"Call Carol before you sign anything. She'll help you."

Jeff shook Ben's hand and congratulated him again before walking away.

"Nice guy," Ben said.

We laughed and headed back into the reception.

Ben and I visited with Lily and the Harbachs while our parents and relatives began disassembling the room.

"How's Margaret?" I asked Lily.

She shook her head. "Not only is her husband in jail, she found out he had been cheating on her and that he was a murderer. There's little comfort in that situation."

"One more horrific tragedy in her life."

"Did he plead guilty?" Ben asked.

Lily nodded. "Both Earl and Harold Henderson took plea agreements. At least there's some closure for the victims' families, but for us...none."

"Lily moved in with Margaret," Evelyn said. "They come over every Saturday."

I smiled. "That was a highlight for me."

"And me," Lily said.

"What is Margaret going to do with Candlewood?"

"She'll be putting it up for sale just as soon as some of the repairs are finished. It's too much for her."

"I can see that it would be."

"We have a new student moving in with us when we get back," Herbert said.

"A young man this time," Evelyn added.

"That's awesome."

"Look what you started," Ben said.

I shrugged. "I don't think I had a whole lot to do with it."

The dishes were washed and in piles for Mom to return Monday morning. The chairs and tables were back in place, the lights and sheers in my parent's van.

"I'm going to change out of my dress," I told Ben.

"I'd rather you didn't."

"I don't want to sit on a bustle for two hours."

"I need to talk to you about that."

"Oh no. Are we still going on a honeymoon?"

"We are. Could you trust me for a couple minutes until we leave?"

"And in the meantime you don't want me to change?"

He shook his head.

When I hugged Dad, I said good-bye to him instead of good night.

"Wait a second," he said. "You're not leaving the planet. We still expect you to call, especially if you need something. Just because you're married, doesn't mean you won't need help."

"Deal," I said.

Dad shook Ben's hand. "Don't hesitate. Ever."

It was still warm outside, and the moon was bright. Ben opened my door.

"We're not going to Milwaukee tonight," he said as we left the parking lot. "We're going to spend tonight at the farm."

"With your parents?"

"They'll spend the night in town with my grandparents."

"I don't understand."

"It cost almost the same to fly out of Madison tomorrow, and I didn't want to feel rushed to leave our reception to get to the apartment tonight."

"So your parents gave us their house?"

"It would be a little awkward with the whole family there."

"I just feel bad that we've put four people out of their beds."

"They were glad to do it."

The farm was dark when we drove in. Ben went ahead of me and opened the door while I stayed at the car determining what I needed to bring in. Thankfully Ben had told me to bring my suitcase for the honeymoon, so he could put his things in, he said. Otherwise I would have left it at the apartment in Milwaukee… which, I suddenly realized, was where the lingerie I'd bought special for tonight was. I grabbed my bag with the clothes and shoes I wore to the church.

"Is that all you need?" Ben asked.

"I think so."

He shut and locked the car door, put the keys in his pocket and picked me up.

"What are you doing?"

"I'm carrying you over the threshold."

"Why?"

"To show you I can."

I laughed. He set me down inside the porch and took off his shoes. Mine slipped off. Once we were inside the house, he locked the door and offered his hand, guiding me through the kitchen, into the living room, and up the squeaky stairs. When he turned on the light in his room, the papers were gone from the top of his desk. His room was picked up, the bed made. One red rose sat on top of a piece of paper on one of the pillows. He grabbed the rose.

"For you, later," he said, putting it on the desk.

He picked up the paper and handed it to me. "For you now."

I unfolded it to see his handwritten note.

"If in the end we look back
And see anything but love
Then we've missed our chance.

If when our years are over
We can't find the faith
That brought us together…

Or if our time leaves
Us without the hope
Of something more than us,

Then we have failed
Not just in some ways
But in every way.

God will not disappoint us. I love you. Ben

I put it down next to the rose and took out the pins fastening my headband. When they were all out, I put my veil next to his tie.

He came behind me and wrapped his arms around my waist.

"I seem to remember you saying something about thanking me later. Any chance this is late enough?"

"Let me think," I said.

"You think," he said, unzipping my dress.

As I stepped out of it, he saw the garter.

"Nice," he said, sliding it off my leg.

"Consider yourself thanked," I said, smiling.

"Oh, no," he said, maneuvering me onto the bed.

I laughed, knowing this was just the beginning. I would be unwrapping Ben for years, but for now I would enjoy what was before me...the soon-to-be seminary student, musician, my husband, Ben.

Bible Study Chapter Sixteen

Confessing our sins

At their last meeting with Pastor Glubke, Ben told Pastor Glubke about his and Meghan's sins. Read James 5:16. Of what benefit is it to confess our sins to each other?

Meghan seemed somewhat embarrassed by Ben's confession. What was Pastor Glubke's reaction to their sins?

Read John 8:1–11. How did Jesus react to the woman caught in sin?

Jesus reminded the crowd of their own sins. When we hear of someone's sin, it is good to remember our own faults and model the grace Jesus had for sinners.

Read Proverbs 11:13 and 16:28. How should we not react to someone's confession of sin?

Where do you find your hope?

What message was Ben trying to portray through the wedding service?

Read Ecclesiastes 4:9–12. Through most of this section Solomon is talking about the benefit of two people, but in the last verse he talks about three. Read Romans 7:18–20. What is the problem that arises when you put two sinful people together, whether it is in a friendship or marriage?

Read Psalm 121:3–8 and Psalm 46:1–3 to see how things change when you add God to the mix. How often will God be with you?

Can you say that about any other person on earth?

Will Ben always be there for Meghan?

Will Meghan's parents or Ben's parents always be there for her?

Read Genesis 29:31 and Exodus 23:25–26. What are the blessings that come only from God's hand?

You cannot go into a marriage thinking your spouse is the answer to everything. Your spouse can make healthy food to eat or go with you to the gym but cannot make you healthy. God controls disease and sickness. Your spouse cannot give you children. Your spouse cannot give you security. Those things come from God and God alone.

What did you think of Matt's toast, or rather, absence of one? Does a toast or a prayer have more power? Why?

Sex God's way

Read Proverbs 5:18–19. Fill in the following blanks.

May you _____ in the wife of your youth.

May her breasts _____ you _____.

May you ever be _____ by her love.

Read Song of Songs 7:1–9. After reading from these two places in the Bible, do you think God wants you to enjoy your spouse's body?

Read 1 Corinthians 7:3–5. Once you are married, your body is not yours alone. Who else does your body belong to?

What does that mean?

Should there be guilt or shame in having sex with your spouse?

God intended that you enjoy sex and reap the fulfillment of sexual happiness within the confines of marriage.

Amber Albee Swenson has a BFA in Creative Writing from Southwest Minnesota State University. Her first book, *Bible Moms—Life Lessons from Mothers in the Bible*, was published in 2007. Currently she is a stay-at-home wife and mom to four children.

Resources

Endnotes
1. *Concordia Self-study Bible New International Version* (St. Louis: Concordia Publishing House, 1986) 947.
2. Ibid., 254.
3. Ibid., 1810.
4. Information from this paragraph was taken from Ibid., 527 and several articles from an internet search of "explain 2 Kings 2:23-24."
5. *Webster's New World Dictionary*, Neufeldt, Victoria. Editor-in-chief. (New York, NY: Warner books, 1990) 156, 380, 472.
6. Norman, Bebo and Ingram, Jason. "I Will Lift My Eyes." <u>Between the Dreaming and the Coming True.</u> Essential Records, 2006.
7. *Luther's Catechism*, Kuske, David.Editor. (Milwaukee, WI: Northwestern Publishing House, 2006) 3.
8. Von Birken, Sigmund (1626–1681). Translation by J. Adam Rimback (1871–1941). "Let Us Ever Walk with Jesus."
9. Knell, Brandon Heath and Cates, Chad. "Love Never Fails." <u>What if we.</u> Reunion Records, 2008.

CPSIA information can be obtained at www.ICGtesting.com
Printed in the USA
BVOW011218230112

281035BV00001B/1/P